"I TOLD YOU I'M NOT THE MAN YOU THINK I AM. YOU'RE STILL LOOKING FOR A HERO."

He started to reach out to her, but he couldn't touch her. "This is the best way, Kathy."

"Best for whom?" she demanded, trying to hide her tears.

"For both of us!" Peter told her. "You're young. You'll get over me."

"Stop saying I'm young! I'm old—old enough to have fallen in love with you!" There, her secret was out. She couldn't lose him now. . . .

"I can't make a commitment, Kathy."

"Are you saying that our being together has been a mistake?"

"Yes. I warned you that it would be."

"Just last night you told me you wanted me . . ."

"I lied."

CANDLELIGHT ECSTASY SUPREMES

TOO CLOSE FOR COMFORT

Ginger Chambers

A CANDLELIGHT ECSTASY SUPREME

Published by
Dell Publishing Co., Inc.
1 Dag Hammarskjold Plaza
New York, New York 10017

Dell ® TM 681510, Dell Publishing Co., Inc.

Candlelight Ecstasy Supreme is a trademark
of Dell Publishing Co., Inc.

Candlelight Ecstasy Romance®, 1,203,540, is a registered
trademark of Dell Publishing Co., Inc., New York, New York

ISBN: 0-440-18740-0

Printed in the United States of America

First printing—November 1985

For Beverly,
who is about to start her way in the world,
and
All the readers of HARBOR OF DREAMS
who wondered what happened to Kathy

To Our Readers:

We are pleased and excited by your overwhelmingly positive response to our Candlelight Ecstasy Supremes. Unlike all the other series the Supremes are filled with more passion, adventure, and intrigue and are obviously the stories you like best.

In months to come we will continue to publish books by many of your favorite authors as well as the very finest work from new authors of romantic fiction. As always, we are striving to present unique, absorbing love stories —the very best love has to offer.

Breathtaking and unforgettable, Ecstasy Supremes follow in the great romantic tradition you've come to expect *only* from Candlelight Ecstasy.

Your suggestions and comments are always welcome. Please let us hear from you.

Sincerely,

The Editors
Candlelight Romances
1 Dag Hammarskjold Plaza
New York, New York 10017

CHAPTER ONE

The raucous cry of a sea gull swooping low overhead caught the attention of the young woman moving slowly along the narrow pier. It was a sound Kathy had been accustomed to all her twenty-one years, but she had missed it for the past four. Florida had sea gulls, but they weren't her sea gulls—they weren't *Texas* sea gulls. They looked similar and they sounded similar, but they were different, just as the scent of coastal air was the same and yet very different in Texas and Florida. She had missed the Texas Bay Area.

Kathy took a deep breath, feeling the heat of the sun kiss her face. She shook her head, letting her long golden curls tickle the exposed skin on her neck and shoulders. Another sea gull swooped and gave a strident cry. *It's good to be back—*

"Home," she murmured, completing her thought aloud.

That word was so sweet. It had so many layers and meanings—so many memories. Home was a place; home was people. Home was the spot where a person's heart ached to be when they were away. And this was home for her.

So many things had changed in her life. She had grown from a questioning, unsure adolescent poised on the brink of adulthood to a questioning, unsure adult poised on the brink of making her way in the world. The questions were different now, but the answers were just as elusive. She remembered the young girl she had been. How many times had her feet made this same journey? Running to see Jason, instinctively knowing that his friendship and counsel were as sure as his hand on the tiller of his boat in a stormy sea.

She stopped near the end of the pier and gazed at the empty slip where *Sunchaser* had been docked. She wished Jason were here now—just as she wished her older sister, Ashley, was. She needed them to talk to. It had been two years since she had seen them—since they had sold the restaurant, repurchased *Sunchaser,* and set out to make Jason's dream of sailing around the world come true. She had seen them off, waving until the sailboat was no longer visible. Tears had been streaking down her cheeks, but they were tears of happiness.

Ashley and Jason's love story had been so beautiful. It was a sample of true love, of sacrifice for that love, of confidence in tomorrow. And she was proud of the part she'd played in bringing them together.

Since they'd been gone, she hadn't lost contact with them. They'd exchanged letters, and throughout her time at the university in Florida, she had received news of their travels and was still able to share in their happiness, still able to feel like a valued part of their lives.

But now it was time for her to start building her *own* life. Only she couldn't begin without visiting the places that had meant the most to her in her earlier life. In some ways the experience was melancholy, making her soul cry out for the two people she loved most in the world; yet in other ways she was able to draw some of the reassurance she needed so dearly. She could hear Jason's voice; she could hear what she knew he would tell her on the eve of her greatest adventure. He would say: "You can be a success at whatever you choose, Kathy. Just remember to step back and make sure that it's what you really want."

And it was. Her very blood was a part of this place. Her spirit was tucked into its heart. What affected the Bay Area affected her. So it was only natural that she would choose marine fisheries biology as her life's work. Her days would be spent researching and protecting the species and ecology that was so precious to the coastal region she dearly loved.

When she thought about her new job, her heart jumped. She was nervous about it—and excited. She had been told that she would be pitched into the field right away, that there wasn't time for tender treatment or slow introductions. She only hoped that she would remember a small part of what she had learned and not disgrace herself or her school.

Kathy shook her head, trying to shake away her doubts. She had graduated near the top of her class, so she should have no difficulty. The only problem that should concern her now was where she was going to stay. All of her worldly possessions were packed away in the back compartment of the Datsun 280ZX Jason had loaned her while he was away.

She needed to find an apartment in the area that was cheap, which was a contradiction in terms. There were numerous apartments bordering the lake that led into the bay. Everyone seemed to want to be close to the water. But the prices! She had already looked at one complex and almost had a heart attack at the price.

Very junior marine biologists weren't noted for high salaries. Maybe she needed to look farther afield—like in Nebraska!

She smiled to herself as she retraced her steps along the pier. There was one place she still had to visit before she got on with her apartment hunting: Claudio's, the Italian restaurant that had been her parent's, and then hers and Ashley's, before Jason came on the scene. In reality it had been her home as well, or rather the rooms above the restaurant had been her home. She wondered how many changes the new owners had made. Would she even recognize the place?

Kathy drove the short distance that separated the marina from the restaurant. And after parking the car, tears came to her eyes as she gazed at the restaurant's exterior. It was still the same as she remembered it! The narrow boards were snowy white; the wooden shutters were a bright green. The new owner had adopted their outside color scheme, just as they had adopted the name. "Claudio's" was still proclaimed proudly on the sign in front.

Slowly Kathy got out of the car and began to walk toward the entrance. Her instinct was to go to the side door, the family entrance, just as she had always done, but she knew she couldn't do that.

She took a deep breath and pulled open the entrance door. Surely she'd encounter some changes; it would be too much to hope that the interior would be exactly the same, too. But it was. The linoleum floor was worn a bit but still shone with care, the ceiling fans were turning slowly, the tables still had red-and-white-checked tablecloths spread over them, and the same white curtains hung at the windows.

Then her attention was caught by a strange sound. She turned just in time to see and hear Mary Morgan O'Day hurrying toward her. "Ohhhhhh . . . Ohhh-hhh . . . I can't believe it! Is it you, Kathy? Oh, my Lord, what am I saying? Of course it's you. You look just like yourself!"

The sturdily built woman enveloped Kathy in a bear hug that left her breathless. "I can't believe it! I just can't believe it!" she cried. Then she let Kathy go and went racing through the swinging door that led into the kitchen. "Iris! You aren't going to believe—"

In an instant both of the women Kathy remembered so well came into the dining room.

"See! Look! It's Kathy!" Mary Morgan exclaimed.

Kathy was grateful that the lunch crowd had not yet arrived. "Hello, Iris. And hello, Mary Morgan," she said, her blue eyes twinkling. Some things never change. Mary Morgan might have some gray hairs beginning to sprinkle themselves through her dark hair and Iris Dawson's features might look even more wizened than before, but the waitress still bubbled over with lovable enthusiasm and the cook still specialized in her crusty old woman act.

"God almighty!" Iris whispered in surprise, her dark eyes running over Kathy's slim body encased in tan shorts and a white top. Then her facade broke and she reached out to give Kathy a quick hug. When she stood back, she made smoothing motions at her apron while she complained gruffly, "You could give a person a little warning, you know."

Kathy laughed. "Aren't you glad to see me?"

Iris harrumphed. "Of course I am."

"Me, too!" Mary Morgan chimed in, unable to keep

silent any longer. She had been literally jumping from one foot to the other and now gave Kathy another hug. "You're a sight for sore eyes!" she exclaimed, then pulled away, her dark eyes aglow with happiness. "And I don't care if you warn us or not!"

Iris ignored the not-so-subtle reprimand. "Have you come to stay?" she asked.

"Yes," Kathy said. "I've graduated from college."

Mary Morgan let out another little squeal. The two women had known Kathy since she was a child, and each felt a certain protectiveness toward her. "You're coming home!" she said. "Oh, I'm so glad!" She glanced at the older woman. "Iris and I were just talking about you this morning—"

"Something good?" Kathy prompted when Mary Morgan paused.

"Oh, of course something good!" the waitress returned. "We were reminiscing about you and Ashley and Jason. The folks who own this place want to remodel." A certain tightness entered her tone. "I think they're crazy! It looks great to me just as it is. I know the hard work that was put into making it look this way. But they seem determined to change it."

"Maybe they have something special in mind," Kathy suggested.

Iris came into the conversation for the first time in several minutes. "How about changing the place into one of those 'fern bars' where fancy people pay fancy prices just to sit around and eat carrot sticks!"

Kathy looked at the cook. "Is that what they want to do?" She could scarcely believe that Claudio's would no longer be an Italian restaurant. "Is business that bad?" she questioned.

"No! That's what makes it all so—so—" Mary Morgan sputtered to a stop.

"What about you two? What will you do?"

Iris answered first. "I'm an Italian cook. I make pizza, spaghetti, and lasagna. I guess I'll have to leave if they want something different." Her brusque voice ended on that conviction, and she walked back into the kitchen.

"Do you really think it will come to that?" Kathy asked, turning to Mary Morgan.

"Who knows? I think the boss's just bored and searching around for something to do." The waitress was frowning darkly as she considered future possibilities. After a moment her expression cleared. "But let's forget about that for now. Tell me what's happening with you. I thought maybe with Ashley and Jason away you might stay in Florida. I know you were considering it at one time."

"I was," Kathy replied. It was hard to be downcast for long around Mary Morgan. "Miami's nice . . . but it's not here, if you know what I mean."

"I sure do!" Mary Morgan responded. "I've lived all my life within ten miles of the bay, and I wouldn't change a minute of it—not for all the tea in China."

"Would you stay on here . . . if it becomes—what was Iris's term?—a fern bar?"

"I guess so. Waitressing is waitressing. I don't mind serving carrot sticks. I'd just hate to see Claudio's change."

The two women became quiet. Then Mary Morgan broke the silence between them by saying plaintively, "I wish Ashley and Jason were here."

"So do I," Kathy agreed.

17

"Have you heard from them lately? The last letter Iris and I received was about six months ago when they were on some little island. I can't remember the name, but it was in the South Pacific . . ."

"I know where you mean, but they've moved on again . . . to Tahiti. They were there the last I heard."

"Tahiti!" Mary Morgan's eyes had a dreamy, faraway look in them. "I've never wanted to travel much—the bug's never bitten me very deep—but Tahiti is a place I'd like to see. It looks so pretty in pictures."

Kathy smiled and teased, "Are you sure it's the island you'd like to see or the men?"

Mary Morgan's smile answered hers. "How about both?"

The front door opened and a small group of people came in. The waitress rushed forward to greet them but not before instructing Kathy to wait where she was.

When Mary Morgan had seated the newcomers and given them their menus, she returned to Kathy. "Have you found a place to live?" she asked her curiously. "I'm asking because something's just occurred to me."

"No, not yet. I just arrived today."

Mary Morgan clapped her hands together. "Then don't bother to look. I've got something for you. And it's perfect."

"I can't afford a lot," Kathy cautioned.

"I realize that. That's why this is so perfect. I have a friend—well, actually it's a friend of a friend—but this friend is looking for someone to condo sit while she and her husband visit their daughter in Australia for about six months. And they desperately need someone to look after their place. They won't charge a penny, but the person has to be trustworthy. And that fits you to a tee!"

"It sounds too good to be true. Why are they having trouble getting someone to do it?"

"Like I told you, they're picky. I've met the couple several times—played bingo with them—and they're a little strange. Absolutely batty over their dog. When it died, they had it cremated and the poor creature's ashes are stored in an urn on their mantelpiece. They want someone they can trust to take care of the apartment and to watch out for the urn."

"Are you making this up, Mary Morgan?" Kathy asked incredulously.

"No, I swear I'm not."

"Is there anything else I should know?" Kathy quizzed half seriously, half in jest.

Mary Morgan motioned for her to wait while she went to take the customers' orders. While she was doing that, another group of people came in, and Kathy automatically helped out by seating them at a table. She had been working in a restaurant in Miami part-time while she was in school, and after all the years she had spent working in Claudio's, she definitely knew the routine.

When Mary Morgan emerged from the kitchen after turning in the first round of orders, she hurried back to Kathy's side.

"Things will be jumping in a few minutes, so I'll make this fast. They seem to have some kind of a problem with one of their neighbors. But I don't think it's anything serious—just minor squabbling. Do you want to go see them?"

Kathy hesitated for only a second. A shrine to a dog's

remains didn't scare her. And the price couldn't be beaten.

"Sure! Why not?"

"Atta girl!" Mary Morgan applauded her decision. She tore a piece of paper from her order book after quickly scribbling down a name and address. "They're a retired couple, so they'll probably be home now. Tell them I sent you."

"I'll do that," Kathy promised. "And thanks."

"Remember, I've warned you. They're a little strange."

The condominium project Mary Morgan directed her to was one of the newer multiple dwellings in the area, but it boasted the settled appearance of having hugged the gentle rise of land beside Clear Lake for many years. The builders had wisely chosen location, architecture, and landscaping. Even the attached marina had a look of permanence, with quite a few of the slips occupied by bobbing sailboats. In all, it was a lovely scene right out of the pages of a magazine, but it was also a scene that spoke of something else: money. Kathy knew that she probably would never be able to afford to live here on her own.

As she parked her car in an empty visitor slot at the front of the complex, she wondered about the couple Mary Morgan had sent her to visit. They might be strange, but they were definitely financially comfortable —which translated into their being *eccentric*, the term reserved for wealthy strange people.

There was a slight smile on Kathy's lips as she walked to the manager's office. She had no idea where the Sinclairs' apartment was located, so she would need to ask.

Kathy was almost to the door when she saw a man approaching the same destination along a nearby sidewalk. Kathy felt an immediate physical attraction to this stranger. *Tall, dark,* and *handsome* were merely words where he was concerned. They didn't convey enough meaning.

As he came closer, she saw that the carved lines of his facial features only got better. And in a lightning-quick assessment she also took in the facts that his thick, neatly cut hair was a warm brown, that his eyes were a fascinating sherry color, that he was somewhere in his late twenties or early thirties, and that the rather conservative three-piece suit he was wearing was covering a body she'd love to see set free.

Kathy didn't realize that she was staring until the man murmured, "Are you going in or coming out?"

That voice! It matched the rest of him perfectly! Vital and alive and extremely sexy!

Kathy visibly jumped, and an indulgent smile lighted up his unusual eyes—which had the effect of catapulting her into uncertainty. Finally she managed to say, "I'm going in."

"Then what are you waiting for?"

Kathy looked from him to the door knob. He reached forward to turn it. Her eyes followed his hand, then moved up his arm, to his shoulder, to his face. Her first impression was still correct: he was the most handsome man she'd ever seen.

"After you," he said softly, only there was an edge of irritation building.

Kathy cursed herself for her juvenile reaction toward

21

him—only it hadn't been juvenile. She knew the difference.

She scraped together what dignity she had left and entered the office. She was very much aware of him as he followed her in.

The manager, an older man who looked as if he rarely smiled, was seated behind a desk in the office cubicle closest to the door. When he saw them enter, he stood up.

"Yes?" he said, more to the man than to Kathy.

The mystery man spoke. "The lady was here first."

The manager's beady eyes shifted to her. "I thought she was with you."

"No."

Kathy decided it was time she spoke for herself. "I'm looking for a certain apartment. Do you have a map?" she asked.

"Certainly," the manager replied, motioning to a side wall.

"Thank you." Kathy moved closer to the indicated map. She pretended to study it, but she didn't have much success since the manager was now speaking to the man she'd come in with, and all of her attention was focused on his reply.

"Mr. Peavey," he was saying, that wonderful voice projecting from that wonderful body, "this is the second time I've had to ask about having my front door repaired."

"It's not been done yet?" the manager responded.

"No, it's not been done yet. If it had, I wouldn't be here. I'm a busy man, Mr. Peavey. I don't enjoy having to ask for something repeatedly."

The manager jotted a note on a sheet of paper, then

he promised, "It'll be fixed by the time you get home from work today."

"I'd appreciate that," the younger man replied. Then, inexplicably, he looked at Kathy again, those sherry-colored eyes sweeping over her. For a moment he seemed frozen, but the moment passed, and he ended up giving her a rather obscure smile before leaving the office.

Kathy stared after him, all pretense of checking the map deserting her. Her body was still reacting to his appeal, but somehow she was left with the impression that he had found her lacking. She looked down at her shorts and loose cotton blouse. Obviously her attire didn't equal his at the moment, but clothing could be changed. And since he lived here, she could see him again!

When the manager asked her if she had found what she wanted, she could truthfully answer that she had. She had also located the apartment.

Strange, eccentric—the words echoed in Kathy's mind as she met the couple Mary Morgan had sent her to see. *Totally off the deep end is a more accurate description.* She couldn't help but wonder if the continent of Australia was ready for them.

To begin with, every available space on their living room walls was covered with pictures of the small white dog that had died and the numerous ribbons he had collected at various dog shows. The scene wasn't totally odd unless you counted the candles that were burning at each side of a huge framed painting of the dog, which was hung over a colorful urn that contained his remains. The fireplace below was rendered useless by the

23

presence of a mound of pet toys in what could only be described as a reinaction of a primitive offering to the dead. Kathy took a deep breath and let it out slowly, wondering what she had let herself in for.

A scant few minutes later, though, she came to the conclusion that the Sinclairs meant no harm. The rest of the world might be a half step ahead and to one side of the path they were taking, but they were blissfully unaware of the difference.

Frederick the Magnificent—the dog—had been the sole purpose of their lives since their daughter had moved away.

"He was our baby," the woman explained.

Kathy knew that transferring emotions to an animal wasn't all that unusual. Psychologically people needed pets, especially when they felt abandoned by family members or acquaintances.

"He's coming back, you know," the woman continued, "but not for some months yet. That's why Donald and I are making our trip now. We want to see Dora and her children, but we also want to be back when Frederick returns."

This was said with total conviction. Kathy could only give a noncommittal murmur.

"Would you like some iced tea?" Mrs. Sinclair asked sweetly, her grandmotherly face lighting into a smile. She had sized Kathy up and was satisfied that she was a person they could trust.

"Ah, yes. Thank you," Kathy responded. She looked at Mr. Sinclair, and he nodded his approval.

As she was serving the tea, Mrs. Sinclair explained what Kathy's duties would be if she stayed in the apartment.

"You must dust Frederick's urn twice each day. And his candles should be lighted for at least an hour. That way he knows we remember him, and he'll be able to find his way back to us more easily." She paused to take a sip from her glass. A few seconds later she confided, "We could have taken Frederick with us—his ashes I mean. But we'd rather not. This is Frederick's home. We'd prefer that he stay here . . . *if* we can find some-one who understands what it means to care for him—which I believe we have. Would you do it?"

Kathy didn't know whether to be complimented or not. But she wasn't stupid. "I'd be happy to care for him, Mrs. Sinclair."

"Irene," the woman corrected.

"Irene," Kathy repeated.

Mr. Sinclair nodded his head in satisfaction.

Kathy stayed with Mary Morgan until she could move into the condominium complex. She saw the Sin-clairs only once before they left. They gave her a key, told her to treat the apartment as her own, reiterated what her duties concerning Frederick were, and then warned her about the neighbor next door.

"He's a rather unusual gentleman, dear," Irene Sin-clair said carefully. "Very confused. He persists in thinking that we park in his parking space. But we don't. All I can say is that he's extremely ill tempered."

"I'll be careful," Kathy promised, wondering what it must be like to live next door to the Sinclairs, especially since the two apartments shared a balcony on the sec-ond level of the development. She promised herself that she would be extra nice to him—if it turned out that he was innocent of wrongdoing.

As she left the apartment, Kathy made a pseudo-casual search for the mystery man she had met the first day, but she didn't see him.

One advantage of not having many possessions is that when it comes time to move, there isn't a lot of work to be done. Kathy put all her possessions in her car and drove to the condominiums the same day the Sinclairs left.

When she pulled into the parking area, Kathy remembered the warning Irene Sinclair had given her. The way Kathy understood the parking arrangements, each tenant's parking slot number and apartment number were the same. She drove slowly, checking for her own, but when she found it, it was already filled by a late-model blue BMW. Kathy looked at it, shrugged, and then guided her car into the visitors' section across the way. The car in the space must belong to the ill-tempered neighbor. She would have a little talk with him later.

The process of moving in took several trips up and down the stairs, and when Kathy finally finished, she stood in the middle of the living room to survey her surroundings. Her gaze wandered to the shrine and she sighed. Then she decided to explore the rest of the apartment before unpacking.

Mercifully the other rooms—two large bedrooms, a master bath and a guest bath, along with a nice-size kitchen and breakfast area—were more normal. A note was sitting on the table with her name written on the front. It was from Irene.

"Kathy," she read, "there's plenty of boysenberry

jam in the pantry. Help yourself. Make our home yours. Don't forget Frederick. Love, Irene and Donald."

Kathy couldn't help but laugh as she read the note. It was perfectly sincere, she knew, but it was so funny! Boysenberry jam? Irene was sweet but definitely an eccentric.

Curious, she moved to the pantry to see what else it contained besides jam. To her surprise it was filled with all kinds of food. The refrigerator was well stocked as well. There was even a cut of roast beef with another note attached to it.

"Kathy," this one said, "I cooked this last night at midnight. I couldn't sleep. Irene."

Laughing lightly and crumpling the cool square of paper, Kathy decided it was time to start unpacking. After only a few moments' hesitation she chose the guest bedroom for her own because she felt uncomfortable taking over the master suite. She brought her things into the room and set about finding space for them. A few articles she brought back into the living room, including some pictures.

She stood back, hands on hips, as she examined the crowded walls. She didn't think she could stand quite so overwhelming a reminder of Frederick. The shrine she wouldn't touch, but the photographs and ribbons would have to go. If she put them away in a safe place in the master bedroom, she could safely rehang them before the Sinclairs' return. But how could she remember where each one was positioned?

Suddenly she got an idea. All she needed to do was to take some pictures—only she didn't have a camera!

Maybe *he* had one—the irritable neighbor next door.

And since she wanted to talk with him anyway, what better excuse did she have?

Kathy gave her head a confident toss. Surely asking to borrow a camera was more original than the old borrowing-a-cup-of-sugar routine.

A spring was in her step as she moved across the balcony and rang the doorbell.

CHAPTER TWO

There was no immediate response to Kathy's summons, so she rang the bell again. When nothing happened, she started to turn away. She had taken only a few steps when she heard the door creak open.

And *creak* was the right descriptive word. It was a high-pitched, distinctive kind of noise that only a faulty hinge can give.

With her back still to her neighbor's door, Kathy's lips curved into an amused smile. When she turned, would Bela Lugosi be standing there decked out in full vampire costume? Was that why the Sinclairs' neighbor was so ill tempered? He wasn't satisfied with the quality of the local blood? Her smile widened, then wavered as she took in the view that greeted her.

By no stretch of anyone's imagination could the man standing there be described as a creature who'd been dead for thousands of years. He was very much alive, from his precisely styled brown hair to his impeccable Italian-made shoes.

Kathy's blue eyes swept over him in disbelief, just as his gaze made a returning assessment of her. It was him —the man she had seen the first day! *He* was the neighbor the Sinclairs were having all the trouble with. Her mystery man was the ill-tempered, irritable neighbor!

Kathy felt his eyes run over her once again, this time in dawning recognition, and once again she was aware that her appearance was wanting. Where she was wearing an old pair of jeans and a Twisted Sister concert T-shirt, he was faultlessly turned out in a dark-blue conservative suit, white shirt, understated tie, and modest —though not inexpensive—cuff links. The crease in his pants was perfect, and his jacket fit his lean, muscular form as if it had been made for him.

To cover her unease, Kathy gathered her pluck and made her smile return. "Small world, isn't it?" she greeted him.

His sherry-colored eyes attached themselves to hers.

"Oh?" he returned, his voice causing a tingle to run all the way to her toes.

Kathy motioned to the apartment behind her. "This is the apartment I was trying to find the other day."

"I see you found it."

"Yes."

A long, silent moment passed between them. Then Kathy took the initiative again by saying, "I'm going to be your neighbor for a while."

His gaze swept over her again, making Kathy's heart begin to beat at an even quicker pace. She babbled on, "I didn't know that you would be my neighbor the other day or I would have asked you where you lived and then I wouldn't have had to look on the map for my apartment—"

"Where are the Sinclairs?" he cut in before she could say anymore.

"They've gone to Australia to tour the country and visit their daughter."

"I hope the natives are prepared," he commented wryly, his features softening into a slight smile.

Kathy gave a quick grin in response because she had had thoughts along those lines herself. "I imagine they're ready for anything . . . even Irene and Donald."

"I should hope so. Otherwise they're in for quite a shock."

Another silence stretched between them. She got the distinct impression that the man wasn't overwhelmed to be talking to her. He was polite and he had even shown a little humor, but he wanted their conversation to end.

Kathy didn't want it to be over. "My name's Kathy Stevens," she said, holding out her hand.

He seemed to hesitate before taking it into his own. The half smile was no longer in evidence.

His fingers were electric to Kathy; hers seemed to be only fingers to him. His grip loosened almost immediately.

She racked her brain for something more to say, and then she remembered the initial purpose of her visit.

"Do you own a camera?" she asked, the sudden question catching him off guard.

"A what?"

"A camera. One of those things where you press the button and a picture comes out."

"I know what a camera is."

"Then why did you—?"

She got no further. His impatience was growing. "I asked because I didn't understand what you said," he explained rather curtly.

Kathy was beginning to feel a little irritated herself. *He may be handsome and have a lot going for him in a*

31

number of ways, but his personality can definitely use some work, she thought.

"If you have a hearing problem, you should get it checked," she suggested with false sweetness. "I understand they're doing marvelous things with hearing aids nowadays. Even the President wears two."

"I don't have a hearing problem," he said. "And I also don't have a lot of time." He glanced at his watch to emphasize his words.

"So who's keeping you?" she retorted, getting into the swing of things.

"You are!"

"Me?" she repeated innocently. "How am I keeping you?"

He took a deep breath and let it out slowly. "Look . . . as I said before, I don't have a lot of time to stand here talking inanities with a young girl. I'm a busy man. I have things to do even if you don't. I have a camera, but it's broken. You're going to have to borrow one from someone else. Either that or go buy one. Okay?"

That was supposed to crush her, she decided. Only she didn't crush so easily. And what did he mean by "young girl"? She wasn't a young girl—at least she wasn't *that* young. He acted as if he thought she was still in her teens!

"I don't exactly have all the time in the world myself," she returned with just as much bite to her tone. "I'm moving in today, in case that fact has escaped your notice. So I'm busy, too. And I'm *not* a young girl!"

He didn't let her go any further. "Opinions are relative. We can agree to disagree."

"Yes," Kathy said with deceptive brightness. "Why don't we."

His eyes flickered. And again, for a moment, she felt something stir their cool depths. But it was gone almost instantly, and he made a move to close the door.

Kathy stopped him with a quick, "Wait!"

He paused, a suspicious look on his handsome features.

Kathy wanted to prick his aura of cool sophistication. And at the moment she had only one device. She tilted her head and asked curiously, "Do you own a blue BMW?"

He frowned slightly. Was he wondering if she had done something to it—like crash into it or something? The thought amused her.

"Yes," he said slowly.

She flashed a grin. "Don't worry, it's safe. At least it is for the moment. But I won't guarantee its condition tomorrow if you park it in my space again."

"Is that a threat?" he asked softly.

Again Kathy experienced a tremor at his words, but it wasn't wholly sensual this time.

"Take it how you like," she answered crisply. Then, after giving a little wave, she retreated across the balcony to her apartment.

Peter Maxwell watched the slender figure disappear from view behind the opposite doorway. *It was too much to hope!* he thought in frustrated disgust. The idea of having an easy, companionable neighbor who would mind his own business and leave him alone could only be a dream if the Sinclairs picked their replacement. In addition she was probably a relative of theirs! Not that she was all that hard on the eye. More than once he had been drawn to the slender curves of her body. But as he

33

had told her, he didn't have either the time or the inclination for any kind of dalliance with flighty teen-agers. He liked his women to be women, to have acquired some experience in the world. If he hadn't already sunk so much money into this place, he would move and be done with the lot of them. But his banker's soul wouldn't allow him to do that. He would stick it out. Maybe the Sinclairs would get lost on their trip. Maybe a giant wallaby would do away with them. Or better still, maybe they would find a whole colony of like-minded individuals and decide to stay there. And send for her! It was a bracing idea.

Peter stepped back and shut the door. He had to get back to the bank. He had already extended his lunch break longer than he should have. But the program he had been working on as an independent project had taken more time to put together than he had planned on. And then he had been forced to stand there and talk with a spoiled, slightly looney child—insanity was probably in the genes!—for no apparent gain.

Peter didn't like upsets in his life. He arose at the same time each day, ate a health-conscious breakfast, read the newspaper from cover to cover—especially the financial pages—showered, dressed, and then went about doing whatever it was that needed to be done. And if something got in the way to disturb his routine, it irritated him. And *she* had irritated him.

A small pang of guilt pricked his conscience about the camera she had requested. He had one and it was in perfectly good condition. Out of contrariness—maybe because she had succeeded in invading his privacy—he had not wanted to lend it to her.

Peter shrugged the guilt away as he turned out the

34

light in his kitchen. She was nothing to him. They were merely neighbors.

Then, against his will, his body responded to his memories of the way the worn jeans had fitted the curve of her hips and the slender shapeliness of her thighs, of the way the brightly colored T-shirt had hugged her nicely formed breasts, of the delicacy of her features beneath a whirl of golden hair. . . .

Peter called a halt to his thoughts. And after needlessly straightening his tie and smoothing his hair, he let himself out of the apartment.

He didn't even glance at the opposite door.

Kathy made a sandwich from the roast beef Irene had cooked the night before. She was still disgruntled by the meeting she had had with her new neighbor, but she tried not to dwell on it. Instead she thought about the job she was going to start Monday with the Parks and Wildlife Department and let that excitement carry her through the meal.

Afterward she decided to get the ordeal at the shrine over with and carefully dusted the urn before lighting the candles on either side for the prescribed hour.

While she waited for the time to pass, she grew restless. Kathy moved from a chair to the couch, then played with the fringe on a Mexican souvenir pillow before running a finger along the colorful satin embroidery thread of the bullfighter's cape.

Suddenly an idea began to form in her mind, and she jumped up to find the local telephone book. Over the last few years, she had lost contact with most of her friends from high school. She had been busy with her life and so had they. She found the *D*'s and looked for a name.

Shortly before seven that evening Kathy was just finishing her final makeup touches before going out to dinner. She and a group of old friends were getting together to celebrate her return to Texas, and they were going to meet at Claudio's. She had showered and put on a lightweight cotton pantsuit. Luckily it was the type that was made to look crinkly because she couldn't find Irene's iron. It wasn't with the ironing board in the laundry nook. God only knew where the woman had put it. Possibly in the freezer!

Her thoughts focused on her mystery man. He didn't look to be the type to be uncertain about where to store any of *his* possessions.

After coming to that conclusion, Kathy felt a twinge of conscience. After all, she had practically threatened him—or rather his car—and had enjoyed doing so at the time because she felt that he deserved it. But now she thought maybe she should apologize.

Kathy's eyes began to twinkle as she wondered how he would react. Would he think that she was just as odd in her behavior as his previous neighbors? Did he think that already? The longer she thought about it, the more appeal the idea came to have.

Kathy hated life to be boring.

Peter was seated in his favorite chair, his eyes closed as he listened to the hum of his personal computer in his study. It was working in tandem with its printer, busily printing out the financial reports he'd been working on since coming home from the bank. His evening was going as planned. His salad was chilling in the refrigerator; later there would be an hour of reading, then a workout at the condominium's fitness center followed by a swim; and finally he would be ready for bed. A nice quiet evening—the kind a man could revel in spending, one where he could think deeply if he wanted, or not at all. . . .

He had just given a deep sigh of contentment when his doorbell rang.

Peter sat up and looked at his watch, then at the door. Who in the world could it be? His acquaintances knew to call before they came. He was careful to live by that credo, and so were they. He frowned as the bell sounded again.

When he opened the door he saw his new neighbor.

"Hi!" Kathy said brightly, as if none of the afternoon's contretemps had happened. "I saw the light in your side window, so I knew you were in."

A thought flitted through Peter's mind about the desirability of purchasing blackout curtains. He remained standing in the doorway.

She was not put off by his unfriendly stance. "I was just getting ready to go out, but I wanted to come over and apologize."

"Whatever for?" Peter asked.

"For this afternoon. I was just getting settled in, and I'm afraid I was a bit short-tempered."

"Don't worry about it," he said, hoping that she would go away. His day had been disrupted enough; he didn't need the evening to follow suit—and from the same cause. The outfit she was wearing fit her body loosely, but his imagination had no trouble filling in the rest. He tried to stop them, but his thoughts took on a life of their own.

37

"Oh, but I do," she contradicted him.

Her eyes were the clearest blue he ever remembered seeing. Maybe it was that halo of curling blond hair arranged attractively around her face. A wisp of her light, flowery perfume made its way to his nose. He shifted position.

"And I don't want you to worry about the camera," she continued. "I've found one. A friend is going to loan me hers."

"Great," he murmured.

Kathy stood there for another moment, a smile curving her lips.

Peter wasn't immune to the fact that she was very pretty. Her nose was a delicate line, her cheekbones were high and classically set, her brows had a natural arch, her mouth was the kind that invited a man's kisses. But something—maybe it was the spark of devilish fun in her eyes—protected her from any form of artificiality.

Peter gave his head a quick unconscious shake. What was the matter with him? Was he hallucinating? It had to be that he was hungry. He had skipped a formal lunch today to work on the program that the printer was now spewing out. To help convince him of the cause, his stomach rumbled.

His neighbor giggled softly. She had heard the sound.

"Maybe I should let you get back to your dinner," she said.

"I wasn't eating," he returned stiffly. He wasn't accustomed to having his personal habits examined—especially not by nosey neighbors who were barely more than half his age.

"Then maybe you should," she suggested seriously,

but there was that devil deep in her eyes. He was almost positive that she was enjoying teasing him!

Color rose in Peter's cheeks. It was a habit he hated —one he thought he had outgrown. But obviously he had not. At least not when he was being laughed at.

"If you'll excuse me," he said stiltedly, indicating with a slight movement of the door that he wished to terminate their meeting.

Kathy did not seem to notice. "What's your name? It's not fair that I don't know yours when you know mine."

Peter knew that if he didn't satisfy her curiosity, she would ask every time she saw him. And he couldn't become a hermit in his rooms.

"My name is Peter—Peter Maxwell."

"It's nice to know you, Peter."

Peter murmured a cool reply and this time was successful in shutting the door.

But he wasn't so successful in shutting her out of his thoughts, and the sole part of his earlier plans for the evening that materialized was his workout—which only seemed to be helpful when he was able to release some of his pent-up tension on the Nautilus machines.

Kathy didn't think of Peter at all that evening. She put him completely out of her mind while she enjoyed her reunion with her friends and caught up on all their news—what they were doing with their lives and so on. It wasn't until she was climbing the stairs sometime around midnight that thoughts of her neighbor returned. And then she childishly stuck out her tongue at his door. It was funny how someone could be so physically appealing and such a pompous pig otherwise. She began to wonder if the Sinclairs just might have known what they were doing concerning him. Still, he was very attractive. . . .

Kathy spent Sunday exploring a wider expanse of the area, renewing additional memories from long ago. She made the short drive to Galveston Island, rode the ferry to Bolivar and back, then returned to the mainland by way of the old highway, which passed through some of the small towns nestled along the bay that she remembered from years past.

When she returned to the condominiums, she saw nothing of her neighbor—not that she actively looked for him again or anything. . . .

The next day Kathy was to start work, so she spent the greater part of Sunday night with butterflies playing tag in her stomach. The fluttering hordes had not abated in any way by morning as she ran a brush through her hair before securing it in a single french braid down her back. To some people her choice of clothing for a first day on the job might seem strange: a tan pair of shorts, a lightweight T-shirt, and a good, sturdy pair of wading shoes. But Kathy knew she needed to be prepared to go into the field that day, and these were the clothes that were appropriate. If she came to work more formally attired, her colleagues might get the wrong impression. They might wonder if they had made a mistake in hiring her. And she didn't want that. She wanted to meet them on their own terms and become accepted by them as quickly as possible.

She stared into the mirror a moment longer, trying to bolster her confidence. *I'm good at what I've chosen to do with my life,* she told herself. She had been an excellent student. And if, for the moment, she couldn't remember the difference between a crustacean and a fish, her memory lapse could be blamed only on nervousness. She just hoped her temporary amnesia would disappear as she drove the short distance to the Seabrook Marine Institute where she was assigned.

Her eyes were large as they stared into their reflected image. She, Kathy Stevens, was about to embark on her life's work. She was all grown up now. For fleeting seconds memories of herself as a young child, as a preadolescent, as a teen, played on the screen in her mind. Looking back, she felt as if she had only blinked a few times and years had gone by. Was she ready to do this? Didn't she sometimes still feel too young and unsure?

Then self-doubt vanished as she lifted her chin and straightened her shoulders.

She could do anything. Jason had taught her that. And this was what she wanted to do: to work in the out-of-doors in her beloved coastal area. What more could she desire?

Kathy turned from the mirror and gathered her keys and purse. When she closed the door to the apartment, she was whistling a happy little tune.

The world was waiting for her. It was up to her to make the first move.

She skipped down the stairs and walked energetically to her car. It was in the proper space now, and the blue BMW was parked next to it.

However, the BMW was not abandoned. Peter Maxwell was leaning just inside his open passenger door, preparing to toss his briefcase inside. He looked over at her, alerted to her presence by the scrunching sound her heavy shoes made on the paved parking area. His top lip curled to one side.

A proper Billy Idol sneer, Kathy thought in amusement. He didn't look pleased to see her, although his eyes did slide down the length of her legs before being pulled back to the task he was performing. Kathy saw the look and was pleased by it.

"Good morning," she called out cheerfully. "It's a beautiful day, isn't it?"

He murmured something in return that wasn't intelligible.

She took in the preciseness of his three-piece suit, of the way it fitted his lean, hard body. As he leaned inside the open door, the material of his pants was pulled tight over his thighs, showing some of their lithe power. She thought again of her first impression of him—that she would like to see that body set free.

When she spoke, a little of that impression filtered through, but it was heavily censored. "Don't you ever get tired of dressing like that? I think I'd die if I constantly had to be so formal."

His eyes resettled on her, and he looked as if he'd dearly love to tell her what he thought of her nosing into his affairs, but proper etiquette prevented him from doing so. "Some people have to work, Ms.—ah—" Peter cursed himself when he stumbled over her name. He didn't want to know what it was. He didn't want to know anything about her!

Kathy grinned. "Stevens. Kathy Stevens. And I realize that. What do you think I'm dressed to do?"

"If I had to make a guess, I'd say grub in the dirt," was his reply as he stood up straight.

"You're not so far off base," she returned. Then knowing that her reply had confused him, she laughed.

The happy sound played against Peter's ears. In spite of all his efforts, he was very aware of her. But she was so young! And she was so opposite to everything he held of value in his life!

He straightened his tie, just as he attempted to settle his thoughts. Her laughter was still ringing in his ears even though it had stopped. He didn't want to look at her, but he knew he must.

Her eyes were twinkling with mischief, her lips curving to expose white teeth. She was still enjoying his previous answer. Peter's breath caught momentarily in his throat. Then he steeled himself to say courteously, "Have a nice day, Ms. Stevens."

Well, at least he knows my name now! Kathy thought.

"Oh, you, too, Mr. Maxwell," she replied just as formally.

Peter felt as if he had one foot in the grave with all the "Ms. Stevenses" and "Mr. Maxwells." But it was better to leave well enough alone. He didn't need complications in his life. And he had more than an inkling that this beautiful creature standing close beside him could be a complication.

Kathy was looking at him as if she knew exactly what he was thinking. But she didn't. Oh, she knew a part. She had surmised accurately that he was feeling uneasy about their formality, but the rest she could only sense. . . .

Unsettled, Peter drew his gaze away from her and got into his car. Kathy did likewise. He waited until she had secured her seat belt and backed out before starting the process himself.

Kathy met with the director of the Institute, Dr. Clifford Smith, and after spending a short time talking with him, she was introduced to the senior biologist who would be her working partner during her initiation.

His name was Eric McMillen, and Kathy immediately felt a kinship with him. His smile was open and friendly, his gray eyes intelligent beneath a swirling mop of short blond curls. He possessed the kind of rugged, individualistic good looks that the people who make television commercials and billboard advertisements scour the country to find.

"Welcome aboard," he greeted her, shaking her hand. His touch was reassuring.

"I'm glad to be here," Kathy returned, meaning it.

Eric glanced at Dr. Smith and winked. "Don't worry, boss, I'll take good care of her."

The director studied him over the top rim of his glasses. "That's what I'm afraid of," he said solemnly. "You've lost the last two trainees I've assigned to you."

Eric laughed. It was a nice sound that came deep from within his chest. "Hey, don't scare her!"

"I wouldn't do anything like that. And I won't even mention our own variety of the Loch Ness monster. I'll let you fill her in about that."

"Thanks," Eric said, his eyes dancing.

"Don't mention it," Dr. Smith replied before shifting his gaze to Kathy, who had been looking intently from one man to the other. The director had been so serious in his office. Was he kidding her now? "It's good to have you aboard, Kathy," he continued. "If you ever have a problem you can't handle, remember: my door's always open. And watch this one." He indicated Eric. "He thinks he's God's gift to the world of women."

Eric made an immediate protest, but it fell on deaf ears as the older man walked away.

Kathy was grinning as he turned back to face her. "Loch Ness monster?" she questioned carefully.

"Our imaginary mascot," he dismissed. Then he motioned to Dr. Smith's departing back. "He's a great guy, but you have to learn when he's having fun. I haven't lost any trainees—at least not yet at any rate."

"That's reassuring," Kathy murmured.

Eric's eyes sparkled. "But I do think I'm God's gift to women. He's right about that."

"Honesty. That's what I like in people," Kathy teased.

Eric nodded approvingly. "You know, I think we're going to get along just fine. I like your style, lady."

"And I like yours."

He gave an appreciative look to her slender form, his eyes staying longer on the shapely length of her leg. "I also like the way you're made. What would you think about having a little something extra on the side?"

Kathy was accustomed to appreciative looks from men and the inevitable follow-up propositions. "No, I like myself just as I am, thank you. A few added pounds on one side of my body would make it very hard to balance."

Eric was silent a moment, absorbing what she said, then he glanced up to meet her smiling gaze. "I thought we should get that out of the way early," he confided. "Set the ground rules, so to speak."

"A good idea," Kathy agreed.

Eric's rugged features burst into a smile of friendly

camaraderie as he put an arm across her shoulders and directed her into another room. "Come on. I'll introduce you to the people who are still here. A lot are out working already, but you'll get to meet them eventually. Then we'll go into the field ourselves. Since you were sensible and came dressed for the job, we'll do some seining in some nice little estuaries I know. Doesn't that sound like fun?"

"It sure does!" Kathy answered happily.

Ten hours later Kathy wasn't so sure of the term *fun*. Every muscle in her body was screaming in protest, and she was famished. She and Eric had taken a short break for lunch somewhere around one o'clock, but she had had nothing to eat since then, and all the hard work that followed had made her ravenous.

The stairs that led to her apartment looked twice as long as they had the days before. She wasn't sure if she could make it.

She took a deep breath, put a hand on the wrought iron banister, and began to pull herself along. She had seined before at school—it had been part of her studies —but never for so many continuous hours. It seemed that she had come to the Institute at one of the busiest times of the year. They had several projects going at the same time, and each required extra attention from the employees. Therefore, some of the regular jobs were being covered by a handful of others—like raw recruits and the people unlucky enough to draw them.

She thought of Eric. Her first impression of him had been correct. She liked him. He had an unfailing positiveness about his work and about life in general that made accompanying him easy. Nothing seemed to get

46

him down. He was always ready with a joke or a quick remark that made the bone-crunching work of the day pass more quickly.

She remembered his approval when she didn't complain, even though there had been a time toward the end of the day when she had almost wanted to cry when he told her that there was yet another spot to be checked. The brotherly clap on her shoulder she had earned upon their return to the Institute had made her silence well worthwhile.

Kathy shivered as she neared the top of the stairs. The sun was low in the sky. The day was nearly done. The wind had picked up from the bay, and her clothes were wet.

The type of seining they had done today involved one person's getting chest deep into the water and holding onto a large pole that was attached to a sixty foot long net while the other person remained in the skiff holding onto the opposite pole. The wader and the skiff moved for a certain prescribed distance, and then the net was hauled back into the small boat where the crabs, shrimp, fish, and whatever were carefully sorted, identified, and counted, with records filled out accordingly.

Of course she and Eric had taken turns going into the water. In between, their clothes had been dried by the sun. But the last time had been her turn, and she had remained damp. Her shoes squished with each step she took.

She was at the top of the stairs, just about to find enough energy to finish covering the remaining distance to her apartment, when the familiar creaking noise of the opposite door drew her attention. She turned toward the sound.

Peter Maxwell was dressed for sport—or at least that was the impression he gave. But to Kathy's tired eyes he still looked perfectly turned out. Did the man ever sweat? His shorts—with their perfect creases—were a dazzling white; his white polo shirt must never have seen a particle of dust. His tennis shoes were either brand-new or they somehow floated above the muck and grime that other people had to put up with while walking. Even the sports bag he carried somehow gave the impression that it repelled dirt instead of attracting it.

He came to an abrupt halt when he saw her, his handsome features quickly becoming a careful blank after a momentary look of shock.

At the moment Kathy didn't feel like dealing with him. She would much rather have limped into her apartment and collapsed into a hot tub of water. But it didn't seem that she had much of a choice.

"Hello again," she greeted, her usual exuberance missing. She felt his eyes examine her. Her exhausted smile became wry.

A reply seemed drawn from him.

"When I said you were dressed to go grub in the dirt, I didn't really expect you to do it!"

"I told you, you were close. Only in this case it was mud . . . and water."

"Good God," he murmured beneath his breath.

Some hairs had come loose from Kathy's french braid and were curling about her face, tickling her nose. She pushed them back, attempting to get them out of the way. She realized she must look a sight, but wasn't he being just a little too fastidious?

"I've spent the day counting fish," she explained.

48

Peter Maxwell groaned inside himself. Was he destined to live next door to a pack of loonies?

"Interesting," he commented.

She looked like nothing more than a drowned rat, standing there shivering in the wind. A spark of chivalry lighted in Peter's chest. Maybe he should offer her something warm to drink while trying to find out exactly what had happened to her. But the small spark was quickly doused. If he was to remain true to his convictions, he couldn't do that. He glanced at his watch as if he were in a hurry to leave.

This time Kathy took the hint and immediately got out of the way.

Without another word her neighbor started down the stairs, leaving her to watch his athletic descent.

For a moment, forgetting everything but her tired state, Kathy wanted to yell out to him that, yes, it *was* interesting—that working for the state Parks and Wildlife Department was the most exciting thing she could think of, that today had been her first day on her new job and she was exhausted, but that she also knew she had handled herself well and made a good impression! But he was gone before the first word could form on her lips.

CHAPTER THREE

Kathy let herself into her apartment and flicked on the light. The myriad of dog pictures and ribbons greeted her. Somehow they weren't so alien now. But she still planned to take them down when she had enough time and energy—which she didn't have either of at the moment.

She went straight into the bathroom, disrobed, and practically fell into a tub of hot water.

Ah, bliss! she thought as she scooted down and dipped her head under the water for several seconds.

Kathy stayed in the bath for a long time, reheating the water whenever it started to cool. Finally, though, her desire for food began to outweigh her need for relaxation, and she climbed wearily out of the tub, wrapping herself up in a big terry cloth robe.

After putting a cup of water in the microwave for coffee, she opened a can of vegetable soup and made herself a tuna sandwich.

After eating dinner, she tidied up and put her dirty clothing in the washing machine. Then she rinsed her shoes as best she could in the tub and left them sitting on top of the clothes hamper to dry. She knew they wouldn't be ready to wear tomorrow morning, but that didn't matter since she would probably spend most of her time seining and they would just get soaked all over again. Wet shoes was a small price to pay for not getting your feet cut on oyster shells or debris or, better yet, suffering the pain of stepping on a sting ray.

The hour was still fairly early, but she knew she wouldn't be going out again, so she changed into a cotton sleep shirt. All she planned to do with the rest of the evening was light the candles, dust Frederick—she planned to keep her word scrupulously—and watch television until the hour of homage was over; then she would be off to bed and, she hoped, more sleep than she had been able to manage the night before.

She was sitting on the couch, all warm and cozy, when she heard a knock at her door.

Kathy jumped, the invasion of sound into the relative quietness of the room startling her. She leapt to her feet and started to the door, but she held back before opening it, caution exerting itself.

"Yes?" she called. "Who is it?"

"Peter Maxwell," came the surprising reply.

Kathy was shocked. She started to pull the door open and then happened to look down at what she was wearing. It wasn't exactly the sexiest thing around, but he was always so formal. And she didn't want to be at a disadvantage once again.

"What is it? I'm dressed for bed."

There was a moment of silence, then Peter said matter-of-factly, "You have a flat tire. I thought you'd want to know."

"A flat?" Kathy repeated, more to herself than to him. She hadn't noticed a problem while driving her car earlier. It must have happened later—after she parked.

"Yes."

51

"Oh, dear!"

There was another hesitation, then, "I just thought I should warn you."

Before she could say anything, she heard him walk away, then the squeaking sound of his door being opened and closed.

Warn her—translate that into: *You're on your own, kid!*

Kathy said good-bye to sleep for the next hour or so. She knew the basic principle involved in changing a tire, but she'd never done it.

Giving a deep sigh, she walked into her room and slipped on a pair of jeans, found her moccasins, then unbuttoned the sleep shirt a few buttons from the bottom and tied the tail into a knot at her waist. The sooner she got on with the job, the better.

A few moments later Kathy was surveying the car. Under the glow of a nearby floodlight it looked something like a sleek panther that had been wounded in its left rear leg. She stared at the flat helplessly, admitting that understanding the basic principles of tire changing and applying that understanding were two *very* different things. She didn't know what to do! Then she remembered the owner's manual that was tucked safely in the car's glove compartment. It gave instructions for everything!

Kathy pulled the booklet free and spent the next few seconds searching through the index and the text for the proper pages.

There it is! Everything was spelled out—with pictures even! Only as she read through the steps, the situation got a little more complicated. Did she have aluminum wheels or steel? That seemed to be important to know.

And there were so many bold-typed **Cautions** not to be overlooked.

She walked to the rear of the car, found the emergency tire hidden in its compartment along with the rest of the paraphernalia that she would need, and moved back to the stricken tire.

She sank to her knees and began. After several false starts Kathy succeeded in getting the car raised and the wheel nuts loosened. She felt ridiculously proud.

She was just examining the emergency tire—the booklet warned that it was to be used only for traveling short distances—and the canister of compressed gas that would inflate it when she became aware of a presence behind her.

Kathy turned to see who it was. When she met Peter Maxwell's intense gaze, she turned back to what she was doing. She said nothing.

A minute passed. She used the time to fit the emergency tire in place.

Finally he said, "I came to see if I could help." He sounded as if it were against his better judgment.

Kathy located the wheel nuts she had removed moments before. "I'm doing all right," she dismissed him.

"I can see that."

She looked in the booklet to check the procedural order it recommended to replace the nuts.

He spoke again. "If you put that on, it will just be a waste of time."

Kathy sat back on her heels and directed another look at him. He was still dressed in his pristine whites, with not a hair out of place. Her answer was dry. "Do you have a better suggestion? This is the only spare tire I see around here."

A glimmer of a smile touched his mouth, and Kathy almost gaped. He was smiling? Him? At her?

"I agree. But if you put that spare on and inflate it, you're just going to have to take it off again tomorrow when your regular tire is repaired. Plus you'll have to replace the gas canister."

"I still don't see a solution."

"I'll drive you to a service station so you can get the tire repaired tonight."

"Is one open?" she asked.

"I know one that is."

"They'll repair the tire tonight?"

"We can ask."

She tilted her head. "And you don't mind doing this?"

"I wouldn't offer if I did."

Kathy didn't fully believe that. Otherwise, why had he left her to it for so long? He hadn't wanted to help her originally. Had his conscience made him do it? A long-forgotten urge to help a damsel in distress?

A slow smile came to play on Kathy's mouth.

Damsels in distress were usually totally incompetent —putting themselves into situations that they had to be helped out of, all the while giving absolutely no assistance to their rescuer. She examined her handiwork. She almost had the job completed—all on her own. But what the man said was true. The booklet did warn that the canister would have to be replaced, and doing that would take time, not to mention money.

"All right," she agreed at last. "Will you wait while I get my purse?"

"I'll be right here."

54

She began to gather up the equipment she had used, but he stopped her by touching her shoulder.

"I'll take care of this," he offered.

The unexpected contact caused a curling sensation in the pit of Kathy's stomach. She hadn't known that he was moving closer; he did it so silently! And she was very much aware of him—of the charged sensation that reached from his body to hers. Of the muscular, masculine legs that his shorts revealed and that were so close to her now. Only she wasn't sure if the feeling was mutual. The first time they had touched, when they shook hands, she thought she had been the only one to feel the electricity. Was it happening that way again? She looked up at him. His features gave nothing away. His sherry-colored eyes were carefully noncommittal.

An eon of time must have gone by. Had he noticed? He didn't seem to, she decided, so as quickly as she could she murmured the reply that was expected of her. "Thanks. I won't be long."

"No problem," he said easily, and knelt to make good on his promise.

Kathy ran along the sidewalk and up the stairs to her apartment. She wasn't sleepy any longer. Not a bit. The charged feeling she had absorbed from her contact with him still remained, and she wasn't sure how much longer it would be before she came back to normal. But in the future—at least for the next couple of hours—she would be careful to be more adept at covering her emotions. Longer than that, she couldn't guarantee.

After extinguishing Frederick's candles she collected her purse from the top of an end table and made sure that she had enough cash to pay the gas station attendant.

Peter sat rather uncomfortably in one of the chairs provided by the service station for people who were waiting for their cars. The smell of oil and gasoline was pervasive in the small room. A calendar espousing a certain brand of spark plugs along with the physical attributes of a pretty girl was tacked on the wall, while varying sizes of engine belts, a clipboard, and several sets of keys were hung on hooks nearby.

He let his glance move to his neighbor as she cranked the handle on a gumball machine. They had been here for at least twenty minutes, and she had spoken barely a word.

"We shouldn't have to wait too much longer," he remarked, trying to reassure her—or was it himself?

Kathy came over to him and offered him a choice of the gumballs she held in her palm.

Peter found himself taking one. As he crunched into the sweet ball, memories of his childhood flooded over him. He shook the remembrances away.

"I really appreciate this," Kathy murmured quietly.

He shrugged.

Kathy looked around the small room. It was not exactly the sort of place she would have expected her neighbor to be familiar with. But then he probably didn't know a thing about the working of a car's engine, so he would need help—just like herself.

Restlessly Kathy walked to the large glass window that looked out onto the pumping islands and the highway beyond. Several cars were being serviced with gasoline.

Peter watched her, his eyes dropping the length of her body, taking in the slim curves of her back and waist, the trim firmness of her derriere, and the long shapeliness of her legs. When she turned, he quickly looked away.

Kathy hesitated a second before sitting in the only other available chair, which was at his side. Normally she was never at a loss for words, but ever since their earlier contact she was uneasy about what to say to him.

"I really do appreciate this," she said, repeating her earlier statement.

"That's what a neighbor's for," he returned.

Kathy latched onto the topic like a person near drowning. "Have you ever helped the Sinclairs?" she inquired.

Peter gave a short laugh. "Not if I can avoid it."

"Then why help me?"

He shifted uncomfortably. "How should I know?" he answered gruffly. "Maybe you bring out the protector in me."

His last remark was made so sarcastically that Kathy frowned. "And you don't like that?" she asked.

Peter said nothing. All his life he had functioned on the idea that people had to look out for themselves because if they didn't, no one else would. But occasionally he had found himself waiving that philosophy—only never when it affected him personally. And this very definitely was affecting him personally.

Kathy was about to say something more when the station attendant came into the cramped room.

"Got it," he said gruffly. "You'd picked up a nail. Big sucker!" He measured it with his fingers.

"Is the tire all right?" Kathy questioned.

"Sure. Right as rain. That'll be . . ." He named a price, and Kathy opened her purse to pay him.

The drive back to the complex was as silent as the ride over. Again Kathy was stricken with an unusual loss of animation. Once, one of her friends had laughingly told her that she could easily strike up a conversation with a fence post if she tried hard enough. But not now. There was absolutely nothing in her head.

Peter parked his car next to hers. Kathy jumped out almost before the car stopped. She was ready to roll the tire over to her car as soon as her neighbor opened the trunk. But he wouldn't let her do it. He hefted the thick tire himself and carried it over to the stricken car. Kathy was then relegated to the sidelines to watch as he finished the project she had started.

When he was done, he dusted his hands and looked at her as if expecting her approval.

Kathy had mixed feelings. She could have done it. She knew she could have. But if she stated that now, she would look ungrateful. And he *had* taken the time to help her get her tire repaired so that she wouldn't have to worry about it tomorrow.

She summoned a grateful smile.

Peter was beginning to wish that he had listened to his first instinct and not come down. When she smiled at him like that, it was so easy to forget his convictions.

"What do I owe you?" she asked, not expecting him to take her up on her offer but doing it out of the politeness Ashley had taught her.

The question startled Peter. Several answers flitted into his mind, but he immediately censored them.

"Not a thing." Maybe what he was feeling was just a momentary weakness, something that would pass in the night. He certainly didn't want any further contact with her. Tonight had been enough—more than enough.

They walked upstairs and separated at the balcony. Neither said more than a rather casual good night.

Peter spent the next day trying to apply himself to his work at the bank. As a senior vice-president he had many duties that cried out for his attention and to which he had always given his all. He had worked his way up in the ranks from teller to the position he held now in a remarkably short time. He knew he had the reputation of being a hotshot, and he was proud of that fact. His career meant everything to him.

That's why he was so shaken to find himself thinking of his neighbor on several occasions that day. He remembered the rounded slimness of her body, the way her hair framed her face, the blueness of her eyes, the curving invitation of her lips. . . .

He stopped himself. There had been no invitation on her lips. That was just his fantasy. And it had to stop. His job came first in his life. He had made that decision a long time ago, and he wasn't going to ruin his future for a pretty little fruitcake with a nice body. His life was structured—planned—and he very much wanted it to go on that way. The sensual side of his nature could be appeased very easily. He had never found it difficult to attract the kind of woman he wanted. The kind who wouldn't cling or get emotional. The kind he could have a brief relationship with one day and forget about the next.

Peter forced himself to read the bottom line of an accounting sheet for what had to be the tenth time, and finally, this time he began to make sense of it.

Things in Kathy's life were progressing satisfactorily. She was totally in love with her job and felt that she was doing well. At least Eric seemed to approve of the work she was doing and underlined his growing trust in her ability by letting her have more responsibility as the days passed.

She was too tired Friday to go out with her friends after work, but she made up for that loss the night after. Then Sunday after lunch, with the aid of the borrowed camera, she took photographs of Frederick's pictures and ribbons and exchanged their layout with one of her own but kept the shrine intact.

Kathy had always loved color and movement, and that part of the room now reflected her taste. Only once she accomplished the minor renovation, she was vaguely dissatisfied. She still liked her keepsakes, but something was wrong and she didn't know what to do to make it right—what to leave up, what to take down. She studied her surroundings a bit longer and then gave up. At least the effect was comfortable—familiar. Maybe later she would be able to tell what it was that was bothering her. And it wasn't Frederick's shrine. That was something else altogether; she was actually becoming a bit fond of the dog, or rather his memory.

She collapsed on the couch and hugged the pillow boasting the embroidered bullfighter. Shortly she was going to have to start getting ready for an open house-type benefit that the local Chamber of Commerce was sponsoring. All the employees of the Institute had been strongly advised to put in an appearance because the money earned from the showing and sale of a well-known wildlife artist's drawings were going to help fund a new preserve along the coast. But she didn't have to get ready yet. She still had some time. The benefit was scheduled from five to nine, and it was just a little after three.

Kathy stared at the ceiling for a few minutes, still experiencing a vague sort of restlessness. Then her head rolled toward the door. She hadn't seen her neighbor since Monday. Was he out of town? Or was he trying to avoid her? If the latter were true, Kathy felt hurt. She wasn't accustomed to having people purposefully keep out of her way. But then he was an odd sort of duck, as Iris would say.

Her lips began to twitch. She wondered what *he* would say if he knew that she considered him odd. Probably laugh in her face. But he had been nice that one time. He had gone out of his way to help her even if he hadn't exactly wanted to.

Kathy's fingers smoothed the glossy threads of the bullfighter's hat. Maybe she should pay him a little call.

The twitch became a smile. He would probably welcome that occurrence as happily as he would receive a visit from the Sinclairs. She could just imagine the look on his face.

She decided to do it.

Soft music drifted onto the balcony from the apartment opposite her own. Kathy heard it as she made her way across the space that separated them. At least he was home.

She didn't hesitate. She stepped up to his door and rang the bell.

Peter didn't hear his doorbell at first. He was busy. Soft lips were yielding to his, and a curving breast was coming to life at the touch of his hand. Then the sound

61

penetrated. Slowly he lifted his head. Cat-green eyes looked sleepily into his as Veronica's dark hair contrasted the fawn-colored fabric of his couch. She was nestled in the crook of his arm.

"Are you expecting someone?" he managed to say, huskily.

"Darling . . . we're in your apartment," she reminded him smoothly.

That was what he liked about Veronica. She was always so cool and sophisticated. Nothing seemed to ruffle her. She was the perfect woman for a man in his position. She wasn't his mistress yet, but she could be.

"Then I guess I'd better see who it is," he murmured, extracting himself from his position on the couch.

He ran a smoothing hand over his hair before opening the door.

Kathy had decided not to let him close the door in her face again. When it opened, she scooted right in, using his moment of startled bewilderment to her advantage. She didn't notice the woman seated on the far side of the room.

"I thought maybe you'd moved," she began brightly. "I haven't seen you all week."

Peter was rendered speechless. All he could do was look at her. She was already in the apartment before he could react to prevent her entrance.

She was looking at him, with those big blue eyes, and he felt a pull toward her that he was beginning to associate only with her—one that involved more than just his body. One that was different from the purely physical sensations he had been sharing with Veronica a moment before. Veronica! His gaze switched quickly to the other woman. Amusement was written on her beautiful features. He looked back at Kathy.

Kathy saw him swallow. "Have I caught you at a bad time?" She asked the question with pretended innocence because nothing would please her more. She enjoyed irritating him.

"Darling"—a low feminine purr caused Kathy to turn—"aren't you going to introduce us?"

Kathy's entire body swiveled until she could see the dark-haired beauty who was languishing on the low-backed couch. Her green eyes looked to be rimmed with naturally dark lashes; her skin was the color and texture of porcelain. She exuded sophistication and experience. She was everything Kathy was not.

Kathy thought fast and then acted. She had wanted to disturb Peter but not like this! She walked with pretended confidence to the woman and held out her hand.

"I'm Peter's neighbor, Kathy Stevens."

The only way to get through this unfortunate situation was to act as if there was no reason to be embarrassed—which there wasn't, if you discounted her rude entrance into the apartment.

Kathy glanced at her neighbor. He still looked stunned. He wasn't going to be much help. The two women would have to see this through themselves.

"And I'm Peter's . . . friend," the woman responded with a proprietary edge, "Veronica Randolph."

She held up her hand and gave Kathy the oddest return salute: her first two fingers allowed themselves to be enfolded in Kathy's. It was something royalty might do but didn't dare. Kathy would rather have shaken hands with a snake!

"I'm apartment sitting for the people next door," she

explained. "Have you ever met the Sinclairs?" She asked the question to fill in time. It would be humiliating to run for cover too soon.

"No, I'm afraid I haven't."

"They're a very nice couple," Kathy continued. She was aware of Peter Maxwell coming to life behind her. She thought he might have coughed, or was he strangling? She didn't turn around to investigate.

"Relatives of yours?" the beautiful Veronica asked politely.

Kathy gave a soft laugh, one she hoped sounded tolerably amused. "Oh, heavens no. I'm just a friend of a friend of a friend."

"That sounds complicated," Veronica replied, her boredom showing openly now.

"Not really," Kathy concluded. Then she turned back to her neighbor. Enough conversation had passed for her to know instinctively that she didn't like the woman he obviously did like. But that was his business, not hers. Now all she had to do was say something—almost anything—and she could leave.

"I was just curious to see if you were home, Peter. When I was looking in my mailbox today, I overheard some people talking about an apartment that had been burglarized. If you weren't home, I was going to keep an eye on your place. Kind of an apartment Neighborhood Watch program, if you know what I mean."

Had that been too much? When she got going, sometimes she *really* got going!

Peter's eyes said he didn't believe what she was saying, but blessedly he didn't give her away. That was the second nice thing he had done for her.

"That's a good idea," he said huskily. "But, as you can see, I'm here."

"Yes." Then, forcing more brightness, she turned to his friend. "It was nice meeting you, but now I have to leave. There are some things I have to get ready for work tomorrow."

"You count fish, I believe," Peter commented softly as he opened the door.

Forget the last nice thing! That erased it! "Yes," Kathy replied, smiling through her teeth, "I do."

"You what?" Veronica questioned, her ears sharp.

Kathy paused. She didn't like having to explain her work to this woman, but she was being forced to. It was either that or have her think that she worked in a fish market—which wasn't something beneath her to do. It was just that since she had the credentials, she was not going to hide them.

"I work for the Texas Parks and Wildlife Department. We do surveys of the aquatic life along the coast. Tomorrow I'm going to start tagging shrimp."

"How awful!" the woman said.

Kathy gritted her teeth harder. She started to stamp across the balcony, back into her own preserves, but Peter stopped her.

"So that's why you were soaked to the skin the other day."

Kathy glared at him. "Yes."

Then she did cross the narrow strip of concrete that separated their apartments. She hoped that she did it regally, but she knew that she hadn't. There wasn't a regal bone in her body.

Kathy closed the door to her apartment with restrained fury. "How awful!" the woman had said. "How

65

awful!" Kathy mimicked. She'd like to take her along and tag *her!*

She continued her march into the bedroom where she threw herself across the bed. *Oh, she's so sleek and sure. So . . . so . . .* Kathy grabbed a pillow and punched it square in its stomach—if it had a stomach—which wasn't the stomach she wanted to punch. She had been so superior. How could Peter want to have anything to do with a woman like that? *Slimy, that's what she is!*

Then, when she realized how absurd what she had just done was, Kathy started to giggle. Her mind played back the entire scene. Peter had looked so funny standing there as if he had been struck dumb!

Tears of laughter came into Kathy's eyes. She was still smiling to herself some minutes later when she stepped into the shower.

CHAPTER FOUR

At the last moment before leaving for the benefit Kathy decided to call a friend. She didn't feel like being alone tonight. She needed reinforcement, and she had no idea when Eric would show up, if at all—even in the face of the direct hint from the director. Eric marched to his own drum, so she couldn't count on him. Toni, though, was always ready for a good time and immediately agreed.

They arrived at the yacht club where the benefit was taking place just before six. The glassed-in room that faced the lake was already crowded, and people were dressed in their best. Kathy glanced down at the dress she had chosen to wear—a soft, rather clingy fabric in a bright shade of pink—and was glad that she had taken extra care with her appearance. She had really enjoyed the excuse to apply her makeup with a more liberal hand and to experiment with her hairstyle.

Toni, with her dark hair and dark eyes, immediately secured a glass of wine for each of them from the waiter who was moving easily among the guests with a tray. She began to sip hers, while Kathy held on to her glass as a prop.

"This is quite a do," Toni whispered, her eyes wide as

she took in the presence of some of the town's leading citizens.

"It's suppose to be," Kathy returned.

Toni giggled. "Are you going to buy a drawing?"

"Are you kidding?" Kathy kept her voice low. "I'm lending them my beauty—that's all I can afford."

Toni giggled again. Then she waved to a friend she spotted in a group a short distance away.

"Did you ever meet Michael Zoras? He moved here around the time you left for Florida."

Kathy surveyed the unknown faces. She was slowly shaking her head when a laugh caused her gaze to swivel slightly to the right. So Eric *had* come. He was standing with Dr. Smith and several of the other people from the Institute.

"Why don't you come meet him now?" Toni was saying. "I'm sure he'd like that. He appreciates beauty."

Kathy gave her friend a wry look and smiled. "Then why don't you go keep him entertained?"

Toni grinned. "I might just do that."

"Good. Because I have to put in an appearance myself. That's my boss over there. I'd better let him know I'm here."

Toni followed the direction of her glance and nodded. "I'll introduce you to Michael later."

"Great," Kathy said as the two women parted.

When Kathy approached her colleagues, Eric was the first to see her. He whistled softly.

"Zounds, woman! I barely recognized you. Is this the same person I work with every day? Not that you're not nice to look at normally," he quickly backpedaled, "but this!"

Everyone chuckled at Eric's uninhibited reaction.

Kathy smilingly turned the compliment back on her partner. "You're not so bad yourself, Eric." She let her gaze sweep over him in his unaccustomed suit before teasingly adding, "Especially with your knobby knees not showing."

"My knees aren't knobby!" he immediately denied with pretended umbrage, which drew protests from the rest of the group.

Finally Eric began to laugh, and small talk ensued until Dr. Smith suggested that they mingle.

Kathy moved over to the group that Toni had become a part of. She didn't see that another person had also joined them until she was practically face to face with Peter Maxwell.

He was talking with a woman—not the one that had been in his apartment—and he was unaware of her arrival. This suited Kathy just fine because she had to try to recover from a double shock: first, that he was here—at the benefit; and second, that if she had thought him attractive before, it was nothing compared with how he looked now. Before, his apparel had always been neat and absolutely correct, whether he was in a business suit or dressed for sport. But now, in a more formal mode of dress, surrounded by others who were equally well dressed, he was absolutely devastating. His hair was combed smoothly; his features shown to perfection. The cut of his dark jacket lovingly followed the lines of his body. He was far and away the most handsome man in the room. And she wasn't the only one who thought so. The woman he was talking to was almost drooling. Every time he smiled down at her, Kathy could see that the woman's knees practically gave way.

69

And Toni was looking at him as if he were a piece of cake that she would just love to devour.

Then he looked up and caught Kathy's shocked gaze. His eyes mirrored the exact same feeling.

Peter heard the woman continue to talk to him, but he couldn't decipher her words. The room was suddenly closing in on him, yet at the same time falling away, until he and Kathy were the only two people left in it.

As if in slow motion, with the background noise suddenly muted, his gaze went over her. No longer did she look the flighty teen-ager dressed in shorts and loose shirts and immaturity. She had evolved into a young woman—one of the most beautiful creatures he had ever seen. Her skin was soft and golden, her delicate features haunting, her eyes twin pools of fathomless blue. . . .

Not a muscle of Peter's face changed. He gave away nothing of what he was feeling. And then slowly the room returned to normal.

Kathy's attention was demanded by Toni, who leaned close and whispered, "Who, my dear friend, is that? Are you keeping a secret from me?"

Kathy tried to smile. She wasn't successful until she was able to drag her eyes away from the man who so dominated the room.

"Who—who are you talking about?" she asked breathlessly. Slowly her heart was returning to a more regular pace, the blood slowing in its reckless assault on her veins.

"That man!" Toni replied rather impatiently. "The one you were looking at and who was looking at you. My God, I've read about things like that happening, but

I've never seen it, or experienced it. *Two pair of eyes meet across a crowded room—*" she quoted.

"Oh, him?" Kathy chose to ignore the last part of her friend's comment.

"Yes, *him!*"

"He's—ah—he's my neighbor."

At that reply Toni took her aside. When they were alone, standing next to a drawing of a crane, she observed, "Surely that's not all he is. You two didn't even speak . . . well, not verbally at any rate."

Kathy didn't want to answer. She moved to take a closer look at the drawing. Toni followed her.

"Isn't this nice?" Kathy asked, trying to keep her vision focused on the bird and not on Peter. She could sense that he was looking at her again.

"Yes, it is. But you're not going to change the subject so easily. I've known you for years, Kathy Stevens. We even shared boyfriends in high school. You owe me. And if he's just a neighbor, why can't he keep his eyes off you?"

Kathy shrugged. "That's all he is. I'm sorry to disappoint you."

"I don't believe it."

"Well, you're going to have to, because that's all he is." She paused, then said, "Now drop it, Toni. Leave it be."

She moved on to the next drawing, and Toni reluctantly followed. "If you weren't my friend, I'd—I'd—" She couldn't find the words she wanted.

Kathy laughed softly, trying to contain her emotions as well as her friend's. "You'd mind your own business," she completed for her.

Toni breathed deeply, her dark eyes flashing, then the

71

humor of the situation caught up with her and she smiled. "You're right. Sometimes I do get carried away." She glanced over her shoulder toward the man who was now talking to another group of people. "Would you introduce me?"

"I thought you were going to introduce me to Michael."

"You want to meet him?"

Anything was better than having to continue to stand there. Or to have to talk with Peter at that moment.

"Of course."

Toni shook her head. "Personally, I'd much prefer to meet your neighbor, but since I promised . . ."

"You're a good friend, Toni," Kathy assured her.

"Why do I have the feeling that I'm being used?" Tony was not easily fooled.

"Because you are." Kathy twisted the truth a little. "I want to meet Michael."

And she did meet Michael, who seemed more than pleased to meet her. But all the while she was aware of Peter. Of the suave way he moved about the crowd, stopping to chat with one group or another, seemingly unaware of the reaction he was causing among the women he favored to speak to.

Peter worked the crowd. It was part of his job. The bank was a major sponsor of the event in cooperation with the Chamber of Commerce, and it was his duty to mingle. But all the while he was moving from one group to the next, he kept an eye on Kathy. He saw when she was introduced to a swarthy young man that some women would find attractive. He saw how the man had definitely found her attractive. He noticed how other men noticed her, with her sweet freshness, her open friendliness, her special beauty.

Finally they could no longer avoid speaking to each other. The woman Kathy had been with for most of the evening saw to that. Toni presented herself before him —Kathy hanging back—and said, "I understand that you and Kathy are neighbors."

Peter flashed Kathy a glance. "Yes," he agreed.

"My name is Antoinette de Angelo. 'Toni' for short."

Kathy felt more than a little uncomfortable in this situation, but she was aware of Toni's speculative gaze and overcame her unease enough to finish the introduction.

"Toni, this is Peter Maxwell."

Peter took her friend's proffered hand, then turned his attention to Kathy. "I didn't expect to see you here," he said, his voice husky.

"I didn't either," Kathy responded, then stumbled on, trying to clarify her meaning, "—expect you, I mean."

Peter's smile increased. "Do you like wildlife paintings? Or does this have something to do with your work?" he asked.

Kathy started to answer, but her reply was cut short by Eric, who came up to her side and planted a quick kiss on the back of her hand, clowning as usual.

"My love," he began in imitation of a bad movie actor, ignoring the people she was standing with, "you're going to have to take me away from all this." He dropped the imitation and added seriously, "Either that or I'm going to freak out. Come on, haven't you had enough?"

Kathy had had more than enough. She gave a soft

giggle even though she didn't feel very up tempo. Now she could add another choice to her list of career possibilities: actress. "I certainly have. Toni, have you?"

Something in her plea must have gotten through to her friend because Toni immediately agreed. Then she ruined it by saying to Peter, "Why don't we all leave? I'll rustle up something to eat at my place, and we can all relax."

Peter's smile had become rather tight.

"No, thank you. I have to stay." His eyes met Kathy's.

Kathy looked quickly away. She didn't look back as Eric hustled her from the crowded room.

The next day was difficult for Kathy. Not only did she and Eric count, measure, and identify the various creatures they found in the seining net, but they also began to tag each shrimp they found, a process that involved slipping a four inch long plastic streamer through the crustacean's tail—leaving two inches on either side—so that later, when the shrimp was recaught, a study could be made as to how far the creature had moved, how fast it had moved, and most important, what portion of mortality existed among the season's hatch. The process was not complicated, but it did take time and care—especially when she hadn't felt up to the day to begin with. As a result she came home that night more exhausted than at any time in the previous week.

But she also brought something with her: a sea anemone that had been caught in one of their hauls. She had kept it in one of the aerated containers they used for the shrimp that were put aside for tagging. The anemone was so beautiful she wanted it to be the first contribu-

74

tion to the saltwater aquarium she was planning to start. However, in the beginning it would have to spend some time in someone else's aquarium—the process involved in stabilizing her own would take several weeks at the very least. After she showered and changed into dry clothing, she was going to call and find someone who wouldn't mind a temporary addition to their tank, then she would set about collecting her own equipment. Originally she hadn't planned to do that for a couple of weeks yet. She had wanted more time to settle in. But life always seemed to have a habit of taking her by surprise, and she had learned to adjust.

She left the sea anemone on the balcony while she went inside to shower and change.

Peter trudged slowly up the stairs, his frame of mind far from the best. Today had seemed particularly long, and everyone around him had been argumentative. The possibility that it was he himself who was argumentative and that his associates were only reflecting his irritability had occurred to him—which didn't help his mood a great deal.

Yesterday had been a disaster. After Kathy's calamitous visit he had not been able to get back into the proper mood, and Veronica had left shortly after. She had planned to accompany him to the benefit, but at the last minute she had decided not to. And he wasn't sure that he was sorry. Then at the yacht club he had been shocked, in more ways than one, by the appearance of his neighbor—which, upon further reflection, he was not pleased about at all because it was safer to write her off as being too young. And to top off the evening he had been stuck with a reminder: a drawing of some kind of furry animal that he had felt compelled to purchase even though he didn't want it, would never hang it on one of his walls, and—most of all—disliked it!

Peter stepped onto the balcony, his mind existing in a dark cloud, his feet automatically turning toward his door. He didn't see the container; he didn't realize it was there—until he kicked it.

Kathy was humming to herself as she heated a can of chili for her evening meal. She was still exhausted, but a shower had gone a long way toward reviving her. Her spirit was also helped by the fact that the first person she called owned a saltwater aquarium and didn't mind a visitor in the least. Now, after a quick meal, she felt that she would be ready to deliver the anemone and then attack the pet stores in the area for her supplies. She had to do something to keep herself occupied.

She had just taken a precipitous taste of the spiced meat, using the spoon she had been stirring with, when she heard a loud, angry knock at her door.

Kathy slowly lowered the spoon. A knock wouldn't surprise her—but an angry knock? She was pressed into action when another urgent summons rattled the door.

Peter stood outside, the bottom of his left trousers leg and his left shoe soaked with water. His jaw was tight. He was spoiling for a fight, and he'd found one. When the door swung inward and Kathy's face looked up at him—the same face that had been causing him so much grief—he let her have it!

"Just what the hell do you mean by leaving a barrel of water sitting right where a person can trip over it? Of all the crazy, irresponsible . . ."

76

His voice trailed off because Kathy was no longer standing before him, listening to his tirade. She had given a little yelp and dashed around his side.

Now, as he turned to follow her movement, she was scrabbling about on the porch, righting the "barrel" and hurriedly, yet gently, scooping something back into it.

"Thank God you didn't step on it," she flung back at him, her blue eyes accusatory.

"If you hadn't left it smack in the middle of the porch, I wouldn't have touched it!" He didn't like the way she was trying to turn the tables, make him feel as if he were in the wrong. Not when he wasn't! "Whatever *it* is!"

"I don't have time to argue," she returned. Then she began to run quickly down the stairs, the container in her hand.

Peter watched her flight, the frown that had been on his forehead etching itself even deeper. Did she think that she could just run away—that she could escape her responsibilities that easily? Without making a conscious decision, he followed her, taking the stairs as quickly as she had.

Kathy ran along a narrow walkway, past several more apartment units and the recreation room. She was headed for the water. The little sea anemone had been through a lot today. First to be caught in their net and then to be left helpless on the concrete porch. She ran along the beginning of the pier that led to the marina. And then, when the pier finally met the water, she stopped and stretched out on her tummy. She knew that what she was about to do might cause her to lose her new pet. Dipping the container into the water to fill it

77

once again might allow the anemone to escape at the same time, yet that was a risk she would have to take. If she didn't, the creature might die.

When she brought the container back onto the pier, she looked inside. It was still there! Floating near the surface, its delicately colored petallike tentacles moving reassuringly.

Kathy gave an exuberant laugh, feeling a wonderful sense of oneness with the world.

Peter was standing a few feet away. He had watched her prostrate herself on the pier, dip the container in the water, and then look curiously inside. Then he heard the laugh she gave and saw the way her face lifted to the sun, her golden hair cascading down her back, her smile radiant. His anger began to drain away.

He walked slowly to her side.

"What is it?" he asked gruffly. He was more affected by her the closer he came, yet he couldn't prevent himself from drawing near. She looked so different than she had yesterday. She was no longer dressed in finery, but she was still beautiful—even more so if that were possible. He felt his mind begin to spin on one level while the rest of him tried to function naturally.

"A sea anemone," she answered, her smile now including him. "We caught it today and I decided to keep it. Isn't it beautiful?"

Peter gave a perfunctory glance into the container before his eyes returned to her as if compelled.

"Very," he agreed. But he wasn't sure if he was talking about the colorful bit of sea life. There was something about her. Something *magical. Yes! That's it.* That was the term he had been unconsciously looking for!

She reminded him of a fairy tale he had been told as a child—a fairy tale about a mermaid. She had that same ethereal quality, that same magical beauty combined with an open innocence and joy. . . .

Peter shook his head, trying to clear the thought from his mind.

Kathy got to her feet and started to walk back up the pier. Peter automatically fell into step beside her.

"I'm sorry I kicked it over," he said, feeling the need to say something.

Kathy shot him an estimating sideways glance. Was he being sincere or sarcastic? She decided on sincere.

"I shouldn't have left it in the way. But I didn't think I had. I thought I put it beside the wall."

"It was probably me." He took the responsibility. "I have big feet, and I wasn't looking where I was going."

Kathy examined the feet in question and gave an amused smile. "Yes, you do, don't you?"

They mounted the stairs and paused on the balcony.

"Do you think it will be all right?" He motioned to the container.

"I think so," Kathy replied. She met her neighbor's eyes. They were a rich, warm brown, touched with a hint of golden shadows. She remembered him as she had seen him last night, talking to all those women, looking so breathtakingly handsome. He was just as handsome now.

"Nevertheless, I feel responsible," she heard him say. It was a distant sound, but it shook her free of her momentary abstraction. She shifted the container from one hand to the other.

"It was an accident." She shrugged lightly, dismissing the incident.

Peter felt awkward about what to say next. All the while they had been walking back to the building he had been busy trying to untangle the widely swinging range of his recent emotions: he had been up and down and up and down in the short space of a few minutes, and now he was feeling a warmth he had never experienced with a woman before, a warmth that was more confusing than anything else he had ever known.

Kathy took the need to solve the dilemma out of his hands. She placed the container back against the wall and teased him, by asking, "Do you think it will be safe now? I'm going out right after I eat and collect the things I need for its new home."

"You haven't eaten yet?" He heard himself ask the question. He seemed to have no control over his tongue.

"No."

She was looking at him with a little frown. Peter saw it but continued, "Then why don't you let me take you to dinner. If you like Italian food, there's a place not too far from here."

Now she really was looking at him strangely. Had his words come out all wrong? He hurried on. "I think that's the least I can do . . . to make up for what happened."

"It was the sea anemone it happened to, not me," Kathy reminded him.

"But I can't take *it* to dinner, now can I?"

"No—"

"So?"

Kathy remembered the chili she had left warming on the burner. If it wasn't scorched by now, it had to be close to it. Thank heaven she had turned the heat down a bit; otherwise the fire alarm would be sounding, smoke would be billowing out from around the door, and the evening would be taking on more of the proportions of a farce than it was already. She thought for a moment, then asked, "Is eight o'clock too late?" It would be too complicated to try to explain all the things she needed to do in the time between then and now, so she didn't try.

"No, that would be fine." Peter didn't question her reasoning, but his stomach gave a rumble at the thought of two more hours without food. To his relief, this time the sound wasn't audible.

Kathy reached behind her for the door knob. "I'll see you later then," she said after successfully opening the door.

"At eight," he confirmed.

"Right."

Kathy closed the door and immediately pressed herself against the cool wood in one flowing motion. His smile unnerved her! She might try to tell herself that she had accepted his offer of dinner because he was talking about going to what could only be Claudio's, but her thumping heart and her weakened knees told a more accurate story.

Peter let himself into his apartment. *Fool!* he called himself. With a growing instinct for his own protection he knew that he needed to stay away from her. So what had he just gone and done? Asked her out to dinner, that was what. He checked his watch. He would have time for a good workout. Maybe if he tired himself out, he wouldn't do anything equally foolish later. He could at least hope that he wouldn't. She was poison for him.

A sense of excitement traveled with Kathy as she stopped off at her friend's house and watched the sea anemone momentarily explore its new environment before contentedly coming to settle onto a rock. It remained with her as she set about getting her tank, filters, crushed coral, and the various chemicals and bacteria that were necessary to achieve the proper water balance—a process she was familiar with because she had been in charge of the aquariums at the university.

She tried to push her excitement away as she changed into something more appropriate to wear to dinner: a muted print dress whose dark cranberry and charcoal colors did interesting things for her hair and skin. But she couldn't disperse the feeling completely. And when the doorbell rang precisely at eight, a growing sense of anticipation washed over her with a vengeance.

Peter was on time for two reasons: first, he didn't have that far to go and second, he had decided over the space of elapsed time that he was placing too much importance on the evening. He was merely taking her to dinner, for God's sake. Nothing more.

When Kathy answered the door, a sparkle in her eyes and a welcoming smile on her lips, Peter's resolve was tested. It was tested even more when she moved ahead of him along the staircase. With each step they took, the light, flowery scent of her perfume rose up to tickle his nose, and for the first time in his life Peter prayed for the quick onslaught of a head cold.

Kathy reacted to her uncustomary nervousness by talking. She had heard from the Sinclairs, she told him. A letter had come only that morning. They were in Sidney and found the natives interesting.

That illicited an ironic laugh from Peter.

Then a silence settled between them, and both were grateful that the drive to the Italian restaurant was short. And, of course, the restaurant was Claudio's.

Peter applied the emergency brake after drawing the car to a stop.

"I've never been here myself," he confided, "but I have friends who rave over it."

Kathy could have said a lot at that moment, but she didn't. He continued, "I've known about this place for years, though. The woman who owned it came to the bank where I was a loan officer and applied for some money to remodel it. Five or six years ago, I believe."

Six. Kathy could have told him exactly. She remembered the day very clearly. Ashley had been so desperate to do anything to try to get business to pick up again. She also remembered how crushed her older sister had been when she had not been able to secure as much financial aid as she had hoped. And it was Peter she had talked with?

"Do you still work at the bank?" she asked, feeling the need to say something.

"Yes," Peter replied. He did not expound further.

"As a loan officer?" she persisted.

"No, I do something different now."

"I'm glad," she decided.

Peter had been ready to get out of the car, but he stopped when he heard what she said.

"You're glad?" he repeated. "I don't understand."

"It must be hard," Kathy said slowly, "having to turn people down sometimes—"

Peter's banker's heart hardened. "Not particularly. I

83

work for a bank, not a charitable institution. We're not in the business to give money away."

Kathy was persistent. "No, but when a person needs money, he can't get it. And if he doesn't need it, he can. Isn't that right?"

Peter had heard that argument before. "I don't make the rules," he said stiffly.

Kathy was looking straight ahead at Claudio's. She remembered that if it hadn't been for Jason and his ability to renovate, she and Ashley might have lost their home as well as their livelihood.

When she remained silent, Peter relented somewhat. "Look, a bank does what it can—what the rules of good banking let it. Basically, the money we're able to lend is money people have deposited, their hard-earned money. They wouldn't like it if we frittered it away . . . if we threw it down a hole with no hope of return. Banks work on trust, Kathy. If there's no trust, there's no bank."

Kathy had never thought of it like that before. Banks had always remained something of a mystery to her. She put her money in; she took it out. In her mind her small nest egg remained stationary, sitting in a nice little stack waiting for her withdrawal.

Then she remembered, too, that Ashley had come home with *some* money lended. She turned to Peter, remorse making her say, "I'm sorry. I didn't mean to sound judgmental. I'm sure you do your best. That you always have."

For some reason Peter had the feeling that there was something more taking place at this moment than a simple conversation about banking. But he couldn't figure out what it was.

He decided it was time to get out of the car, and he opened his door and stood up. The cool night breeze blowing off the water felt good to him. It helped him to regain his composure. He felt as if he had been knocked even further off edge, and by something he didn't understand.

He walked around to the passenger side and helped Kathy out. Once inside they had to wait briefly at the reservations desk while another couple that had entered before them was seated. Then it was their turn. A woman dressed in what could only be described kindly as a gypsy costume seated them at a table. Kathy was looking at her with some amusement. Peter couldn't believe his eyes. One gaudy color clashed merrily with another.

The woman gave them their menus and told them that a waitress would be with them soon.

Kathy could hardly suppress a giggle. She recognized the woman as one half of the pair who had bought Claudio's from Ashley and Jason. She knew the woman liked to think of herself as the arty type, but just how far was she planning to take it? She certainly looked ridiculous in the gypsy regalia.

And then Mary Morgan presented herself at their table, a long-suffering expression on her face. She didn't look at the couple at first, just readied her pad and pencil to take their order. Kathy had to squeeze her arms against her stomach to keep from laughing out loud.

Peter was reading the menu, but his eyes widened as he gazed first at Mary Morgan and then at Kathy, who looked as if she were about to explode.

He was about to ask Kathy if something was wrong when Mary Morgan saw Kathy herself.

"Saints above! Would you look at this! Just look at this!" the waitress burst out. "Kathy, I don't think I can stand much more. This is what she came up with today. *This!*" Mary Morgan displayed her own gypsy costume. A thin veil was on her head, and fake gold coins swung from a belt at her waist, while a series of chains fluttered on her wrist. "I'm surprised she doesn't make us go barefoot. She probably would if she thought she could get away with it. She said we were to try this to see if it worked before she decided to change the place over. Why doesn't the woman let well enough alone?" Her last remark was said in a hissed voice, not any the less heartfully felt because of its lower level of volume.

Kathy tried to smother her amusement, but it was difficult. She had to start more than once before she could say, "You look very nice, Mary Morgan."

"Nice, schmice! I feel like an idiot. I'd rather be fired than wear this thing!"

Kathy grew suddenly serious. She knew that each penny the waitress earned was sorely needed.

"Don't do anything stupid, Mary Morgan," she warned.

"I won't. Why do you think I'm still here?"

By this time Peter had come to the obvious conclusion that the two women knew each other.

He cleared his throat. That drew their attention.

A tinge of color entered Kathy's cheeks. She knew she wouldn't be able to keep her identity a secret much longer—not with Mary Morgan around.

"Mary Morgan, this is Peter Maxwell. Peter, Mary Morgan O'Day."

The two people nodded at each other, Mary Morgan giving him the quick once-over as she had any new "boy" that Kathy had brought home in the past.

Kathy covered her amusement by smoothing a tendril of hair back behind her ear. If ever there was a case for mistaken terminology, that was it. Peter was no *boy*. He was very definitely a *man*. But that fact didn't seem to phase Mary Morgan.

"Mary Morgan has been my friend almost all my life, Peter. In fact, she helped raise me."

The waitress's eyes were still narrowed on Peter's face. Kathy couldn't tell whether or not she approved of him.

"That's right," the older woman said at last. "Me, Iris, the cook, and Ashley . . . Ashley is Kathy's sister. We all had a hand in raising the child. And she turned out pretty good, even if I do say so myself."

Peter remained stationary in his chair.

"And we did it right here," Mary Morgan continued, sharing the information as Kathy knew she eventually would. "Right in this very restaurant."

Peter shot Kathy an inquiring look. She shrugged.

"You lived here?" he asked quietly.

"Upstairs," she answered.

"And your sister—"

"Owned Claudio's," she finished for him. "She's the person who came to you for a loan. It really is a small world, isn't it?"

The last was said to add brightness, to lighten the atmosphere. Mary Morgan had been called to another table, and for the moment, they were alone.

Peter was aware of their earlier conversation. "I did give her what she wanted, didn't I?"

"Yes . . . some of it."

Peter was relieved. "Thank God for small favors," he murmured.

"That's what we thought," she teased.

"But she doesn't still own the place now." It was a statement, not a question.

"No." Kathy let her eyes survey the room before coming back to rest on him. "She and her husband sold it . . . to the first gypsy you met." She smiled slightly. "Then they did what other people only dream of doing: two years ago they set off to sail around the world."

"What about you?"

"I was in college, getting my degree."

"Have you had it long?" he asked. He was quickly doing a mental recalculation. When he first met her, he had thought her barely out of high school—seventeen at the most. At the benefit he had been forced to acknowledge that she was somewhat older. But not old enough for a degree!

"I graduated this spring," she informed him.

That would make her over twenty. Old enough. He shifted in his chair, trying to divert the sensual direction of his thought. He was supposed to be keeping a distance between them—one he couldn't afford to let down. As a shield he picked up the menu and glanced at it again. "Well, since you're the expert, what's the best thing on the menu? Or has it changed since your sister sold the place?"

"No, it's the same," she replied slowly.

"Does coming here make you miss her?" He was quick to pick up on the tinge of sadness in her answer.

"A bit. But what worries me more is that Claudio's probably won't be the same for long. The new owners

88

are thinking about changing it to another kind of restaurant, to attract a different sort of clientele."

"Why should that bother you? You're out of it now. What they do with the place is their business."

Kathy drew a small circle on the tablecloth with the end of her spoon.

"Because of my friends who work here," she said simply.

"Won't they be kept on? If they still serve food, they'll need help."

"You've met Mary Morgan. She might want to stay, but I don't know if the owners will let her, not with the kind of place they're thinking about opening. And Iris . . ." She shook her head. "No, Iris would never stay, and of her own choosing."

"That's not your problem."

"But it is!"

The conversation was cut short by Mary Morgan's return.

"Sorry that took so long. Some people can't make up their minds. They changed their order four times! Now, what will you two have?"

Peter made a motion of concession to Kathy.

She pursed her lips and thought. Then she said, "For a while when I was a kid, I thought I'd die if I ever ate lasagna again. But I've kind of missed it. Bring us some lasagna, Mary Morgan, and . . . a salad." The last time she had been here with her friends, they had ordered the largest pizza in the house.

"What kind of dressing?" the waitress prompted.

"Blue cheese," Kathy returned.

"Just squeeze a little lemon on mine, please," Peter said.

"Are you watching your weight?" Kathy teased before she could stop herself. It was something she would have said to any one of her friends but not to him.

Peter was startled, then laughed slightly. "No, not particularly," he hedged.

"Good." Kathy grinned. "Because the lasagna is a killer. It's delicious—but talk about calories!"

"It doesn't seem to have hurt you," he said.

Kathy looked down at her trim figure, which caused him to look down as well. For someone so slim, her breasts were fully rounded, and the dark material of the dress couldn't disguise that fact.

When she looked up, she saw where his attention was centered, and her breath caught momentarily in her throat.

Peter looked quickly away.

From that moment talk between them became sporadic. They were helped by the arrival of the salad and then by the lasagna. Eating kept them busy even though neither was really in the mood for food.

Finally the ordeal was over. Peter paid the bill with relief. All he wanted to do was gain the safety of his apartment—alone. No, what he really wanted was to suavely ask Kathy in for an after-dinner drink and have his wicked way with her while she had her wicked way with him. But he knew that would be asking for trouble. At the moment his feelings were too unstable. He had to find some way to gain control of them.

It wasn't as if he hadn't controlled worse in his life. Being dragged through one of his mother's divorces after another, from one stepfather to the next, had taught him that it was better not to get too connected to people

90

because the separation that inevitably followed was too hard. He had never understood his mother or the men she married. She seemed to be eternally restless, and her husbands never seemed to be able to meet her needs.

Peter reaffirmed his intention to resist Kathy's appeal. He could do it.

CHAPTER FIVE

Kathy slid a sideways glance at Peter as she sat beside him in his car. His profile was one of the nicest she'd ever seen. His nose was straight, his chin was firm yet curving, his lips were finely drawn with more than a hint of sensitivity that he seemed to want to stamp out at any cost.

She turned her eyes and stared at the road ahead. The man intrigued her. Normally she was a good judge of people, but she just couldn't figure him out. One minute he was friendly—warm even. And the next he was quiet, withdrawn—just as he was now. Just as he'd been since she had caught him looking at her breasts in the restaurant.

Warmth rose to Kathy's cheeks as she remembered how she had felt at that time. She hadn't felt shy; men had looked at her breasts before. But never had she felt as if she had been physically touched by a man's eyes.

She stole another glance at Peter. What would he say or think or do if he knew the effect he had had on her?

Peter's fingers tightened on the steering wheel. With every fiber of his being he was aware of her. If he could do it and still retain a grip on his sanity, he would laugh at his determination to resist her. The task was next to impossible. Not when she was sitting so near, her thigh only a short reach away. Peter knew his only salvation was to end the evening as quickly as possible.

Kathy frowned when the car came to an abrupt halt in its allotted space. Her frown deepened as Peter set a quick pace along the walkway and stairs. Then after mumbling a word of parting, he started to walk away. The old expression about a horse racing for the barn door flitted through Kathy's mind.

Something—was it a streak of stubborn perversity?—made her call after him. "Peter?"

He stopped in midstride.

She summoned her friendliest tone. "Would you like to come in for a cup of coffee? That's all I have to offer, I'm afraid. The Sinclairs don't keep anything stronger, and I haven't stocked up myself yet."

Peter turned, his features expressionless. "No, thank you."

"Are you sure? It would only take a minute to make." Kathy smiled.

When he said nothing, Kathy's smile changed to a mischievous grin. He was being so distant at the moment. What would happen if she challenged him a little? Without further thought she covered the distance between them and reached up to give him a quick kiss. At first the kiss was a tentative meeting of their lips—all she had meant for it to be from the beginning. She held herself back, intent to pull away immediately. Then, without warning, the situation changed for her. She began to tremble slightly, the scent of his cologne making her feel light-headed. When she swayed forward, her hands coming up to steady herself against his chest, that was when it happened—when the quick kiss became something so much more. She was aware of his warmth, of his strength, of the magnetism that had drawn her to him from the very beginning.

Kathy put everything she had into that moment, all the earnestness her body had to share, all the budding passion. Her lips moved, parted slightly, and moved again.

When she pulled back, her eyes were large in the starlight, her breathing disturbed. She had to will her legs to continue to support her while she looked into his eyes, trying to gage what effect the kiss had had on him.

Kathy had always been attractive to the opposite sex. She had had many boyfriends in high school and college. She had been kissed many times. But none had affected her as profoundly as Peter. And she had been the one doing most of the work!

Peter stood transfixed. It was everything he could do not to jerk Kathy back into his arms and finish the job she had started. Still, somehow—miraculously— he was able to resist that clamoring urge. He had to. It was a case of his survival pitted against hers.

Emotion was rampaging inside him. He could still feel the silent plea of her soft lips; he could still taste the sweetness of her breath. The brand her breasts left against his chest was still burning. . . .

He drew an uneven breath before saying huskily, "You didn't have to do that. I don't expect payment for a nice evening."

Kathy hadn't thought of it that way at all. The thought had never entered her mind. What she had done, she had done because she wanted to. But if he thought otherwise, she was content to let him—especially when she still wasn't sure of his reaction.

"Some men do," she said softly.

"I'm not one of them."

Kathy met his steady gaze. The richness of his eyes looked to be lighted by a flame, but she couldn't be sure. Not in this half-light.

Suddenly a confused sort of shyness overcame her. She gave a half smile, one that was a mixture of desire and hesitation. She looked down at her folded hands and then back up at him. "It was a nice evening, Peter. Thank you."

That hide-and-seek smile was nearly Peter's undoing. He had been through so much, and that smile almost destroyed his resolve.

"My pleasure," he said, trying to affect a tone of exaggerated gallantry that would disguise the huskiness in his voice.

They parted without saying another word.

Kathy thought about Peter for hours after she went to bed that night and then again when she got up in the morning. She didn't come to any conclusions, though, except to admit that she was more than a little interested in him, which was an understatement. Each time she remembered how it felt to touch his lips with hers, a delicious warmth would steal over her.

She devoted even more than her usual attention to her appearance before leaving the apartment the next morning—brushing her hair until it shone, leaving it down from its usual braid, taking more care with the application of liner around her eyes, and even adding a little natural shadowing to her lids. But her care came to no avail. Peter's apartment had a closed, empty look, and when she walked to the parking lot his car was already gone.

When she arrived at the institute, Eric was waiting for her.

"You look extra special this morning," he pronounced, his gray eyes crinkling at the corners as he anticipated his own teasing. "Are you planning to vamp someone here? Or is this just a practice run?"

Kathy tried not to smile. "I'm not out to vamp anyone, Eric," she denied. "I just felt like doing something a little different, that's all."

"You're talking to a man who knows women, don't forget. I know a campaign to get attention when I see one." He tilted his head. "Who's the lucky guy?"

"No one you know," she retorted quickly.

"See? I told you," he said with a triumphant grin.

Kathy swung into step beside him, and they walked toward the pickup truck they used in their work. Eric was still grinning as he started the engine and headed for the spot along the bay where they were scheduled to sein.

Kathy had to raise her voice to be heard over the noise of the engine and the wind rushing in through the open windows. "For a man who says he knows women so well, you're certainly not doing things right in your own life."

Eric glanced at her. "What do you mean?" His voice was loud as well.

"Sue!"

"What about her?"

"If you knew as much as you think you do, you'd see that she wants you to make up your mind." Eric had spent the past few days pouring his heart out to Kathy

96

about his trials and tribulations with his live-in girl friend.

"I *have* made up my mind."

"Oh?"

"I'm going to stay just where I am!"

Kathy made an exasperated sound. "But that's not making up your mind. Sue wants to get married. Right?"

"Right."

"And you're not sure. Right?"

"Right."

"So how does staying where you are resolve anything?"

Eric's rugged features beamed. "Because we keep the status quo. We might get married eventually but not right now."

"You might lose her. Have you thought about that?"

"Sue?" Eric looked genuinely astonished. "Sue would never leave me. She loves me too much."

"Don't take her for granted, Eric."

"Hey . . . lighten up! I'm not worried."

Kathy shook her head slightly. In the short time she had known Eric they had already become fast friends. Wading through muck and mud together for hours on end had a way of telescoping time. She liked Eric. She liked him a lot. She only hoped that he would wake up to the reality of his relationship before it was too late.

Kathy was tired that evening, but little by little she was becoming adjusted to the long hours of hard work.

As she topped the stairs to her apartment she glanced at Peter's door. Was he home? She paused for a moment, debated about going over to see, and then decided not to. If she was going to vamp him, as Eric had accused her of wanting to do, she certainly was no longer in the proper condition. Especially not since she had slipped earlier in the day, dunking herself completely in the water. Her hair was in the rebellious mass of ringlets it usually formed after becoming wet, and she could swear that a piece of vegetation had somehow worked its way into one side of her bra.

Kathy gave a reflexive rub to the affected side. That was when she heard a footstep on the walkway approaching the balcony.

Peter's mind was detached from what he was doing as he neared the stairs to his apartment. It had been like that for most of the afternoon. And for the first time in what seemed to be ages, the cause was not his neighbor. No, today his concern centered on another woman: his mother. She had called today to tell him that she was getting married again. *Is it number seven this time or number eight?* Anyway, in a couple of weeks she would be stopping in Houston before going on to Los Angeles to meet her prospective bridegroom; she wanted to see him again.

Peter had very mixed and volatile feelings about his mother. Every time she came to visit she left a wake of disruption in her path. Like a tornado she swooped down out of an unsuspecting sky only to be gone just as suddenly, leaving him to pick up the scattered pieces of his life. And right now he felt as if there were already too many pieces of his life in disarray.

A slight noise came from directly above him, drawing his attention. He looked up just in time to see Kathy's slender figure scuttling along the balcony toward her door.

Peter started to turn on his heels, to take a walk around the condominiums, to get his mail—anything. She was one of the scattered pieces of his life that needed to be dealt with. Only he wasn't up to dealing with her now, if he ever would be. Then he saw a head slowly appear over the railing. It was Kathy: blond, beautiful, and completely bedraggled.

I'm caught! Kathy thought woefully, groaning silently. She should never have peeked to see if the person approaching was Peter. She was angry with herself for her curiosity. Now she had to say *something!*

"Hi," she settled upon. It was all she could manage.

"Hi, yourself."

"You just getting home?"

Peter nodded.

"Me, too," she said needlessly.

She felt his eyes go over her. "Don't say it," she hurried on. "I know I'm a mess."

Peter wasn't thinking that at all. He was wondering how it was that some women have to spend hours in front of a mirror to achieve a desired result and Kathy managed to look wonderful even under the worst of conditions.

Kathy grimaced, uncertainty making her say things she should have left unsaid. "I fell in," she explained. "I was getting out of the skiff to take my turn in the water when something moved under my foot . . . and I fell in."

"What was it?" he asked.

"Under my foot?" She shrugged. "I don't know. Possibly a sting ray or a flounder."

"And that doesn't bother you?"

Kathy frowned. "I don't understand."

Peter gave a half smile that made her reach out to the railing for support.

"No, *you* wouldn't," he murmured, marveling once again over how different she was from other women.

Kathy's grip tightened. She wasn't sure if she was being insulted or not. It was difficult to tell with Peter.

Peter stuffed his hands into the pockets of his trousers and rocked back on his heels. This had to be the zaniest balcony scene ever played. Instead of pledging eternal love, they were talking about creatures of the deep! His smile widened.

"What is it?" Kathy asked suspiciously. "What's so funny?"

Peter looked up at her, his eyes sparkling with amusement. "It's just that you're a very different sort of person."

"Thank you." Her reply was sardonic. That was just what she wanted to hear—and from him: she was *different!*

He saw her irritation. "No," he said quickly, "I mean that as a compliment."

"Oh, sure you do," Kathy returned. "I believe you. And if you have any handy pieces of swamp land in the desert for sale, I'll be glad to talk to you about buying one later." She paused. She didn't like being laughed at. She wasn't accustomed to it. "You know, I think the Sinclairs were right about you. They said you were a hateful man."

"The Sinclairs can't find their way out of a lighted broom closet!" he clipped, beginning to share her irritation.

"They're a *very* nice couple!" Kathy retorted adamantly. She knew the situation was getting out of hand fast, but she seemed unable to do anything to stop it.

"I didn't say they weren't *nice!*" he defended.

"You implied it!"

"I did not!"

Kathy's emotions had made a complete turnaround. If there had been a handy potted plant around, she would have happily lobbed it onto his head. Then she realized where he was and that he had been standing on the sidewalk throughout the entire conversation.

"Are you planning to stay down there all night?" she snapped.

"If I want to, I will."

"Then why don't you?"

"I may!" he declared stubbornly.

Kathy glared at him before rushing into her apartment and slamming the door behind her.

For the next few minutes Kathy reveled in her anger. He was hateful and obnoxious and superior! And then she began to see how childishly they both had behaved.

At least *she'd* been dressed for the part! He hadn't. That was what made it all so funny, if you looked at it from a detached point of view.

Kathy showered, ran a comb through her damp hair, changed into a clean pair of jeans and a baggy shirt, and searched through her collection of keepsakes for something to give him as a peace offering. She settled on a branch of coral.

After fluffing her hair as best she could, she licked her lips, cradled the coral in her palm, and went to his door.

Peter had collapsed into his favorite chair and was rubbing his aching temples. His jacket was lying in a partial heap over the arm of the couch, his vest had fallen to the floor, and his tie was undone, as were the top buttons of his shirt. He was trying to make his mind a blank, but he was not being successful.

Then he heard a soft knock at his door. He stayed where he was for several seconds. He knew who the caller was.

Kathy knocked again and called, "Peter? Are you there? I know you're not still on the sidewalk because I looked."

Peter rubbed his temples one last time and then buried his face in his hands. When he looked up, he was smiling. Only Kathy would say something like that.

Peter got to his feet and opened the door.

Kathy stood outside, looking maybe fourteen in her oversized shirt, with her hair in damp disarray around her scrubbed face. But he remembered the body beneath. It was not the body of a fourteen-year-old.

She was solemn, but he could see that her straight face was taking some effort.

She held out the coral. "I'm sorry," she apologized. "You're not a hateful man."

Peter looked at her gift and then into her eyes. They were the color of a bright summer sky.

"Don't make too rash a statement," he murmured. "You might want to take it back someday."

Kathy grinned. "Well, then let's change it to say that you're no more hateful than the rest of humanity."

"I'll go along with that."

Kathy proffered the coral again. "Take it. I want you to have it."

Peter held out his hand and had to catch his breath as Kathy's warm fingers brushed against his own in the exchange.

"Thank you," he said quietly.

"You're welcome."

Peter awkwardly continued to stand in the doorway.

"I apologize, too," he said at last. "But I don't have anything to give you."

"I don't expect anything. And anyway, it was mostly my fault. I took offense where none was meant."

He looked at her closely. "Are you sure you're not related to the Sinclairs?"

Kathy reacted suspiciously. "Why?"

"Because if I say something about them, you get angry."

Kathy shrugged. "I guess I just feel I have to protect them."

Peter snorted. "Well, don't. Believe me, they're batty, but they can take good care of themselves. Before their dog died, they used to sic him on me whenever they'd see me."

"You knew Frederick?" Kathy's eyes widened.

Peter grimaced. "I had the pleasure."

Kathy looked at him. "What did you do to him?"

"Nothing. Absolutely nothing. I think the dog just instinctively knew that I didn't like him."

"Or his masters."

"Or his masters," he confirmed. Then he reneged. "It's not so much that I dislike them. I just can't make them understand. Mrs. Sinclair insists that the number on her parking space is to the left of the space. I can't convince her that the number is *in* the space."

"Did you know that they think Frederick is coming

103

back?" Kathy asked, trying not to grin in anticipation of his reaction to the news.

"They what?"

"They think Frederick is coming back."

"From where?"

"From"—Kathy waved her hand in the air in an all encompassing gesture—"from wherever he is now. 'Journeying,' I think Irene called it."

Peter nodded his head slowly. "Yep. That sounds like them."

"Would you like to see his shrine?" She didn't think she was being disloyal to the Sinclairs. She had grown to like the dog. Maybe if Peter saw how much his neighbors truly loved their pet, he might gain more insight into their feelings.

"Shrine?" Peter repeated. He looked at her disbelievingly.

Kathy grinned, her eyes sparkling with enjoyment. "Come on." She moved toward her apartment.

Peter took only a second to place the piece of coral on a nearby bookshelf before following her out of the apartment.

When he entered her living room, he couldn't help but see the monument to the dog. There was Frederick, in all his glory, his black eyes looking impudently out of a rather crudely executed painting. Peter watched as Kathy moved to light the candles on either side of the mantelpiece.

"I have to do this once a day and let them burn for an hour. Irene and Donald think it will help his spirit find its way back." She looked over her shoulder to make sure that he was watching. "And this"—she pointed to the urn—"holds his ashes."

"Good God," Peter declared under his breath.

Kathy stood back and surveyed the shrine. "It's silly, I suppose, but I think it's really their way of keeping his memory alive. They don't want to admit that he's dead. They must have really loved him."

Peter dragged his eyes away from the urn. "You really *are* an unusual person."

Kathy tilted her head, a frown creasing her brow. "Why?"

"To do this."

"I get the apartment free because I do it."

"But you respect their feelings."

She shrugged.

"Most people wouldn't," he continued.

Kathy disagreed. "Oh, I don't know. I think they would. People have a way of living up to the good others expect of them. The Sinclairs trust me. I'm only living up to their trust."

Peter said nothing, but his mind was busy. Truly he had never met a person like Kathy before. She was loyal, sincere, trustworthy. . . .

He shifted position. He had to get his mind off of Kathy. He looked about the room, trying to find inspiration. He found it in the aquarium equipment.

"What happened to the sea anemone? It didn't die, did it?"

"No, it's perfectly fine. I took it over to a friend's house until I could get my aquarium set up. It'll be a few weeks before I can bring it home. I was planning to start work on it tonight." Then, on the spur of the moment, she offered, "Would you like to help? They're really a lot of fun."

"Ah—no. No, I . . ."

While he stumbled with his words, Kathy quickly accepted his decision. "Sure, yeah. I understand."

Peter saw her disappointment but steeled himself against it. If he stayed, all hell might break loose. And he didn't want to fall into anything with her—like a bed. Oh, he wanted to; his body wanted to. It was taking the first steps already. But he wouldn't let it happen.

To help counteract the physical clamor of his body, Peter took a step backward. Only it wasn't a full step and it was rather halting because he was fighting both his mind and his physical drive.

Kathy was quick to notice his action. "Are you all right? You look kind of funny."

"I'm fine," he tried to assure her, but there was a funny tightness to his words.

Kathy didn't hesitate. Memory of the last time someone had almost fainted in her company leaped into her mind. Then it had been Ashley exhausted from overwork. She rushed forward. "Have you been getting enough sleep at night?" she inquired, her solicitousness instinctive.

Kathy began to direct him back to his apartment. He wanted to groan aloud. If he wasn't getting enough sleep at night, it wouldn't be hard to find the cause. But he wasn't going to tell *her* that.

"I'm fine, really," he protested.

"No, you should rest. Did you eat lunch today?"

"No."

They were at his door, and Kathy pushed it open. She clicked her tongue in reproach. "Well, you should have. Now, sit down and let me take care of dinner. I'm not a great cook, but I can open any can in town."

Since his apartment looked to be a carbon copy of

106

hers, Kathy thought she knew where the kitchen was located. She left Peter sitting in a chair and hurried down the short hall.

In the kitchen Kathy leaned into the pantry. There wasn't a can in sight! She blinked her eyes and then started to go through the packages and containers one by one. When she was done, she stood back, her hands on her hips. *Good grief! He's a health-food freak! Now what can I make for him?* She had promised him a meal, but she didn't know beans about preparing health food.

Beans. Beans! She rerummaged through the pantry until she found a bag of dried navy beans. They couldn't be that hard to cook. She was just beginning to read the instructions printed on the side of the package when Peter appeared in the hallway.

"What are you doing?" he asked curiously.

Kathy tried to block his view.

"Me? Oh, I'm—I'm—"

Peter came toward her. With very little difficulty he moved her aside. He picked up the plastic package and weighed it in his hand.

"This doesn't look like a can," he said, one eyebrow lifting.

"You don't have any cans."

"Do you know how to cook beans?"

Kathy decided honesty was the best policy.

"No, but it can't be *that* hard."

Peter agreed. "Oh, it's not. But feel them." He fingered a stonelike bean. "They stay like that for hours."

Kathy lifted her chin. "So you admit it's easier to have them precooked—in a can. They don't even have to be heated if you don't want to take the time to do it."

107

"But they don't taste as good, and they're not as good for you."

"Who says?" Kathy challenged.

Peter sighed. "Let's not get into another argument. Look, in the refrigerator is a salad I made this morning. There's plenty enough for two."

"I'm not a rabbit," she said stubbornly.

"I realize that."

"Do you not eat meat either? No, you do, because you ate the lasagna at Claudio's and it had meat."

Peter couldn't resist. "I was slumming."

Kathy still considered Claudio's her possession—if not in law, then in spirit. A slur against the restaurant was a slur against her. "Take that back!" she demanded, instantly resorting to anger.

"Aren't you going to serve me?" Peter was having fun. It was a dangerous kind of fun, like skating on the thinnest of ice, but the danger added to the thrill. He liked the way Kathy's eyes flashed, the way her cheeks blushed, the way her breasts—even covered by the loose shirt—rose and fell in her agitation.

"No! You look as if you can take care of yourself now. So do it!"

She started to brush past him.

The floor space of the kitchen was only as wide as the doorway. Peter blocked it.

Kathy looked up at him. At first the look was one of command. She wanted him to get out of her way! And then, as she continued to meet his level gaze, the ambience of the situation began to change.

The challenging laughter that had been in Peter's sherry-colored eyes slowly faded. The smile that had been on his lips faltered and disappeared. He looked down at Kathy. And nothing—not his good intentions or his knowledge that he would probably live to regret what he was about to do—seemed more important than the simple fact that she was near.

Kathy's heartbeat accelerated. Anger had been its cause at first, but that anger seemed to have instantly evaporated. She knew what was about to happen, and she couldn't make herself move away—because she *wanted* it to happen.

Peter closed the distance that separated them, and his hands rested lightly on her ribs. Almost in the same movement his head lowered.

Kathy gave a soft gasp, not from surprise but rather from anticipation. Her eyes fluttered shut as his face neared. She could feel his breath on her skin.

The kiss was gentle at first, exploratory. Then, as she began to respond, his mouth began to harden, alternately coaxing and demanding, coaxing and demanding, moving on hers, lingering, teasing, taunting, until eventually, her senses inflamed, Kathy was willing to yield him anything that he wanted.

She moaned softly as the warm insistence of his tongue slid between her lips, touching her own tongue, beginning to duel with it. Only it was the kind of duel that produced no casualties, just splendor. Her knees felt as if they were about to give way, but he pinned her back against the refrigerator, molding his hips to hers, making her aware of his arousal. His kisses moved along her cheek to her ear where delicious sensations coursed through her body at his touch; then suddenly—urgently—his mouth came back to cover hers again.

Kathy's fingers spread over the muscles of his shoulders, of his back. She could feel them as they tensed and moved. She could feel the heat of his body, his latent strength. She pulled on his shirt, wanting it to disappear.

Peter's breath was ragged when he moved back slightly. His eyes were burning as he looked down at her. Then, unable to stop the fire that was scorching through his system, he buried his face in the hollow of her neck, his tongue sliding over the soft skin, his hands beginning a throbbing massage of her breasts, her waist, her hips.

Finally his mouth found hers again as she gave another soft cry of pleasure.

Kathy didn't know whether she was going to survive this moment. And she didn't really care. It wasn't as if she hadn't wanted it, hadn't dreamed of it. But it was so much more than she'd expected. Peter—even in her wildest dreams—was more than she'd expected. Every nerve of her body was tingling with a sensual life that he had ignited. She loved the feel of him against her, the driving need that fanned the flames of their desire. Her fingers threaded through his thick brown hair, reveling in the strength of it. She pulled his head closer, her own mouth giving as much as it was taking of their devouring passion.

Then something—a sound outside? a voice inside?—broke them apart. And for several seconds all either of them could do was look at the other in stunned silence.

Still in his arms Kathy remained under the influence of his persuasive lovemaking. If Peter had wanted to continue, she was more than ready. But it was Peter who slowly began to extricate himself.

As he stepped away, Kathy felt as if a part of her soul

had been torn from her. She wanted to cry out in protest, but something made her hold back.

With trembling fingers she tried to straighten her baggy shirt.

Peter smoothed his hair and cleared his throat. He tried to speak, but he didn't know what to say! Should he apologize? And for what? She had been just as caught up in the moment as he. She had enjoyed it just as much as he had. "I—ah—" he began but quickly broke off. He couldn't believe the depth of the emotion he had experienced with her. He was accustomed to being turned on by women. But with Kathy it had been more—just as he always had known it would be. And that's what he had to reconcile himself with later. Much later. Only right now he had to say *something*. He gave a short laugh that didn't ring completely true and murmured, "That was an interesting way to end a disagreement."

As reality began to sink in and passion lessen, Kathy's cheeks became flags of pink. She had never gone so far so quickly with someone who in reality was little more than a stranger. But, then, never before had she ever felt such an instantaneous response!

She didn't know what to say. But since he had come up with something, so would she. "You're right!" she agreed and tried to laugh, too, but the sound was shaky.

Peter made himself relax—at least as much as a man in his situation could relax. He had been to the guillotine, laid his head on the block, felt the blade slice through his neck, and come out alive. Or rather, he thought he was alive. Maybe he wasn't, and he just didn't know it yet.

He cleared his throat. "Look, I don't know what happened—" he was beginning to say when she interrupted.

She had been in the process of trying to push her hair back into some semblance of order when she stopped, her hands frozen in the air. Now he was sounding as if he regretted it! And she couldn't match that because she didn't regret it.

"Oh, don't you? I thought it was perfectly obvious."

Peter gave a partial smile that was hard won. Control of the situation was fast slipping out of his hands. Then he had to laugh at his display of ego. What made him think that he had ever been in control? Certainly he hadn't been when he kissed her.

"Yes," he admitted at last, "I guess it was."

Kathy's knees quivered, and it was only through a strong effort of will that they didn't give way.

"I liked it," she stated honestly. There was no use in pretending otherwise. He knew. He could tell. But somehow putting it into words was important to her.

Peter said nothing. His eyes moved to hers, were caught, then he dragged them away.

When another moment passed and he still had said nothing, some of Kathy's fragile confidence deserted her. She ducked her head and started to walk away. Only once again he stopped her, this time by placing an arm across her path.

Kathy looked at him, startled. She could smell the faint, lingering fragrance of his cologne mixed in with his own special scent. It made her want him to hold her close in shared passion.

Peter saw the erotic message in her eyes, and it was all he could do not to do what she wanted. Finally he forced, "It won't work, Kathy."

"What won't work?" she whispered.

"This . . . us!" he said.

Kathy studied his handsome features, trying to read his expression.

"I didn't know there was an *us,*" she said huskily.

"There isn't!" he exploded, frustration lending support to his words. "At least there shouldn't be! We're two very different people, Kathy. Two totally different people. Our attitudes about the world are different. The way we see things." If he had stopped at that point, Kathy might have gone away partially convinced. But he didn't. He made the fatal mistake of continuing. "I'm a busy man. I can't take time to get involved now —especially with someone like you."

Like you! What did he mean by that? First he wanted her, then he didn't. It was hard to keep up with him!

"Are you trying to tell me you didn't enjoy what we just did?" she asked, trying to keep her cool, trying to ferret out exactly why he was so determined to push her away.

"Hell no! A dead man would have enjoyed it!"

Satisfied at least to some degree, Kathy tried another approach. She wasn't exactly overwhelmed with it, but the woman did pop into her mind, so she decided to use her. "I suppose you like it better with Veronica," she taunted.

Peter took a stab in the dark. "She's definitely more experienced."

"That's not necessarily something to be proud of!" Kathy shot back.

"At least she's not an impulsive child!"

This time Peter's accusation hit too close to home.

"I'm *not* a child!"

"But you are impulsive, Kathy! I could take advantage of you. It would be so easy."

"Then why don't you?"

"Because I have to live with myself!"

"I wouldn't complain."

Peter ran a harried hand over his cheek and jaw. Then he said flatly, "I wasn't wanting to do this. I didn't want to hurt you. But you're not leaving me much choice. What happened was a mistake, Kathy. A mistake! I can't take it back. I can't change it. But I can see to it that it never happens again."

Kathy felt as if she had been battered. Her shoulders slumped. Her chin quivered. She didn't understand why this was happening. She knew that he had wanted her. She was experienced enough to realize that. So why was he doing this? She reached out to touch his arm. "Peter —" she said softly.

Peter moved so that her hand failed to reach its destination. "I didn't ask you into my home, Kathy. I'd appreciate it if you'd leave." His voice held little feeling.

At that, Kathy decided she had had enough. Never before had she stayed in a place where she wasn't welcome, and she wasn't going to start now, no matter how much it hurt to leave.

This time as she started to walk past him, Peter didn't move a muscle. He wasn't going to interfere. He had said what needed to be said—what had to be said. Yet the feeling that remained wasn't very pleasant.

CHAPTER SIX

Kathy was late for work the next morning. Eric started to tease her, but after taking one look at her puffy face, he decided not to. And he didn't press her for any details. She would tell him if she wanted; and if she didn't, he would accept her decision.

She didn't say anything about her personal life, but during the next few days, she attacked her duties with a ferocious zeal that must have given some comfort to her troubled mind and spirit.

For the next several days Peter went about his work at the bank with a cool detachment. But inside, where no one could see, his emotions were churning. He had done the right thing. The situation had gotten out of hand, and he had put a stop to it. So why did he miss her?

Friday evening Kathy made arrangements to go out with a few of her friends and promised herself that she would have a good time. To aid in that goal, she slipped into one of her prettier dresses, put on extra makeup, and then surveyed the results. A spark was in her eyes, a flush was on her cheeks—and no one else would know that their cause was determination and not excitement.

115

She had made up her mind about Peter: she was going to cut him out of her life completely. If he didn't want anything to do with her, she didn't want anything to do with him. She had managed to get through twenty-one years without him; and she could easily continue.

That thought was with Kathy all evening. While she talked, while she laughed, while she danced. Maybe that was why she drank a few too many piña coladas. Kathy didn't have a good head for liquor, so she usually stayed with nonalcoholic beverages, or, if pressed, she would have one drink at the most. Tonight, though, out of defiance she didn't stop with one.

As a result everything became so funny to her! She would giggle at the slightest provocation. She thought it was hilarious that Toni had to help her up the stairs to her apartment because her feet couldn't seem to negotiate the climb on their own. Also the fact that her key wouldn't fit properly into the lock brought on another fit of giggles.

In Kathy's mind she was perfectly all right, and she was quick to assure her friend of that fact when she was asked if she needed further assistance.

"I'm fine!" Kathy said. "In fact I've never been so fine in my life!"

Toni laughed. "Sure you are."

"I *am!*" Kathy insisted as she collapsed onto the couch.

Toni shook her head. "What you are, Kathy, is tipsy. And what I suggest is for you to get yourself straight to bed."

"But I feel too good to go to bed!" Kathy complained.

"I know, but do it anyway."

Kathy smiled and waved to her friend as she left.

When she was alone, Kathy stared at the empty room. Suddenly she didn't feel so wonderful anymore. What she really wanted to do was cry. Huge tears formed in her eyes, flooding them. She sniffed, feeling miserable.

She didn't understand why Peter didn't like her when everyone else did.

Kathy rubbed a cascading tear from her cheek.

He's just so difficult!

Another tear followed the first one's path and had to be wiped away.

Someone should tell Peter exactly what kind of person he is. Going around ignoring people. Kissing them and then ignoring them.

She tried to get to her feet but wasn't successful the first time. When she tried again, a rather ungraceful effort, she finally achieved her goal. Her next goal became the door.

Kathy pulled it open and made her way unsteadily across the balcony to the opposite apartment.

Peter was lying in bed. He wasn't asleep—that being a state that had evaded him lately. Over the past few days he had been winning his rest only after a long struggle, and tonight the struggle wasn't over yet.

He looked at his watch. It was a quarter to one. Thank God he didn't have to go to work tomorrow. He didn't know how much longer he would be able to hold up. Something was going to have to give, but he didn't know what.

Restlessly Peter sat up. Maybe if he tried yoga. He

117

was just assuming the proper position when a loud, incessant knocking broke the stillness of the night.

Peter sat unmoving for a moment. Then as the knocking continued, he slid from the bed, put on a robe to cover his nudity, and walked carefully toward the noise.

One look through the window that butted against his door showed Peter that his visitor was Kathy.

His lips thinned. He was annoyed with himself for the way his heart jumped and with Kathy for being the cause.

When he opened the door he was ready for blood. Couldn't she understand that he wasn't going to get involved with her!

Kathy's blue eyes were vivid as she glared angrily at him. Then they began to change as her features crumpled. Moisture collected, pooled, and then somehow, miraculously, held in place.

Peter's initial irritation changed to immediate concern. "Kathy? Has something happened? What is it? Tell me."

Without thinking he scooted her indoors. When she said nothing, just continued to look at him in that slightly unfocused way, he repeated his earlier questions, only with more intensity. He ended by demanding, "Tell me, Kathy!"

Kathy sniffed and tried to pull away from his unconsciously bruising grasp.

"Don't . . . you're hurting me," she complained.

"I'll do more than that in a minute if you don't tell me what's happened!" he clipped.

Reaching into the foggy recesses of her mind, Kathy remembered why she was there.

"You—you—brute!" she burst out.

Peter froze into stillness.

"You—you—animal!" she accused.

Slowly his fingers loosened. When she lost his support, she swayed.

Peter's concern changed into suspicion. "Why do you say that?" he asked.

"Because—because—you don't like me!"

The statement was somewhere between a wail, a question, and an accusation.

Peter folded his arms and looked at her. Finally he said quietly, "You're drunk, Kathy."

"No, I'm not!" she returned, trying to hold her chin up. "I'm—I'm—" The word Toni had used popped happily into her mind. She grinned proudly. "I'm tipsy!"

"Go home, Kathy."

"No! I came here for a reason, and I'm not going until I—until I . . ." Her voice trailed away as she began to look confused again. Then she said, "Until I tell you everything I want to tell you."

"You can do that tomorrow."

Kathy gave her head an exaggerated shake. "No. No, I can't. You won't let me."

Peter had to smile. Even in this state she had a freshness about her—an innocence.

"I promise I'll let you . . . if you can remember what it is you wanted to say." The last was added under his breath.

Kathy shook her head and came forward until she could grasp the lapels of his robe.

"I want to say it now. I want . . ." Her fingers tightened, a vaguely surprised look came into her eyes, and after a moment, she slowly began to wilt toward the floor.

Only Peter's quick action prevented her from falling all the way. She was sprawled in his arms when he called irritably, "Kathy!"

He looked down at the lolling head, at the closed eyes, at the beatific smile that had come onto her lips. It was no use. She had passed out.

Peter's mouth settled into a grim line. Just what he needed. Just the bloody hell what he needed! He adjusted his grip on her body, shifting her until he could swing her up into his arms.

His quick, angry steps made short work of the balcony. He wanted to be rid of her! Even in this unconscious state he found her appealing, which told him the depth of his folly.

He stopped at her door and tried to turn the knob. The door was locked. He tried again, hoping that he had been mistaken. It remained locked.

In frustration Peter turned his back to the door and leaned against it. He wanted to laugh at the irony of the situation, but laughter wouldn't come. He banged the back of his head lightly against the wood. Then a thought occurred to him. Maybe she had been carrying a purse. He hadn't seen her holding one earlier, but he hadn't exactly been looking.

He shifted Kathy's position once again and began to recross the balcony. As deadweight she was heavy. Fast on the heels of that thought, he wondered what someone would think if they had happened along a moment before and saw him carrying a limp form across the narrow space and then saw him turn to carry it back. He'd probably be lucky if they didn't call the police!

Peter paused to peer into the darkness. Then, smiling faintly to himself, he reentered his apartment. Kathy hadn't moved in all the time he'd been carrying her, nor did she stir when he deposited her on the couch.

After ten minutes of searching for the missing purse, he finally had to admit that there was not one, which meant that there was no key.

He ran his fingers through his hair and glanced at the inert form on his couch. He could call the apartment manager and possibly try to get a key, but how would he explain his need for it? Not to mention the fact that it was after one in the morning, and the manager was a crusty sort who wouldn't appreciate being awakened.

Peter absently drummed his fingertips along the back of his favorite chair. Then he came to the only conclusion that was available to him: *She'll have to spend the rest of the night here.* A rush of blood surged through his veins. He contained it somewhat by adding:—*in the spare bedroom.* Then he chided himself, *She's passed out, for God's sake!* It wasn't as if he were keeping her here to seduce her—which he couldn't do even if he wanted to!

Peter's jaw squared before he went over to the couch, picked her up, and took her to the room he used as a combination office and extra bedroom. Once there, he laid her gently on one side of the bed. Then he sat at her feet and brought her legs onto his knee to remove her shoes. *Make it a quick job—get it over with.* But when his fingers came into contact with the shapely flesh, he paused, his gaze going over the entire woman. She was so young, so beautiful. In sleep her face was so vulnerable. The dark lashes against a curving cheek, the small straight nose, the soft responsive lips above a chin that

121

held just the slightest intimation of a cleft. He hadn't noticed that before. His eyes remained on the indentation and on her lips. Then, calling himself to task, he finished the job he had started: the removal of her shoes. When he was done, he shifted her under the turned-down coverlet and pulled it up over her shoulders.

Her blond hair was splayed out over the pillow, looking like the texture of spun gold. Peter touched a soft curl. Was she a mermaid? A beautiful sea creature who would sacrifice her most precious possession to gain the love of a mortal?

Peter shook his head, dismissing the fairy tale from his childhood. He dropped the curl as well as his fanciful speculation and moved quietly toward the door.

Yet he couldn't dismiss the loveliness of her features or the sensitivity of her expression. That stayed with him, even as he reminded himself frequently of the honor of her trust.

Kathy knew nothing until the next morning when a voice prompted, "Hey . . . wake up! If you stay asleep much longer, I'm going to start charging you rent!"

One blue eye pried itself open. What she could see of the room wasn't familiar. Then slowly a little bit of yesterday evening returned to her. She had been with her friends; they had been dancing. *Am I at Toni's house? No.* She could almost swear that Toni had brought her home last night. She had a vague memory —and anyway, the voice had been masculine.

"It's about time!" the voice intruded once again.

Kathy turned toward the doorway and squinted her eyes. "Who—" she started to ask when the form straightened away from the doorjamb and she recog-

122

nized Peter. Her mistified tone changed to one of shock. "You!"

Peter smiled slightly. "Yes, me."

Kathy struggled to sit up, but she got no further than lifting her head, which she gingerly had to lower when it became evident that it was in danger of exploding.

"Aaargh!" she groaned, putting a hand to her face.

Peter watched her movement, his body reacting in spite of himself. She had been hard to resist unconscious, but awake!

"What—what am I doing here?" she got out weakly at last.

"You locked yourself out of your apartment."

"I did?"

Peter nodded, his eyes not showing any of the emotions he was feeling. His hands were stuffed in the pockets of his slacks. He felt it was better that way; otherwise they would be all over her.

"But how . . . ?"

She seemed to be having trouble forming the words, so Peter helped. "How did you get here?" he supplied. Then he answered his own question. "You wanted to tell me something."

Kathy blinked. "I did?" Somewhere in a far corner of her mind she remembered something about that, but it was encased in too much fog to break through.

"But you didn't have a chance to say it—or at least not all of it. You passed out. Alcohol doesn't seem to agree with you."

The last was said very tongue in cheek. If Kathy had felt better, she would have challenged him. But, as it was, something else he said held her attention.

She lifted her upper body carefully, using her elbows

for support. "What do you mean, 'not all of it'? What did I say?" As she began to focus on what had driven her to drink earlier in the evening, the warm heat of embarrassment rose up to encase her body.

"It really wasn't very logical," he replied.

Kathy wanted to run groaning from his apartment to hers. But first of all she didn't know if she was capable —her head still felt like a fully expanded balloon; and second, if her apartment was locked, what good would it do her to run to it?

"What did I say?" she whispered, hoping for the best.

Peter's sherry-colored eyes examined the floor before lifting to ensnare hers.

"You accused me of not liking you."

"Oh, God." Kathy moaned softly. It was worse than she thought! If she lived to be a hundred, she would never—ever—touch anything stronger than a glass of water again! She tried to save the situation by struggling to her feet. "You were right when you said I don't hold liquor very well. More than one and I'm gone." She snapped her fingers and tried to laugh. "You must have thought that was the funniest thing you'd heard in years!"

"Not really," Peter replied steadily.

Kathy busied herself by brushing at some of the wrinkles in her dress. She was willing to do anything not to have to look at him.

"Well, I'm sorry," she apologized. "I promise I won't inflict myself on you again."

Peter watched as she began to search for her shoes. She seemed to be avoiding looking at him. Finally he said, "Kathy . . ."

Hearing her name coming softly from his lips caused

a riot of jangled emotion to shoot through Kathy's body, but she pretended nothing was happening.

"Surely I was wearing shoes when I came in," she said more to herself than to him.

"They're under the edge of the bed."

After finding her shoes, she sat down on the disturbed coverlet to put them on.

She tried to keep a steady stream of one-way conversation going. "I suppose I'll have to go to the manager to get a duplicate key. I just hope he doesn't ask any questions." She stood up. "Are you sure I didn't bring a purse? But, no, if I had you wouldn't have had to put me up last night. I—"

Kathy tried repeatedly to put on her shoe, but her fingers were trembling so badly that the best she could do was fumble with it. When the shoe tumbled from her grasp, Peter was at her feet, bending low to help her.

Kathy looked down at his bent head. She wanted to reach out and touch the thick strands of his hair, to feel the vibrant texture, to have some form of contact with him. But she curled her fingers into her palms and held them tightly. He was doing this only to aid in her departure. He wanted her out of his apartment—just as he had the other day.

Peter's fingers reached out to curve around her ankle. He had the shoe in his other hand, ready to direct it onto her foot. Then, slowly, his hand began to move, eventually sliding up the delicate curve of her calf. Her skin was so smooth and warm and enticing!

Kathy froze in position.

Peter continued his exploration. He had wanted to do this last night. His fingers moved to the sensitive flesh at the back of her knee, the inside of her knee, the beginning of her thigh. . . . Then his gaze lifted.

She was looking down at him, her eyes wide. Her eye makeup was smudged, he noticed, with more of it on the fine skin under each eye than on her lashes or lids. But to him, she had never looked more appealing. She was so precious and young and in need of love. Like his beautiful mermaid.

Peter was unable to withstand such an onslaught. He had fought so hard, so valiantly, but now he was forced to concede the battle. And as the forgotten shoe dropped softly to the carpet, he didn't care. To the victor belongs the spoils, the old saying goes. Only who was to say who was the victor and who was the defeated? And sometimes weren't the spoils that were won worth the subjugation of everything else?

Kathy held his gaze until his nearness made it impossible. Then as the warm urgency of his lips pressed against hers, a searing heat exploded throughout her system. Her pulse began to race madly, her senses reel. She gave back kiss for kiss, holding onto him madly, uncaring of anything but what was taking place at the moment.

He leaned forward, causing her to fall backward onto the bed, his body moving with her, turning so that he wouldn't crush her. As they lay side by side, his fingers threaded through the silken strands of her hair.

Kathy looked into his eyes and saw the flames she once had imagined there. An equally torrid blaze was consuming her, prompting her to assist him in every effort for closeness that he made. She held still as he loosened the buttons on her dress so that he could pull the material away. A small breath of pleasure greeted the sliding away of her slip and bra to expose two perfectly formed breasts.

Peter gazed at what his plundering fingers had exposed, and then he bent to slide his lips over a curving mound, bringing the rosebud peak to tingling hardness.

Mindlessly, he continued to worship her, letting his tongue draw sensation upon sensation from both of her breasts.

Then he pulled slightly away to look at her, his eyes glittering.

Kathy stared back at him, her breathing ragged, her bones melting under the heat of their mutual desire.

When he spoke, she didn't understand him at first. The passion-filled blood coursing through her veins was roaring in her ears. He was forced to repeat what he said, his voice thick, "Does this answer your question, Kathy?"

"What question?" she whispered, barely able to find her voice.

"The one you asked last night"—he dipped his head once more to nuzzle her erect nipple before moving closer to her waist, kissing her through the material that remained there—"about my not liking you."

Kathy had to take several deep breaths in order to respond. "But you said—"

Peter shifted position until he was leaning over her, his eyes on a level with hers. "Never mind what I said," he murmured huskily, stilling her words. Then his lips moved to continue feasting upon hers.

Kathy didn't wait to be given that directive twice. Responding to the almost unbearable needs welling up within her, her arms curved about his neck, straining him close.

When Peter hurriedly discarded his clothing while she finished removing hers, she didn't stop to question if what she was doing was right, if she was ready for what was to follow. From the beginning she had instinctively sensed that he was the man she had been waiting for.

Then, as overheated flesh met overheated flesh, there was no more thought given to anything but the burning quicksilver flames that demanded immediate satiation.

Kathy was hesitant to meet Peter's eyes when eventually he pulled away from her to lie by her side.

She was still caught up in the tumult of emotion of the minutes before, but she was also coming back to earth rather quickly.

They had done it. *She* had done it. She was no longer a virgin, although the fact that she was one before had never bothered her. She didn't think she was the only one left at her age, and if she was—well, she never worried about it. Not since she and Jason had had their talk about her not letting herself be pushed into doing anything that she didn't feel comfortable doing. Well, she hadn't been pushed today, and the thought was deeply exciting.

Kathy looked shyly at the back of Peter's head. Her fingers reached out to touch the soft brown hair. He had given her so much—made her initiation so sweet. She had heard horror stories in the past, and none of it had come true for her.

Peter lay still. He couldn't believe what had just happened! He hadn't planned it. He had thought about it, yes. He almost had been obsessed. But when he awakened her, he hadn't expected events to culminate in this! He had planned to offer her coffee and maybe some orange juice and see her on her way. Only it hadn't worked out that way. And it had been her first time!

He hadn't expected her to be virginal. God, when he had realized it, he could scarcely believe it! He had tried to pull away, but she hadn't let him. She had wanted him to continue—and that had made him go completely out of control. He hadn't been able to think rationally anymore. He had merely reacted.

He felt her tentative touch. Then came her soft voice. "I—ah—I've never done that before, Peter."

Peter wasn't sure what to say. It had been a long time since he had made love to a virgin, and then he had been a virgin himself.

When he hesitated, Kathy rushed on. "Are you disappointed? I mean . . . I know you value experience."

Peter turned onto his side so that he could look at her. He realized his mistake immediately when it was all he could do not to pounce on her once again. She looked so lovely with her golden hair spread out on the pillow and her golden skin completely exposed.

His words were thick when he assured her, "I wasn't disappointed." That she was asking that showed her inexperience. She had made love with him so naturally, so joyously, he hadn't missed any of the more practiced moves. He reached out to stroke a golden curl. Then he began to wonder if possibly she hadn't been ready to be made love to for the first time. Maybe he had forced her, at least in the beginning. He hadn't given her much opportunity to protest.

"Kathy—" he began, his tone hinging on regret.

She stopped him immediately, guessing what he was about to say. "No," she whispered, touching his lips softly with her own and then pulling back to smile at him, a wise, sweet upturn of lips that still managed to portray innocence, "don't say it. I wouldn't change what happened for the world."

Peter was beguiled by that smile. "You wouldn't?" he repeated.

Kathy shook her head. "No."

"Why?"

"Because you're special, Peter."

His voice was husky when he asked, "Why do you say that?" He knew this was the wrong approach, that it would be better to treat this situation in as sophisticated a manner as possible. To try to get out of it without being too personal—*too personal!* Since when had his dealings with Kathy not been personal? And now this! The prospect of this happening had haunted him all along. And now he was trying not to be too personal?

Then an equally irrational thought popped into his brain: was it possible that he could play with fire and not get burned? Could he do it? Could he form a relationship with her and walk away from it unscathed?

Kathy's reply brought his attention back to her. "I just know it. Otherwise I wouldn't be here. I have good instincts about people."

Peter didn't move for several seconds. He remembered something she had said to him about people living up to the good other people expected of them. But it wasn't like that for him. He couldn't trust that line of reasoning.

He pulled away, he stood up, and after looking at her another moment, he left the room.

Kathy watched him as he walked away, her eyes drawn to his lithe form. Just as she had speculated, he was quite well built with long muscles that heredity had provided and exercise had perfected. He had a beautiful body—one she wanted to experience again.

When he didn't come back immediately, Kathy forced herself to get out of bed and dress. Her headache from first awakening was almost gone. *Is sex a good cure for a hangover?* She gave a nervous giggle. Would the world be interested in knowing that? But a lingering lethargy still had hold of her body. Her every nerve ending seemed to glow as well as want to rest and savor the experience. She didn't want to move unless it was to have Peter make love to her again. Then she would move, more than before, because now she would know more.

Kathy had to locate her shoes again. This time they weren't neatly placed under the edge of the bed. She found one, but the other was missing. She carried the high-heeled shoe in her hand as she traced Peter's steps.

He was sitting in the living room, a maroon robe wrapped securely about his body, and he was smoking a cigarette.

Kathy didn't know what to say at first, so she commented on that. "I thought you were a health nut." She motioned to the cigarette.

"There are a lot of things you only think you know about me." His reply was distant.

"I know that I like you," she said simply.

"That could be a mistake," he returned, then laughed shortly. "That *is* a mistake."

Kathy came closer to the chair and knelt at his knee. Reacting by instinct, she placed her head on his thigh.

"I don't think so," she disagreed.

Peter drew deeply on the cigarette, coughed, and then smashed it out. "This isn't a game, Kathy."

"I know that."

"And whatever it is, I think it should end. Right now, before—"

"Before what?" Kathy raised her head to look at him. "Before one of us gets hurt?"

"I was thinking of you. I won't get hurt."

"You said you like me. I'm not naive enough to think that a man has to like a woman before he makes love to her, but"—she studied him—"I think you had to like me."

Peter reacted with impatience. "Stop assuming that you know me! You don't!"

"I'd like to learn about you."

Peter stood up to pace the room. Kathy remained on her knees, her eyes following his movement.

"You're much too young for me," he said at last. "I'm thirty-two and you're what? Twenty? Twenty-one?"

"Twenty-one," she replied. "And what does age have to do with anything? You're always bringing it up, but I don't think you really believe what you're saying. You didn't think I was too young a few minutes ago."

She had him there. Peter gave a muffled moan.

Kathy rose to stand next to him. Her hand reached out to make soft contact.

Peter refused to look at her. He was fighting another war within himself—one in which he was the only combatant.

"It won't work, Kathy," he warned.

Kathy gazed at his set jaw. She could already feel the

rigidity of his body from touching his arm. Had she made a mistake? Was most of the liking on her side?

Her fingers slowly dropped away. She turned away.

"I—" She stopped, unable to go on. Then she made herself continue. "My shoe. I could only find one. When you find the other, just—just leave it outside my door. You don't have to bother to knock. I'll find it."

She sounded so sad, so forlorn! Peter's heart twisted. She started to walk away. *What am I doing?*

Kathy got no farther than the door. Peter came up behind her and dragged her back against his hard body.

"No!" he whispered hoarsely as he bent his lips close to her ear. "This is stupid. It's the most stupid thing I've ever done in my life, but I can't let you go. Not like this!"

Kathy was aware of the power of his desire as her slim back was pressed close against him. Her body reacted in kind, and she turned, her arms going up to encircle his neck, her mouth raised for his kiss. Peter didn't disappoint her—his mouth crushed down on hers, insistent, demanding, and yet sensitive to her every response.

Both were shaken when the kiss was done.

"You do things to me, Kathy," he rasped, his words thick. "Things that take away my better judgment."

Kathy was breathless. "I know. You do them to me, too."

Peter pressed his forehead to hers, trying to get his thoughts back into some kind of order so that he could say what had to be said. It was crazy! He was crazy! For all his adult years he had stayed away from women he couldn't control his feelings with. And now, here he was, getting ready to open himself to one he could control nothing with. To open himself wide. There was only one faint hope, one out.

He cleared his throat. "There's one thing, Kathy. One thing that you have to agree to if this is to continue."

"What?" she whispered. She would have agreed to anything.

"There can be no strings. When you want to end it or I want to end it, the other agrees immediately . . . with no hurt feelings or recriminations."

"Agreed," Kathy said lightly. At the moment the price didn't seem too high to her. She was living for the here, the now. She wanted Peter; she wanted him physically, and she wanted to get to know his mind. He was the first man she had felt this way about. She would deal with tomorrow's problems when they occurred, if they occurred.

Peter held back for another few seconds, his eyes studying her intently. Then, unable to restrain himself any longer, he joined their lips and welcomed the sensual need that instantly flared up between them.

CHAPTER SEVEN

Because their apartments were so close together, Kathy did not so much move in with Peter as she did creep in. One day this possession was transferred from her apartment to his, and the next day another possession would follow the same path. Peter felt uncomfortable using the Sinclairs' apartment, so she, keeping true to her promise, still spent some time there each day carrying out her duties honoring Frederick's memory.

"I feel like I'm living with Jacques Cousteau!" Peter complained teasingly by Tuesday of their first week together. Kathy had brought a number of her keepsakes over by this time, and of course they all pertained to the sea.

"Do you mind?" she asked impishly. The fact that she was sitting in his lap with only a towel wrapped around her freshly showered body and running the tips of her fingers over his chest before dipping ever so tantalizingly lower gave her a bit of confidence.

"Are you kidding?" Peter responded, his body beginning to stir. "Not when he looks like you."

Kathy giggled. "Thank you."

"You're welcome," Peter replied before bringing the marauding fingertips up to his mouth where he pretended to nibble each end in preparation for what was to follow.

At work Eric couldn't get over the change in Kathy.

"Hey! Give me the name of the elixir you're using. I could sure use some of it myself."

"I've told you what you should do. You just won't listen to me," Kathy reproved smilingly.

Eric scratched his head in puzzlement. "Now, what was it you said I should do? Move to Timbuktu? Go for a long walk on a short pier? Find myself some locoweed and eat it? Was it any one of those choices?"

Kathy laughed at Eric's buffoonery.

"No, you idiot!"

"Then let me think. Aha!" His face brightened. "Now I remember. It had something to do with Sue."

"You're getting warmer!"

"And I'm also going to be a daddy!" he announced.

Kathy blinked. Surely she hadn't heard him correctly. "You're what?" she asked.

"I'm going to be a daddy. Well, technically I already am, but we're going to have to wait till the thing's hatched to say that I really am."

"Sue's pregnant?"

"Done up right and proper."

"When?"

"Sometime late next January. We stand a chance of hitting my birthday on the twentieth."

"That's a nice present."

"Yeah."

Kathy hesitated, then asked carefully, "Am I getting an invitation to the wedding?"

"Am I getting one to yours?" was his quick come-back.

Kathy frowned. "The situation is completely different."

"What makes it different?"

"The baby, you idiot!" This time the derogatory tag was not made in fun. She was glad that she and Peter were taking precautions so that the same thing wouldn't happen to them when neither was ready for it.

Now it was Eric's turn to frown.

"I'm still not ready to get married."

"But Sue's pregnant!"

"She doesn't have to be married to have the kid!"

"No," Kathy returned hotly, "but it helps!"

The two of them glared at each other over the top of the pickup as they stepped out to start their work. Then, gradually, both of them realized the futility of their argument. They were friends who disagreed. Neither could persuade the other to their point of view. They might try, but if they were unsuccessful, the friendship shouldn't die because of it.

They both began to smile.

"Come on," Eric prompted by way of backing down. "Maybe if we try hard, we can get off early this evening."

"Sounds good to me," Kathy agreed. She thought of Peter and goose bumps ran up and down her spine. But they were pleasant goose bumps.

The secretary Peter worked with most closely at the bank was slightly in awe of him. In the past he had rarely noticed her as anything more than an efficient machine. But recently, just the beginning of this week,

137

he began to smile at her, say "good morning" and mean it, and even be understanding if she flubbed up a report. In effect he began to treat her as if she were a living, breathing human being. The result was that awe evolved into adoration. In a quick few days she decided that she would lay down her late middle-aged life for him if he asked her—although like Romeo and Juliet, their romance was not fated to be. But he was so handsome, especially when he smiled, which he seemed to be doing a lot these days.

Normally Peter was the first to arrive at his apartment after work each evening, and he would spend the time preparing a quick nutritious meal for them to eat later and then getting in his daily five mile jog that Kathy seemed to have no interest in sharing. "I get enough exercise on the job, thank-you-very-much," she told him the first time he had asked if she wanted to go. But today, when he arrived home, she was already there. He could tell that by the aroma of meat cooking.

She met him in the living room, a spatula in one hand, a dishcloth in the other. After a quick kiss she stepped back defensively.

"I know. You don't eat meat. But I'm dying for a hamburger. I'll make you one, too, if you want, but I can't look another bean sprout in the eye!"

Peter began to laugh at the part defiant–part pleading picture she made. He didn't examine his feelings too closely. He promised himself he would not. But Kathy had a way of making him enjoy each moment, and he liked that. She could make him laugh when no one else could.

"A hamburger sounds fine," he decided. "I haven't had one in months, but I like them . . . on occasion."

Kathy pulled a face. "I don't know how you stand it."

Peter drew her into his arms, careful to avoid the spatula. "And I don't know how you can stand rock music. All that noise!"

"It's not noise!"

Peter's head swooped, and Kathy didn't protest any longer. She loved the feel of his lips on hers, the hunger his touch ignited in her belly, the lingering fragrance of his cologne combined with his own natural scent, the feel of his hard-muscled body.

"Are you still ready for that burger?" he teased softly when he released her mouth.

Kathy's blue eyes began to sparkle. "Yes, but only because I know I can have you for dessert."

Peter grinned. "Having come to know a little bit about you, which am I? Chocolate fudge or caramel creme?"

Kathy licked her lips. "Oh, definitely a combination of each!"

Peter laughed and let her go. He followed her into his kitchen.

Kathy hummed a little tune to herself and smiled at him frequently as she prepared the rest of the burger makings: pickles, tomatoes, onions, lettuce.

"Do you want cheese with it?" she asked daringly, knowing that she was pushing him but doing it anyway because she loved to tease him.

"No, thank you. There's enough cholesterol in the meat."

"Do you mind if I have cheese?"

Peter hesitated. Damned if he didn't mind! One side effect of being so close to Kathy was that he was beginning to feel protective of her, to want the best for her. But if he admitted that, he would also have to admit that she was getting too close. So instead, he chose to ignore it—to just let them drift along.

"No, not at all," he said eventually.

Kathy grinned. "Good. But I don't happen to like cheese on my burger. I just wanted to see what you'd say."

After their meal—enjoyed by both—Peter put on a Mozart recording and sat with Kathy on the couch. She was curled up against him. He found the experience pleasurable. He had had mistresses before, but he had never just spent time with them. With Kathy, this, along with everything else, was different.

He ran his fingers along the soft skin of her arm, marveling at the smoothness. She gave the impression of being so delicate, and yet from the work she did and from his own personal observation, he knew she was strong.

Kathy tipped her head and smiled up at him. It was a dreamy kind of smile—happy, content.

"You look pleased with yourself this evening," she murmured, reaching up to sweep a few loose strands of hair away from his forehead. This was fast becoming a ritual with her whenever she was feeling particularly loving toward him.

He returned her smile. "I am."

"Why?"

Peter shrugged lightly. "I don't know."

Kathy's eyes began to twinkle. "It wouldn't have anything to do with me, would it?"

Her teasing was infectious. Peter caught the baton and carried it forward. "Should I sell you for what you're worth?" he asked. "Or should I sell you for what you *think* you're worth?"

Kathy tried to look outraged. "Peter! How dare you!" She sat forward in his arms and pretended to pummel him with her fists. Then she stopped and affected deep thought. "Well, since it would be good business practice, definitely sell me for what I think I'm worth. An extra million or two wouldn't hurt."

Peter chuckled delightedly and tightened his arms until she was lying unprotestingly against his chest. "And what would you do with a million dollars? Try to buy the Bay Area and turn it into a wildlife refuge?"

Kathy made a face. "No. That would take more than a million and upset a lot of people." Then she did think seriously. "You know what I'd do? I'd buy Claudio's back from the people who bought it from Ashley and Jason and give it to Mary Morgan and Iris."

Peter's look turned to one of curiosity. "Why would you do that?"

"So they wouldn't have to worry about job security."

"Then they'd have to worry about running the place."

"True. But that's a nice kind of worry."

Peter let Kathy settle back into the crook of his arm. "I got the feeling from you that your sister didn't enjoy worrying about it."

"Ashley worried about everything."

"Including you?"

"Including me—especially me."

141

Peter looked down at her bright head. "I can imagine. You must have been a handful!"

Kathy laughed softly. "I wasn't that bad. Just the usual teen-age stuff."

"Boys, booze, partying?"

"Not booze. I didn't touch the stuff." She struggled to sit away from him so that she could look at him with earnest eyes. "That night . . . last week. I never get drunk, Peter. That night was unusual. I—I was upset about you. I didn't think that you liked me and that hurt. Normally, I don't drink anything. When I was a baby, my parents . . . Ashley's and mine . . . were killed in a car wreck caused by a drunk driver. I don't know if I don't drink very much because I can't handle it or if there's some deep psychological mumbo jumbo involved. Anyway, I don't want you to think that you've hooked up with a lush."

"I never thought that."

"Good." Kathy settled back against him, liking the feel of his body close to hers. It was both comforting and deliciously unsettling at the same time.

Peter thought about what she had told him. "So who raised you?" he asked.

"Ashley. She dropped out of college to take over caring for me and the restaurant."

Peter whistled softly. "That was quite a load to tackle so young."

"Yes. I didn't see it that way at first, but Jason helped me to understand."

Her voice softened imperceptibly whenever she said her brother-in-law's name. Peter felt something inside of him stiffen. He refused to put a name to it.

142

"Jason"—he repeated the name—"you think a lot of him, don't you?"

"Well," Kathy confided happily, "I did find him first." When Peter said nothing, she explained, "I introduced him to Ashley—only she didn't like him at first. She thought he was a pervert."

"And was he?"

"Good grief, *no!* He's just the kindest man around, that's all, with the greatest capacity to see inside of people. He understood me when no one else did. Ashley eventually found that out and fell in love with him."

"Like you already had, right?"

"Right. I love him . . . but as a brother. That's all I ever felt for him. Like he was an older brother or possibly a father. Kind of a mixture, if you know what I mean."

Peter nodded. He did know what she meant. It was easy to give affection when you craved parental love so badly. He remembered a certain stepfather—the one who had told him the story of the mermaid. He had seemed to understand all the confusion taking place in his young charge's mind and soul. But he hadn't stayed around for long. That marriage seemed to last the least amount of time of any of them. But Peter never forgot him—or the aching void he lived through afterward.

Kathy had continued speaking. He caught her last words. ". . . sometime. I think you'd like each other."

Peter started. "What?"

Kathy repeated patiently, "I wish that you and Ashley and Jason could meet sometime. I think you'd like each other."

"Yes," Peter agreed, but a ghost from his past had been released, one that froze his soul. One that made

143

him pull away. He didn't like to be reminded of the losses he had suffered—and what was worse, could possibly suffer again if he wasn't careful.

He disengaged himself as quickly as he could and stood up. Kathy looked at him, puzzled. She could sense the tension that had come over him.

Peter made a jerky movement as he stuffed his hands in his pockets. "I—ah—I think I'll take a shower. It's been a long day."

He didn't wait to hear a reply as he walked quickly into the bathroom.

Kathy's gaze followed his retreating back. She didn't know what had happened, but something had. And it was something he wasn't prepared to talk about with her yet.

Kathy experienced a vague premonition. She shivered, but it wasn't from coldness.

That night was the first time since they initially made love that they weren't intimate. Kathy lay in bed next to Peter, pressed against his back, feeling his steady breathing, unable to break through to him. It was as if there was an invisible wall hovering between them, one she could do nothing to scale.

Peter lay awake, wholly aware of Kathy's warm comfort only a hand's reach away, but he wouldn't make the move. He *couldn't* let himself—not tonight.

He tortured himself with the reasons why he should never have let her near him. Physical need wasn't enough. It wasn't an excuse. He should never have touched her. He should have moved away as soon as he knew he felt an attraction.

In the morning Kathy awakened to find Peter's arm curled around her. In sleep he had pulled her near. She placed her palm tentatively on his chest, loving the feel of him. She moved it ever so slightly.

That touch was enough. Peter was in a light sleep just prior to awakening, and when he felt the gentle smoothing motion and recognized it as coming from Kathy, he reacted like a man recently faced with starvation.

He rolled over, capturing her body beneath his, and he began to kiss her roughly, wildly, as if his very life depended upon the nurturing only she could give him.

Kathy responded instantly, her fingers digging into the flesh of his shoulders—his back—pulling him to her, reveling in the need they shared.

They were both late for work that day, but on the plus side, some of the uneasiness that had existed between them the night before had dissipated. Peter refused to think of anything except the sensual enjoyment he received from Kathy's body. He also dwelled on the sense of peace he found with her. And Kathy tried to think only of this morning, of the hunger he had shown for her, of the way he held her afterward, as if she might somehow disappear.

When they came into the other's presence again that evening, it was as two lovers might who had been separated from each other for days on end. They went immediately to bed, not speaking of their private concerns but showing affection in ways they were unable to convey with words.

Afterward Peter lay back on a pillow while Kathy rested her cheek against his chest. His fingers twirled strands of her hair, enjoying the golden silkiness.

Kathy sighed, a sated, relaxing release of breath.

Peter's fingers tightened momentarily, wordlessly agreeing with her satisfaction.

She moved her knee to cover one of his long, hard thighs. "That was nice," she murmured, putting her feelings into words at last as she nuzzled the tip of her nose against the sensitive skin at the base of his neck.

"An understatement," Peter agreed, bowing his head toward her.

They were quiet for another short length of time, neither wanting to move or to speak.

Kathy gave another little sigh. *Oh, how I enjoy being with Peter, making love with him. It's so . . . so . . . indescribably enjoyable!*

Then a reminder of last night came to sully her happy contemplation. *What happened between us last night? What sets off his withdrawal from me?* She had asked herself that question all day today, and the only conclusion she could come to was that it had something to do with her family. She had been talking about Jason and Ashley, and soon afterward he had pulled away.

A slight frown creased her brow as she continued to lie against him, her forefinger making abstracted circles in the fine hairs growing on his chest.

Peter never talked about himself. Never. He could have been hatched from an egg, or a test tube, for all that she knew about him. Did he have surviving parents? A sister or a brother? Maybe both?

Kathy sighed again, which made Peter begin to chuckle. Her finger stopped its movement. She didn't understand what had caused his amusement. "What is it? Did I miss something?" she asked.

Peter tipped her chin upward and teased, "I was laughing at you. You keep sighing. Are you bored?"

Kathy's eyes crinkled into a smile. "And what if I said that I was?"

Peter stole a quick kiss. "Then I'd have to find a way to amuse you."

"That sounds interesting."

"Ummm. Very," he agreed.

Another kiss was taken and then another until there was no question of theft.

Finally Kathy broke away laughing. "Okay. Okay. I give up!"

Peter's eyes were glowing as he returned, "Are you still bored?"

Kathy shook her head vigorously.

"Good," Peter said as he settled back against the pillow once again. He drew Kathy close against him.

They lapsed into another silence. But as had happened before, Kathy broke the spell. "Peter?"

"Ummm?"

"You've never said very much about yourself."

"That's because there's not much to say."

"Oh, there has to be!" Kathy struggled onto her elbow so that she could see his face. She liked to watch people's eyes when she talked to them. Their changing expressions added a great deal to any conversation.

Peter folded one arm under his head and looked up at the ceiling. "I'm just a regular guy, Kathy. No different from any other."

"So then you didn't just hatch from an egg!"

Peter began to smile. "I'd like to confess something to you, Kathy."

147

"What?" she asked breathlessly, prepared for anything.

"When I first met you and you made statements like that, I thought you were as crazy as the Sinclairs."

"I'm not crazy!"

Peter grinned wider. "I know that now . . . I think."

Kathy pretended to pout. "I'm not. I'm just—just—"

"Impulsive," he completed for her.

"Yes!"

"Don't worry. Maybe you'll grow out of it."

"But I don't want to grow out of it! Anyway, I'm already grown, as if you hadn't noticed."

Peter's eyes dropped to her breasts. He trailed a finger along their curving lines. "I've noticed," he returned, his voice slightly husky.

Kathy playfully slapped his hand. "You're changing the subject," she accused.

"You choose your subject, I'll choose mine." He reached for her again, but Kathy evaded him.

"I *have* chosen my subject! And you're it! Peter, I'd like to know more about you! I mean . . . after all . . ." She motioned to their positions in the bed.

Slowly the amusement faded from Peter's eyes, and he sat up, swinging his feet to the floor.

"I've already told you. There's not much to tell."

He started to rise from the bed, but Kathy stopped him by quickly getting to her knees and wrapping her arms around his waist.

"Please, Peter . . ." she entreated. She felt the tension in him. It was the same immediate onslaught of strained emotion that had come between them yesterday. Maybe she should have said nothing, but then again, that wasn't her way.

Peter didn't reply, but neither did he try to get up again.

Kathy was encouraged by his nonmovement.

"Is your mother still alive? Is your father?" she questioned.

No perceptible physical change came over him, but Kathy sensed a further tightening. Of his emotions?

"My mother's alive. My father died when I was eight."

"Do you have sisters and brothers?" Getting information from him was like pulling teeth! But at least he was talking.

"No, just myself. Thank God," he added in a murmur that she could barely hear.

She cocked her head, as if in doing so she could add volume to his last words. "Did you say, 'Thank God'? And why would you say that?"

Peter determinedly removed her arms from his middle and stood up.

His change of subject was just as direct. "Are you hungry?" His mouth was smiling slightly, but his eyes were not.

Kathy gazed up at him. She didn't want to eat. She wanted to listen while he talked. But she knew better than to press her point. He was sensitive to her questioning, so it was better to let the matter drop. She certainly didn't want to put any distance between them again.

Taking his rather heavy-handed cue, Kathy slid her feet to the floor and stood up in one energetic motion. "I certainly am! Do you have any ideas for dinner? Like broiled brussel sprouts? Or—I know! Steamed cabbage leaves!"

Her return to her usual teasing manner allowed some amusement to creep into Peter's eyes.

"Would you eat that if I agreed?"

Kathy put a horrified expression on her face, as if she had tasted the most foul tidbit of food.

Peter laughed. "Then why don't we go out to eat tonight? I can order my brussel sprouts and cabbage leaves, and you can order a nice, big, juicy steak."

"Agreed!" she cried, and the cry turned into a whoop as Peter whisked her from the floor and twirled around the room with her in his arms.

When they had completed one circuit, they collapsed back onto the bed laughing. It was sometime later before they began to dress for dinner.

CHAPTER EIGHT

Kathy wasn't aware of when it happened, but as the days went by she realized she had fallen in love with Peter. One moment she had been living her life, enjoying each moment that presented itself, not concerned with love—as in *Love* with a capital *L*—and the next, she realized that it had occurred. She loved him. She loved him as much as she loved Ashley, as much as she loved Jason—even more. Peter had come to mean everything to her.

She was sitting on the pier in front of the condo complex, her feet dangling above the water. Her discovery was like a miracle to her—all warm and beautiful. If life were a movie musical, she would be running up and down the nearby grassy knoll singing her heart out to the sky above.

Kathy swung her bare feet, trying in vain to skim the surface of the water. She only had one problem and that was Peter. *Should I tell him? Or should I just coast along, pretending nothing has happened, and wait to see what the outcome will be?* Kathy wished she had someone she could talk to.

She leaned back and reached into the pocket of her shorts for the forwarded letter she had received earlier in the day. Ashley and Jason were still in Tahiti. She would give just about anything if they were here.

Kathy examined the contents once again. It was upbeat as Ashley's letters usually were—happy, ecstatic—and filled with all the everyday occurrences that made up their lives. The only thing that was different was Jason's added note. It was written in pencil and looked to have been hastily scribbled. It read: "We think we might have a surprise for you, kid! Hang on. We'll let you know as soon as we can!"

Knowing Jason, the surprise might be anything. And if it wasn't that they were coming home soon, Kathy decided that she didn't want to know.

She wasn't aware that she was no longer alone until a step sounded close by on the wooden slats of the pier.

She turned and saw that her visitor was Peter. He was dressed in his pristine white shorts and shirt. She thought he was at the Fitness Center working out. At least that had been what he said he was going to do, and she had wondered if he was getting tired of her. *See what love can do?* she asked herself. *It starts pulling on your imagination, making you think things you wouldn't ordinarily think!*

He sat down beside her, looking out over the calm water. After a long moment Kathy felt his glance switch to her.

"You taking a busman's holiday?" he asked softly.

"A what?"

He shook his head in mock sadness. "A busman's holiday—a person spends all day driving a bus, and when that person goes on vacation, he takes the bus! See? Get it?"

"I get it," she answered noncommittally. Kathy was

happy that he was here, but she wished that he had stayed at the Fitness Center. She needed to think.

"I mean, with you spending all day in or near the water—"

"I said I got it," she returned a bit sharply.

"Well, all right! Sorry I brought it up!" He sounded offended.

Kathy immediately apologized. "No, I'm the one who's sorry." She placed a hand on his knee. "I didn't mean to snap. I just—"

"It's okay."

"No,"—her eyes were large—"I truly am sorry."

Peter looked into those beautiful blue eyes, eyes that were a reflection of so much in her soul, and he felt his heart give a flip-flop. He quickly looked away. A sea gull seemingly hanging suspended in the sky served as a good subject.

"It's okay," he repeated.

Kathy continued to look at his profile. Finally she said, "You didn't stay at the center long."

"No."

"Too crowded?"

"A bit," he answered. Peter kept his eyes on the bird that was now dive-bombing an unsuspecting fish. He couldn't tell Kathy that he had started to exercise and had felt a sudden demanding need to come back to her. No, he couldn't tell her that. He could barely admit it to himself.

"Too bad," she commiserated, looking down at the water lapping against the pilings.

Peter's gaze turned back to her. He saw the letter that was still in her hand.

"That from the Sinclairs?"

Kathy shook her head. "No, from my sister, Ashley, and Jason."

"They still on their boat?" he asked. Kathy had told him about *Sunchaser*—how it had been sold and later repurchased.

"Yes."

Peter noted the downward tilt of her mouth. He reached out to run a finger along the soft skin of her arm.

"You miss them, don't you."

"Sometimes," she admitted, then turned to look at him. Without thinking she asked, "Don't you sometimes miss your mother?"

Peter's hand pulled back.

"I mean," Kathy hurriedly continued, trying to fill the breach, "you love her, don't you?"

Peter didn't want to discuss his mother with Kathy. He didn't want the two of them to mix in his mind. One was locked shut in one compartment; one had taken over the rest. Still he felt compelled to answer her question. "Yes . . . I love her."

Kathy decided that now was the time to probe further—at least just a little bit further. "Does she live near here?"

"No."

"In the state?"

"No, New York—at least at the moment."

"Did you live in New York?" Kathy had never been able to place a regional accent with Peter. His speech pattern was television-commentator Midwest.

"I've lived everywhere, Kathy."

She laughed cautiously. "Surely not everywhere. You're not old enough."

"It felt like everywhere."

Kathy suspected that she had made another breakthrough.

"You moved around a lot?"

Peter sighed with exasperation. "You certainly do ask a lot of questions!"

Kathy grinned mischievously. "That's the only way to get answers." Then she repeated, "Well, did you? Move around a lot?"

Peter stood up. Kathy quickly scrambled into position beside him.

"When I was a kid, I did. Now, that's enough. I don't like to talk about myself."

"Don't be so modest. You're an interesting subject." She tried to tease him back into more confidences.

"I'm not a species of fish, Kathy, to be put under a microscope and studied."

"I realize that."

Peter looked down at her, at her golden hair, her golden skin, her sky-blue eyes, and any resentment of her probing questions evaporated.

"I know you do," he said softly as he held out a hand. "Come on. Let's go back to the apartment and see what we can do to entertain ourselves."

A twinkle of immediate understanding grew to life in those same sky-blue eyes. "You mean play a game? Like Trivial Pursuit?"

A slow smile tilted his lips. "I mean play a game, but not *that* kind of game."

Kathy pretended innocence. "Are the rules very hard? I'm a quick study, but—"

"You'll manage," he interrupted.

Kathy continued her teasing. "Will it be fun?"

"You can give me your opinion afterward."

"Oh."

Peter smiled down at her. His hand was still extended. He was waiting.

Kathy didn't make him wait another second. With a trusting little laugh she placed her hand in his and then swung into step beside him.

Later that night Peter stared unblinkingly into the blackness of his room. Kathy was asleep at his side, her regular breathing and still body something he had been waiting for so that he could have some time alone to think. But now that he had the time, he couldn't form the thoughts.

His hand automatically reached for a soft golden curl. It was so much like silk! His fingers crushed the vibrant hairs and then released them, holding the curl gently. He fully expected the aroma of crushed flowers to assail his nostrils. Roses, lilies. . . . He drew his hand away and gave a deep sigh.

He didn't know where this relationship was going to end! She was so young, so guileless, so fresh to the world. Tragedy had struck early in her life, but she had known nothing except loving support afterward. Whereas he—

No, he didn't want to think about his past. That wasn't what he needed to examine. He needed to consider the future, the path he was going to take—not the one he had already followed.

But whenever he thought of the future—a future without Kathy—his mind rebelled. And that fact scared him.

Take tonight—when he had preferred to be with her

rather than at the gym working out. And it wasn't just because she was beautiful, willing, and a fantastic partner in bed. He had wanted to be with her. Just to talk to her, if need be.

Peter wished he had never gotten himself into this situation. He was damned if he did and damned if he didn't. If he woke Kathy up and told her to go back to her own apartment—that their association was over—like he should do, he didn't know if he wanted to live with the emotional fallout. She was fast becoming part of his life. But he couldn't commit to her. He couldn't commit to any woman. He was too much his mother's son.

In her sleep Kathy must have unconsciously felt some of the turmoil that was stirring his soul because she rolled toward him and gave his flat stomach a soothing pat while murmuring unintelligible words of comfort.

Peter's body remained completely still. He didn't want her to awaken. If she did, she might notice his discontent and wonder at the cause. And he couldn't explain it to her when he couldn't explain it even to himself.

By morning Peter had himself under control. *Kathy's young, but she knows what she's doing. I warned her. She knows the score. She isn't stupid.* He told himself this as he shaved. But when he sat down at the table opposite her for breakfast, he hid behind the newspaper so that he wouldn't have to look at her bright freshness.

She didn't allow that evasion for long, though. "Peter?" she called.

"Ummm?" He tried to concentrate on the financial

157

page, attempting to make sense of another giant corporate takeover.

"What do you think of my uniform?"

"Humm? Uniform?" He kept his nose pointed at the newsprint.

Kathy solved the problem by simply removing the paper from his grip. It was up and away and neatly folded beside her plate before he could say a word.

"Now"—she smiled, satisfied—"what do you think of my uniform?"

Peter examined the bright-blue material and the shoulder patch that bore the insignia of the Parks and Wildlife Department.

"Are you going to jump into the water in that?"

Kathy started to giggle. "No."

"Then why . . . ?"

She sighed patiently. "I told you last night. I'm going on a creel survey today."

"For all I know, you could need scuba gear to do that."

Now Kathy really did laugh. "A *creel* is a basket or pouch that a fisherman uses to put his catch in. I'm going to the fishing piers and boat ramps in the area to interview the people about the fish they've caught. If they'll agree, I measure them, record their type, see where they were caught . . ."

Peter couldn't resist. Kathy had a way of taking him out of himself, making him see the absurd.

"The fishermen or the fish?" he asked.

"What?" Kathy said blankly.

"Just who are you going to measure, record, and so on? The fishermen or the fish?"

"Why the fish, of—" she began to answer earnestly.

158

Then, when she realized what he was doing, she jumped from her chair and came around to plop herself in his lap.

"Just for that"—she tried to sound stern—"you're going to have to pay a forfeit."

Peter let his troubles slide away. Whenever Kathy was this close, he couldn't resist her—which was the root of his problem. But at the moment he didn't care.

His eyes were lighted by a lazy glow. "Just what do you have in mind?"

Kathy looked at her watch. "Well, if it weren't so late, I could think of any number of things. But . . . I'll settle for a kiss."

Peter pretended to consider her choice. "Is it proper to kiss an officer of the state?" His eyes dropped to her uniform.

"I could take it off," she volunteered.

Peter laughed. "No, you'd better not. We'd both be late for work again."

Kathy ruefully agreed. "You're right. I'll keep it on." Then she began to smile. "Now about this dilemma— If the officer of the state agrees, I don't see where there would be any crime in—"

Peter didn't let her finish. His body could stand no more teasing. He wanted to kiss her. He wanted to feel the assurance of her lips against his, the touch of her body.

The kiss was much more than Kathy had expected. She drew back, her eyes wide, her breathing disturbed.

"White man speak with forked tongue," she accused him at last.

Peter looked at her puzzled, his own breathing erratic. He wanted to do more than kiss her now.

"You said we'd be late for work," she explained. "That we couldn't—"

Again he interrupted her flow of words. "I'm willing to chance it if you are."

Kathy's eyes were sparkling with mischief. "You? A stuffy old banker?"

"Even stuffy old bankers need love."

Kathy looked at her watch once again and then, grinning, pressed her lips to his in a manner that informed him she didn't care about time in the least.

As luck would have it, Kathy wasn't late for work. And since Peter had a shorter distance to travel than she, she knew that he wasn't late either.

She walked into the Institute humming a pleasant little tune and greeted everyone she met with a happy smile. She knew she probably should be worried—about whether she should tell Peter that she loved him; about whether he would come to love her; and if he didn't come to love her, about how much longer they would be together—but for the life of her, she couldn't lower her spirits to wallow in self-doubt and questioning. At the moment her life was wonderful!

Kathy had always been an optimist. To her the psychological glass was always half full instead of half empty. Worry had its place but not at the expense of enjoying today.

Then, too, certain changes had come over Peter since they had become lovers. At first he had held himself back—been aloof to a degree in their everyday give-and-take. It wasn't something blatant; it was just something she had sensed. But slowly, as time began to pass, the aloofness was no longer evident. Yes, he still withdrew

160

occasionally, especially when she questioned him too closely. But even considering that fact, she had made some headway in learning more about him. She knew he was an only child, that his mother lived in New York, that he loved her. But she had also learned that there had been problems in his life. Problems he was reluctant to talk about with anyone. Problems that still affected him even though he was a strong adult male, successful in his job and independent in his life-style.

Walking into another section of the Institute, Kathy made contact with the person she was to assist in the creel survey. Eric was scheduled for a week's vacation, so this was a perfect opportunity for her to learn a different aspect of the organization's work.

The woman she was assigned to help was not much older than Kathy, but she had been involved in the examination of the area's marine population through the creel survey for some time. She certainly knew her way around the fishing piers and the fishing marinas. She was friendly, efficient, and a good representative of the Parks and Wildlife Department.

"We women have to stick together," Paula said shortly after they had gathered the needed equipment and forms and started off for the first boat ramp. "This is still too much of a man's world for us not to."

Kathy felt a bit of a pressure not to let Paula down. And when the day was finished and they had returned to the institute, she was confident that she had been successful. At least Paula was still happy to have her around, even going so far as to call a cheery, "See you tomorrow," before leaving for the day.

As Kathy climbed the stairs to Peter's apartment, she contrasted the way she appeared today to the way she appeared after seining. She was more tired emotionally with the strain of learning a new job and temporarily having a new partner, but at least she didn't end the day looking like a drowned rat! The official Parks and Wildlife uniform was required when meeting the public, and she enjoyed looking like this sometimes. She wondered if Peter would appreciate the change.

She was smiling in anticipation of seeing him when, before she could insert her key, the door swung open and there he was standing before her.

"Well, hello! I didn't expect such service!" she greeted happily.

And then her happy smile began to fade. Peter wasn't smiling; his features were stiff.

"Peter?" she started to question, her voice hesitant.

Something was wrong. He was standing in the doorway, blocking it.

Kathy absorbed his body positioning on one level—*He's trying to keep me from entering!*—while another part of her mind grappled with the cause.

"What is it? Has something happened?" She couldn't keep the concern from her voice.

Then a movement behind him caught her eye. She looked around his shoulder. A woman was standing a few feet away. A beautiful woman with dark hair styled full and free, her figure as slim as a model's. She also wore her clothes like a model did—with class and panache and a careless grace.

Kathy blinked, not understanding what was happening. Her gaze transferred to Peter. She formed a silent "Who?" with her lips.

Peter's mouth tightened. He was just starting to make a reply when the woman behind him called out, "Peter, darling. You're being very rude. Why don't you let the young lady come in?"

Kathy was held by the strange look in Peter's eyes. She thought she detected flashes of pain and dread as he stepped aside and motioned for her to enter.

When Peter closed the door, she could feel the tension that existed in the room. It was flowing in waves between him and the woman. *Who was she?*

Kathy didn't know what to do. Should she excuse herself and go into the bedroom to change—a convenient excuse to leave these two to whatever business they had to conduct—or should she pretend that she was merely a visitor paying a friendly call?

Once again she looked at Peter. But as had happened before, he was of no help. Only this time Kathy felt compassion for him. Whatever this was, it was serious.

She decided to play the situation by ear. She pasted a smile on her lips and in her eyes and greeted the other woman.

"Hi. My name is Kathy Stevens. I'm—ah—I'm Peter's neighbor."

The woman smiled, and she became even more beautiful. "And I'm Laura, Peter's mother." She extended her hand.

Kathy's eyes must have grown larger in surprise because the woman gave a tinkling laugh. "I know. I don't look old enough to have such a big, lumbering son. But I assure you I am."

Kathy could see the resemblance now. The same nose and chin, the same coloring. Only, as Laura claimed, she didn't look old enough to have a thirty-two-year-old son. She looked forty at the most.

Kathy placed her hand lightly in the extended hand of the woman. Then her glance switched back to Peter. He had said nothing. Looking at him, she reviewed the description his mother had made, and she immediately became defensive. She would never call him big and lumbering. Big, yes. But not lumbering! She bit back the sharp words that flashed through her mind. Maybe she was jumping to too quick a conclusion. Parents sometimes had the most embarrassing ways of talking about their children.

The woman turned to her son. "Peter? What about that drink? You were going to get me one, remember? And you?" she said, turning to Kathy, "would you like something? Peter is in one of his moods. I told him I was coming, but he seems to have forgotten. Sometimes I think he'd like to forget all about me and the fact that he has a mother. But since I'm still stubbornly alive—"

"Mother!" Peter spoke for the first time, his admonition harsh.

Kathy saw that color had crept into his cheeks. He was embarrassed as well as angry!

"Well, darling, I'm just telling the truth. You always put such emphasis on that."

Peter's jaw clamped shut. Then he said tightly, "This isn't necessary, Mother."

Laura laughed. "You mean airing our dirty linen? Oh, Peter, don't be silly. I'm sure Kathy is interested. Aren't you, my dear?"

Kathy felt color come into her cheeks as well—and from the same cause. No wonder Peter didn't like to talk about himself or his family!

"I—I—" she stammered.

Laura smiled at her. "It's all right. It's not as if you're a stranger."

"She shouldn't have to be subjected—" Peter intervened only to be interrupted.

"You're not trying to tell me she doesn't live here, are you, darling?" his mother said. "I'm not blind. First of all, she has a key—that's rather obvious." Kathy had forgotten the key in her hand and looked down at it helplessly. His mother continued, "Second, there's an extra toothbrush in the bathroom and a bottle of perfume. You've not taken to wearing perfume, now have you, Peter?"

Peter looked ready to kill, and Kathy wasn't sure which one of them he wanted to do away with first.

Laura went on. "So, she might as well know some of our contretemps. At least as far as those that will affect her."

"Nothing will affect her," Peter ground out.

Laura lifted a perfectly drawn eyebrow. "Oh?"

Kathy shifted position uncomfortably. She wished she was outside the door again; she would go directly to the Sinclairs' and lock herself inside.

"Well"—Laura looked at her, examining her with those pale-green eyes—"that's too bad."

Peter stalked to the rarely used wet bar on one side of the living room. He poured his mother's drink and delivered it to her.

"Thank you," she said sweetly, then made herself comfortable on the couch.

Kathy had never felt so ill at ease in her life. She and Ashley had occasionally fought, and she had occasionally resented her older sister, but they had never experi-

165

enced charged emotions like Peter and his mother shared.

"I—ah—" She tried to get Peter's attention. He was looking at the floor, a dark expression creasing his features. But when she spoke, he looked up. "I think I'll go next door. I have to take care of Frederick. You know—"

The look he gave her was hard. Still, had she seen a momentary plea for her not to leave? When he spoke, though, there was no entreaty in his manner. "Yes, I know. And I agree that that would be a good idea."

Kathy hesitated before leaving. If he truly didn't want her to leave . . .

Peter's mother broke into the silence that followed his statement. "It was nice meeting you, ah . . ."

"Kathy," Peter supplied steadily.

"Kathy. A nice name." She took another swallow of her drink. "You can come back later, Kathy. I don't bite. And I wouldn't dream of depriving you of my son's company overnight."

A thoroughly maddening person, Kathy thought in summation. She seemed to enjoy digging at Peter constantly.

Some of Kathy's fighting spirit returned. It had been in abeyance because of momentary shock. "I fully intend to return, Mrs. Maxwell. I—"

Trilling laughter broke into her sentence. Laura almost spilled the remains of her drink as she seemed about to convulse. "Darling! I haven't been Mrs. Maxwell for almost thirty years! Hasn't Peter told you? I'm another Zsa Zsa Gabor! I'm working on husband number eight now! At least I will be as soon as I get to

California. I've only stopped in to see Peter to get his blessing!"

"You don't want my blessing," Peter said coldly. "You never have."

Laura smiled sweetly and held up her glass in a mock toast. "Dirty linen, darling," she reminded him.

Peter's entire body was still, but his eyes were blazing.

Kathy wasn't sure if she had made the right choice. Maybe she should stay, just to keep these two apart.

Laura glanced from her son to Kathy and—as if she had the ability to read minds—she said, "Run along, dear. Peter and I enjoy our little tiffs. We've never physically gone for each other's throat, at least not yet. And we've known each other for quite a few years."

Peter didn't look at Kathy. His gaze was riveted on his mother.

Without saying another word Kathy stumbled from the apartment.

Once she was inside the Sinclairs' rooms, she fell back against the door. Her heart was thumping as if she had run a race. Her mind was reeling. She had never met a woman like Peter's mother. Sharp-tongued, spiteful, needling! Didn't she care at all about her son?

Kathy paced the room. What was happening over there now? She wished that she could be a tiny fly on a particular wall.

167

CHAPTER NINE

Peter's eyes were still blazing as he approached his mother, his fists clinched.

"That wasn't called for, Mother. Kathy has nothing to do with you."

Laura looked up, unafraid. "She seems to have a lot to do with you, though. She's the first woman you've actually lived with, isn't she? Oh, I know you've had mistresses. But she's different. Just how special *is* she to you, Peter?"

Peter didn't answer.

Laura sighed. "Well, from what I saw, I approve. Are you going to marry her?"

Peter warned tightly, "Don't push it any more than you already have. I don't need your approval, just as you don't need mine."

Laura slid the nearly empty glass onto the low table before her. "No. That's true. But then you've never approved of me. I suppose I should stop trying—"

"Trying to what?" Peter cut her off. "Don't make me laugh. You've done exactly as you wanted all of your life. You haven't cared what anyone else thought or felt or needed. You're a selfish bitch, Laura. Selfish and disloyal and—"

Laura was on her feet in a second; in the next a hand

168

struck her son's cheek. The harsh sound surprised them both.

They were breathing quickly, their eyes locked. Then Peter took a step back, his palm going up to cover his stinging cheek.

"You may stay here tonight, Mother," he said formally, his voice carefully controlled, "but tomorrow I want you to leave."

Laura's green eyes flickered momentarily with some emotion, and then she said quietly, "My flight leaves in the morning. I hadn't planned on staying any longer."

"Good," Peter returned. Then he turned and walked away while his mother started for the bar.

A soft knock sounded at Kathy's door. An hour had passed since she left Peter's apartment. And during that time she had been sitting in the growing darkness with only the glow from Frederick's candles providing light.

When the knock came, Kathy jumped. Then she was off the couch and running to answer the door. Maybe it was Peter. Maybe she would be able to help.

But it was not Peter who was standing outside. It was his mother. Kathy was tempted to close the door in her face, but something—curiosity?—made her hesitate. And that hesitation was her undoing.

"Hello, Kathy. I was hoping that this was where you live." She laughed uncertainly. The laugh was completely different from the one Kathy had heard earlier. She continued, "Or, rather, where you used to live."

Kathy could not see much of Laura's face in the vanishing daylight, but what she saw looked older, exposing all of her fifty-odd years. But any compassion that might have welled within her was immediately squashed. This woman had hurt Peter, and it was Peter who she loved.

She said nothing. Laura was still standing at the doorway.

"May I come in?" she asked.

Kathy remained unmoving.

"Please?" she added, and it was the loneliness in her plea that broke Kathy's resistance.

Kathy nodded and moved out of the way.

Laura's gaze widened as she took in the strangeness of Frederick's shrine, but she said nothing.

"Sit down if you like," Kathy said stiffly.

"Thanks." Laura dropped with tired elegance onto the couch.

Kathy sat in a nearby chair.

"Peter went for a walk," his mother informed her.

"Oh?"

"That doesn't surprise you, does it?"

"Not really."

Laura studied her for a moment. "You don't like me very much, do you?"

Kathy's lips were tight as she replied, "I don't know you well enough to judge."

The older woman broke into a smile, and a flash of her earlier personality showed through. "Don't lie to me, darling, or your nose will grow."

Kathy's features didn't change.

Laura sighed deeply and found the bullfighter pillow Kathy often held when she was disturbed. The fringe seemed to act as a panacea to taut nerves.

"I didn't come here to fight with him. Do you believe that?" When Kathy said nothing, she went on, "But it just seems to come naturally to us. It has since Peter was twelve."

"Does that bother you?" Kathy asked at last. She was still smarting for Peter because of the woman's earlier barbs.

"Would you believe me if I said yes?"

"No."

Laura gave a brittle smile. "No wonder Peter admires you—you're painfully honest when pressed."

"And loyal," Kathy added, letting the woman know exactly where she stood.

Laura's eyes narrowed. "Do you love him?"

Kathy reacted with anger. "What I feel isn't any of your business!"

"I'm his mother."

"You don't act like it!"

"Exactly what *is* a mother?" Laura demanded, becoming angry herself. "Someone who kisses every little scratch her child gets? Who pats him on the head and tells him that everything will be all right with his world when she knows perfectly well that it won't?"

"That wouldn't necessarily be a bad way to behave!"

"You're not old enough to be an expert!"

"Age has nothing to do with it!" Kathy retorted. "I get tired of people always talking about age! I may be young, but I wasn't born yesterday. I've formed opinions about life—valid opinions!"

Laura's green eyes were snapping with fire, then suddenly the flame went out. She collapsed against the rear cushion of the couch and said softly, "You're right. I apologize."

Kathy was left with fight still in her. She wanted to continue to argue with the woman, continue to make her point. But upon being given an apology, the wind was fairly taken from her sails. She lifted a hand in helpless appeal and then stood up to pace. She couldn't stay still any longer.

She didn't realize that Laura had been watching her steadily until the woman commented, "I'm glad you love him."

Kathy stopped pacing. "I didn't say that I did!"

"I'm a practiced hand at falling in love, Kathy. Believe me, you don't have to put what you feel into words. I already know."

When Kathy still refused to confirm her suspicion, the older woman continued, "I'm glad you love him because he needs someone like you."

"You didn't give me the impression that you cared earlier," Kathy accused.

Laura smiled weakly and patted the bullfighter pillow back into place on the cushion beside her.

"Peter and I aren't a typical mother and son. We've been through too much together, most of which is my fault, I suppose." She looked up, impaling Kathy with her gaze. "I'm not exactly stable emotionally. I suppose you've guessed that."

Kathy had never had a conversation like this one! She wasn't accustomed to people—strangers, really—examining their failings publically. She slowly sank back onto the chair. "I—ah . . ."

Laura laughed. It was the same tinkling laugh Kathy had heard when they first met. Only some of the hard polish was gone.

"Have I embarrassed you? I apologize again, if I have. My last shrink was very proud of me, actually. He said I was finally beginning to open up and see myself as

I actually am." She paused, her eyes lighting with laughter. "I hated to contradict him, so I didn't, but I've known myself all along. I just can't seem to do anything about it, that's all."

Kathy's feelings had gone full circle: from being willing to like the woman to disliking her intensely to being willing to like her again, with certain reservations. She cleared her throat and said, "Would you care for something to drink? Coffee or tea, I mean? I don't have anything stronger."

"Coffee would be very nice, thank you."

After heating a water-filled cup in the microwave, Kathy brought it, along with the necessary accoutrements, into the living room.

"I hope you don't mind instant," she said, still feeling slightly uncomfortable in this woman's company.

"No, not at all," Laura replied.

Kathy watched as Laura prepared her drink. Her fingers, like Peter's, were long and slender, but where the son's nails were buffed until they shone slightly, the mother's were painted a deep bloodred.

"Peter always was a difficult child," she began after taking a sip of the hot liquid. "He didn't like moving around, which, of course, we did a lot. He resented it, in fact. But"—she shrugged her shoulders slightly—"what could I do? My husbands always seemed to be traveling men."

Kathy remembered what Peter had said about living everywhere. And she definitely had been left with the impression that he had not enjoyed it. "Have you really been married eight times?" she asked, needing something to say.

"Seven," Laura corrected. "The one coming up will be number eight."

"Oh."

Laura smiled slightly. "You don't approve of me either, do you?"

Kathy tried to hedge once again. "Really, I'm not in a position to judge—at least not about that."

Laura was quick to take up the qualification. "But you do judge me about Peter?"

Kathy's chin lifted. "Yes."

"And what do you think?"

"I think you enjoy watching him suffer."

"Just as he enjoys watching me suffer!"

"I don't believe that."

"You don't believe he enjoys needling me?" The green eyes were beginning to snap again.

"No, I don't." Kathy stood her ground.

Laura pushed the cup away, her fingers folding into each other convulsively. "I'd like to believe that myself, but I don't. Peter hates me."

Kathy shook her head. "No! He doesn't. He told me."

The green eyes lifted. "He's talked about me?"

"When I asked."

"Under protest, I would venture to guess."

"Under protest."

Laura gave a shaky sigh, seemingly out of character. "He probably only said it to keep from shocking you. How many sons actively hate their mothers?"

"I don't know. But I do know Peter. At least I know his character."

"You saw the way he talked to me!"

"I also saw the way you talked to him!"

"He blames me for destroying his life!"

"He's only thirty-two. He doesn't look destroyed to me."

"But he is! On the inside. You don't know—You didn't hear—"

There must have been a terrible exchange after she left, Kathy surmised, for Laura to come to her looking so tired and defeated.

"People say things they don't mean when they're angry," Kathy tried to console her.

Laura was silent a moment, then asked, "How old are you Kathy?"

Kathy answered warily, "Twenty-one."

She continued to be subjected to intent appraisal. "You're very wise for twenty-one," the older woman said at last.

Now it was Kathy's turn to shrug lightly. "Like I said, I've learned a few things along the way." She remembered a time when she was so angry at Ashley and how she had said things, done things, just to hurt her even though she loved her dearly.

"I wish I had been so wise when I was your age." Laura smiled and then laughed. "I wish I was that wise now!"

Kathy had to smile with her as she denied, "I'm not wise. Most of the time I just luck into things."

"Like my Peter."

"Like your Peter."

One of the slender hands with bloodred nails came out to grasp Kathy's wrist. "Be patient with him, Kathy. I don't know whether he loves you or not, or if he'll let himself. But for his sake—for my sake—don't let him close you out of his life."

Kathy's heart leaped and then plunged. She didn't like to think about Peter closing her out, building barriers, putting up walls.

"And now I should go," Laura announced, slowly standing up. "I'm leaving in the morning. I—ah—my flight is scheduled for then."

"A short visit," Kathy murmured.

"That's all Peter and I can stand of each other." There was laughter in her wry comment, but behind it were tears.

Kathy wanted to reach out to the woman, say something to help, but there was nothing more she could do. The problems between Laura and her son were years in the making. If they were to be solved, really solved, it might take just as long to rectify them.

When Kathy was once again alone in the apartment, she walked over to the candles and blew them out. Then she moved slowly through the darkness, shedding her uniform as she went. What she needed now was a warm shower and time to absorb all that had happened. This had been anything but an uneventful night. And it wasn't over yet.

A little before ten o'clock Kathy crossed the balcony to Peter's apartment. She didn't know whether she was doing the right thing, but instinct told her that she was. Besides, earlier she had told Laura that she would return. She just wondered how Peter would react. Would he want her there—spending the night—while his mother was present? She knocked softly on the door.

After her second knock the door swung open. Peter's eyes were stormy. The storm didn't abate when they focused on her.

176

She tried to pin a smile to her lips.

Peter stiffened. At that moment he would have given anything he possessed to draw Kathy into his arms. He needed her! He needed to feel the reality of her, the warm flesh and blood of her, to aid in dispelling the nightmare he always seemed to be drowning in whenever he and his mother engaged in one of their yearly love fests. But he couldn't let himself reach out. Not now. Not yet.

Kathy looked up at him and could read nothing in his expression. He looked frozen in anger, in indecision, in bitterness.

"I was lonely," she said softly, hoping to break through to the warm, gentle emotions that she knew existed within him.

So am I! Peter wanted to cry out. But he said through tight lips, "It's late, Kathy."

"I know."

"Mother's already in bed. She was tired."

From the cold, hard look of him, they'd probably had another angry exchange.

"I didn't come to see your mother," she told him, her gaze taking in the fact that he was still wearing the vest to his suit, but it was unbuttoned, and his tie was still in place, although it was loosened—visible signs of the emotional upheaval he was experiencing.

She took a step forward.

Peter almost took one back, but he stopped himself just in time. He was virtually trembling with his desire to hold her.

Then she touched him. One small, delicate, capable hand reached out and came to rest lightly on his chest

—and he could keep himself aloof no longer. A quick intake of breath signaled his immediate thaw.

Kathy responded instantly as well, pressing her body to his, rejoicing in the crushing power of his embrace, the feel of his lips against her neck, her cheek, her eyes, and finally her mouth. But even as she celebrated this victory, she realized that it could be fleeting. Tomorrow might bring other skirmishes, ones in which she might not fare so well. But she would deal with it when it came. She couldn't think about the possibilities of what might be when the present was so sweet.

Then, somewhat awkwardly, they broke away from each other, although contact still remained through Peter's hands at her waist.

When he spoke, his voice was low and ragged. "I needed that."

"So did I." She smiled tremulously, still caught up in her feelings of the moment before.

Peter pulled her inside and closed the door. Then, unable to resist, he kissed her once again.

When the kiss was over, he looked nearer to being his old self than at any time since that evening had begun.

"I didn't expect you to come back," he said quietly.

"I told you I would." She made the familiar gesture of smoothing back his hair.

"No, you told my mother you would."

"I was telling you, too." She dropped the soothing hand onto his shoulder. "I wasn't sure you'd want me."

"I want you."

At the fervency of that reply Kathy began to giggle. "I know. I can tell."

Peter had softened enough to smile. Then his smile disappeared. "But I don't think you should stay."

"Why not?"

"I just don't."

"Your mother knows I've been staying with you."
She didn't add that they had talked or what they had
talked about.

"I realize that. And she's no one to pass judgment on
another person's actions. It's just—"

"I'm not ashamed of what we're doing, Peter,"
Kathy said calmly, interrupting his hesitancy of speech.

"I never thought you were. Otherwise you wouldn't
be here."

"So?"

Peter looked down into her upturned face. How
could he explain to her the mixture of emotions he was
feeling? How he wanted her to stay so badly he could
taste it—not for sex necessarily. He could control his
basic urges at least to some degree. No, tonight his need
of her was more for companionship. He needed an an-
chor, a rudder, something to help him control the hurri-
cane he was embroiled in. But there was another concern as well—one that was even more prominent in his
thoughts: he wanted to protect her good name. It was a
very old-fashioned feeling for someone who prided himself on being very much a man who was accustomed to
thinking only of himself and his needs and his desires.

Peter swallowed. He felt as if he'd been hit right in
the pit of his stomach. *God! What a time to discover that
I'm falling in love! As if I don't have enough troubles
already!*

Without realizing it he started to shake his head.
Then the words followed. "No, Kathy."

"But you wanted me to come!" she protested.

"Now I want you to go," he said evenly. "I don't want you in the middle of this."

Kathy's first reaction was anger. There he was! Changing back and forth again! And then maturity took the upper hand. He had what he thought was a good reason for not wanting her to stay, and it wasn't up to her to force him to change his mind. Oh, she could do it. A lingering touch here, a special kiss there. But that would be using sex to get what she wanted, and she wasn't that type of person. She had too much respect for herself and for him.

Her clear blue eyes continued to hold his. Then her voice came clearly. "All right. I can handle that."

Peter gave a slight smile. Had he wanted her to put up a fight that he wouldn't have arranged to win? "Atta girl," he said bracingly, both for her benefit and for his.

Kathy reacted with mock annoyance. "I'm *not* a girl!"

" 'Atta woman' sounds ridiculous," he forced himself to tease.

Kathy smoothed a finger down his cheek and stood on tiptoe to let a short kiss follow.

"One day I just might tell you something, Peter Maxwell," she confided softly.

He didn't ask her what that something was. And she didn't volunteer any more information. The time was not yet ripe.

Then after a longing look, Kathy hurried out the door, not stopping to think until she got to her lonely bed where she lay the remainder of the night in restless slumber because the long, lean, muscular body of the man she loved was not nearby.

CHAPTER TEN

Kathy overslept the next morning. In the confusion of tearing into a fresh uniform, grabbing a quick cup of coffee to help her wake up, and searching all over for her car keys, she was able to keep thoughts of Peter and his mother somewhat at bay.

But as she raced out of her apartment, she couldn't help the contemplative glance she gave his front door. Was his mother still there? Or had her plane been an early one? And was Peter still at home? Had he taken part of the morning off to transport his mother to the airport?

Kathy didn't think that either of the latter possibilities was true. In all likelihood they had parted, or would part, company this morning after yet another bitter confrontation, and he would go to work, trying to pretend that nothing had happened while his mother went to the airport in a taxi. She knew Peter; he would do that.

As she continued to look at the door, Kathy wished that she had X-ray vision like the comic book Man of Steel. A toss of her head told her that she was being silly. Maybe it was the loss of sleep she had suffered last night taking an early toll. As it was, she didn't know if she would be able to stay awake all day. She wondered what Paula would say if she went to sleep while in the process of measuring a redfish. Then she sheepishly admitted that she already knew what Paula would say.

That thought was enough to make her hurry. She didn't need to be any later than she was already.

Kathy functioned better that day than she thought she would. She was tired and sleepy and more than a bit distracted on occasion, but she was able to cover any lapse so that Paula never knew the difference. Buying such control, though, was taxing, and when the workday at last drew to a close, she greeted it with more gratitude than usual.

All the way home Kathy thought of Peter. And when she thought of Peter, she thought of his mother and of the strain that existed between them. They were like two combatants locked in a battle that was continued out of reflex. Each inflicted pain that mounted on previous pain, and neither seemed able to solve the cause.

When Kathy pulled into the parking area, she saw that Peter's BMW was already in place. With quick economical movements she parked and then hurried along the sidewalk to the stairs. She wanted to see him. But when she went into his apartment, she found that he was not there.

Half an hour later Peter wearily climbed the stairs. His workout hadn't made him feel one bit better. He raked a hand through his hair as he started to unlock the door. It squeaked open before he was able to turn the key.

Kathy stood inside the room, her eyes full of concern. He looked away from her as he stepped inside and dropped his sports bag onto the floor.

When he didn't look back at her right away, she called, "Peter?"

Peter resisted the tempting sound of her voice. If he had wanted to hold her close last night, it was nothing compared with what he wanted to do now. But he made himself walk to the bar, where he opened a bottle of Perrier water and poured some of the sparkling liquid into a glass.

A frown creased Kathy's brow. "Peter?" she repeated. A knot of fear was beginning to form in her stomach.

Peter took a long drink before turning to her, and when he did, his gaze was guarded.

Kathy's knot tightened. Something was wrong. Something was very seriously wrong. "Your mother? Did she have an accident? Is she—"

Peter let her go no further. "My mother's perfectly well, as far as I know."

At the coldness of his tone Kathy recoiled internally. He was talking to her as he had in the beginning, when he didn't know her, when he didn't care to know her.

Peter saw the flicker of pain in her eyes, and it was all he could do to keep up his front. But this was something he had to do—for her sake as well as for his. He loved her or, rather, he thought he loved her. But for how long? As long as his mother had loved each husband she eventually left?

"Then . . . " Kathy quickly composed her face, putting on a smile that she didn't feel. "Then what's up?" she asked brightly, covering her fear. "You look as if you've met the Ghost of Christmas Past or something."

Peter didn't crack a smile. "Christmas Future would be more accurate," he replied.

"And did he tell you anything?" she prompted, more for something to say than as a means of gaining an answer.

Peter replaced the glass on the bar. "Yes."

"What?" Kathy refused to let her knees buckle.

"It's over, Kathy."

"Your mother's visit?" She purposely misunderstood. "I know. She left this morning."

"Not my mother," Peter clipped.

"Then what?" She knew. But if she put it off, made it more difficult . . .

"Us," he said, tolling the death knell to her happiness.

"No!" She reacted instinctively.

"Yes!" he contradicted.

Kathy turned away. She couldn't keep the happy look plastered on her face. Not any longer. Neither could she continue pretending stupidity.

"No," she repeated softly. It was a moan.

Peter started to reach out to turn her around, but he quickly withdrew his hand. He couldn't touch her! If he did, all would be lost.

He took a deep breath. "When we entered into this agreement, we made a deal. Do you remember?"

"No," Kathy lied, her throat tight. Her back was still to him. She couldn't look at him.

Peter reacted impatiently. "We agreed that either of us could end our association at any time and with no recriminations."

Kathy was silent for a moment, then she whispered, "But why?"

184

Peter moved away from the bar. Everything had happened too quickly for him! Too intensely! He had to reinstate the distance between them.

"This is the best way, Kathy," he said at last.

"Best for who?" she demanded.

"For both of us!"

Kathy turned, her blue eyes were moist with tears. "I think I deserve a better explanation than that." Her voice was shaking.

Peter struggled to keep a wall of insensitivity around him. It used to be so easy! He had ended affairs before, and he hadn't worried about what effect his decision had on the woman. Not that it had *had* any effect because he had chosen carefully. But with Kathy . . .

"I've told you all along that I'm not the man you think I am. You're young, Kathy. You're still looking for heroes."

"No, I'm not! And stop saying I'm young! I'm old . . . old enough to have fallen in love with you!"

Kathy hadn't meant to say that. As the words came out, she looked just as appalled as Peter.

"Oh, God!" Peter groaned.

Kathy decided to make the best of a bad situation. Her secret was out and by her own lips, so it wouldn't do any good for her to deny it. "It's true. I admit it."

"You'll get over it."

"What makes you so sure?"

Peter's lips pulled into a bittersweet smile. "Years of practice. Watching my mother operate is an education unto itself."

"I'm not like your mother."

Peter's sherry-colored eyes grew hard. "No, you're not. But maybe I am."

"I don't understand." *Keep him talking,* she thought desperately. *As long as you keep him talking, you stand a chance.*

"This—us—" He waved an expressive hand. "What we've had together has been good. But it won't continue that way. One day you'll get tired of me, or I'll get tired of you."

"I love you! Didn't you hear me? When you love a person, you don't get tired of them!"

Peter's tone was becoming angry, his exasperation growing as was his need to end this confrontation.

"I can't make a commitment, Kathy. It's as simple as that."

"How do you know? Have you ever tried?"

"No." His lips were pressed grimly together.

"Then you can't know!"

Peter ran a hand through his hair in a gesture of futility. *This has to end. I have to convince her.*

"Listen to me, Kathy," he said with false patience, "I don't want to hurt you—"

"I know you don't!" Kathy interrupted. "I know you better than you think, Peter. You don't like to hurt anyone!"

"Stop making me out to be some kind of saint!" he rebuked heatedly.

"I'm not!"

"You are! You're trying to make me into something you imagine I should be! But I'm human, Kathy. Very human. I have human faults. I make mistakes."

"Are you trying to say that you think our being together has been a mistake?"

Peter didn't, but he saw his opportunity and seized it.

"Yes, that's exactly what I'm saying. I warned you that it would be."

Kathy's body flinched as if he had hit her physically instead of emotionally.

Peter compounded the lie. "I've been thinking about this for a long time."

Kathy contradicted him. "Last night you told me that you wanted me."

"I lied."

"I don't believe you!" Tears were welling in her eyes.

"Then believe this. I want it to end, Kathy. I want it to be over. Whatever passed between us before is no more."

Kathy was beginning to tremble. She didn't believe him. She couldn't believe him! "But I love you," she whispered, hanging on to one last thread of hope.

"I don't believe in love and neither should you," he said flatly, "not if you don't want to open yourself up to a lot of pain."

Kathy's bottom lip was quivering. "I'm in pain now, but I still love you."

Peter had to turn away.

Kathy gazed at his back through a haze of tears. She wanted to go to him, to touch him.

"Peter," she called softly, achingly.

When he neither moved nor replied, she drew a bracing breath and after a series of seconds passed, she continued with only a slight waver. "I'm not a psychologist, but I think you're afraid of love, Peter. It's not that you don't believe in it; it's that you're trying to hide from it. You may not love me. I realize that. But one day you might come to love someone, really love them, and when you do, I hope you don't—" Her voice broke

187

but she soon had it back under control. "I hope you're not too blind to see it."

Peter kept his back to her, but his fists were clenched and his knuckles were white.

She was speaking again. "I'll collect my things tomorrow—after you leave for work."

Then she was gone. Peter heard the familiar squeak of the door and its soft closing.

He remained immobile for an unknown length of time.

The next morning Kathy waited until after she was sure that Peter had left before entering his apartment.

For a moment she stood unmoving, assimilating the room. Peter's presence was still there, left behind him in a wake of aftershave and charisma. He was as real to her as if he were standing inches away.

Kathy closed her eyes and drew a shaky breath. His mother had practically begged her not to let him close her out of his life. But what could she do? He didn't love her, that much was obvious. He didn't even act as if he liked her very much! And that was what hurt the most. Had all their time together been for nothing? They had been happy. She knew they had been. They had laughed and talked and made love.

He had to have felt something for her!

So what had made him change?

There was only one supposition: his mother's visit.

Kathy thought of the woman, of her bloodred nails that she seemed to enjoy putting into her son's back. Then she remembered the softer side of his mother, the concerned side. There was enough distrust on both sides

188

to weigh a load of guilt. But how had Kathy ended up carrying it all?

Kathy gathered most of her possessions and carried them back to her apartment. Purposefully, though, she left her favorite nightgown hanging in the closet. It would be a good excuse to come back tonight to talk to Peter. She wasn't yet satisfied that he wasn't merely reacting to his mother's visit. She just couldn't believe that he didn't care.

And then she made herself go to work, although her heart wasn't in it. After what seemed like an endless day, it was finally time to go home. Even the drive to her apartment seemed to take an interminable amount of time.

She became aware of the knots in her stomach as she pulled into her parking space. Somehow her legs mechanically moved—as if possessing a life of their own —and she suddenly found herself inside her apartment, almost holding her breath.

The rest of the evening was a blur. She was only aware that her ears were attuned for any sign of movement on the balcony—one step, one squeak from the door. But even she had to admit a setback when the hands of the clock reached two thirty and he still had not come home.

It was a bleary-eyed young woman who presented herself at work the next morning. Paula took one look at her and persuaded her to stay at the institute to get some paperwork done instead of working in the field.

Tears rushed to Kathy's eyes, her emotions were so strained and close to the surface. But she quickly blinked them away. Most of the people at the institute concluded that she was coming down with a virus. There was no need to tell them otherwise.

She did the necessary paperwork, asking questions whenever needed, but her mind was almost completely on Peter.

His absence from home last night had brought the nightmare closer to reality. Maybe he wasn't reacting to stress. Maybe he meant what he had said. And if he did, how would she be able to handle it?

It was with relief that Kathy's gaze sought and found the blue BMW as soon as she drew into the parking area. Her heart gave a corresponding leap. Then she became nervous. What if he wouldn't open his door to her? She had left his key on the bureau dresser in the bedroom so she would have no way to get inside unless he let her in. And what if he just handed her the nightgown and shut her out again?

Devils of uncertainty were new to Kathy. She usually decided on a path and stuck to it. But rejection was also something new to her. She wasn't sure which course she should follow.

Giving in to her nerves, she went to her apartment first. Then, after sliding her perspiring palms up and down against the blue material of her uniform any number of times, she gathered some confidence and went to knock on his door.

The door was opened immediately. Had he been waiting for her to make the first move toward a reconciliation?

His sherry-colored eyes said differently. They coursed over her with no feeling.

"Yes?" he asked. The intervening weeks since she moved in had dissolved into nothing.

Kathy tried a smile. It was a weak shadow of her former efforts. "Hello, Peter."

He returned no greeting.

"I—ah—I wanted to talk with you." She decided not to mention the gown. Leaving it as an excuse to see him again didn't seem like such a good idea—in fact it seemed juvenile.

"I'm busy."

"Oh, I know you are," she agreed quickly. She could hear a familiar Mozart melody playing softly in the background. Some weeks ago she had no education in the classics; now she could identify a number of pieces. "It would just take a minute," she said. Then she tired of sounding as if she were begging. "I think you owe that to me, Peter."

Peter unwillingly stepped back to let her pass. Again his body was ramrod straight. "All right. You're in," he said when she halted in the middle of the room. "What is it?"

Kathy turned to look at him. "I can't believe you're doing this to us, Peter." She hadn't meant to start off with that sentence. She had been going to work it in later.

"Believe it," he returned coolly.

She decided that since she had already thrust a toe into the cold water, she might as well plunge in completely. "But I *know* you have some kind of feeling for me!"

"You're wrong."

"But we were so close!"

"You mean in bed?" he interpreted, then he gave a

harsh laugh that pierced her heart. "A beautiful woman isn't hard to make love to, especially one who practically throws herself at a man."

"I didn't do that!" she denied.

Peter's features were grim. "Grow up, Kathy. You never made one word of protest. Not one."

Kathy's gaze faltered. What he said was true. She hadn't protested. She had just happily accepted everything as it came.

Seconds passed before Peter continued speaking. "You only think you love me because I'm the first man to make love to you. You won't feel that way for long. I guarantee it."

Her gaze lifted. "Are you advising me to go out and find another lover?" The question was incredulous.

"It's an idea I plan to follow myself."

Her blue eyes were large and unconsciously pleading. "You mean you could just go out and—" She couldn't finish.

"Liaisons are temporary, Kathy. They come and they go. Get used to it."

Tears escaped from her eyes and rolled down her cheeks as she silently shook her head in disagreement. "No, I never will."

"Suit yourself," he shrugged. "What you do is your business."

Kathy was a fighter. Normally there was no cause for which she wouldn't do battle to the death if she thought she stood a chance. But in this instance, when he had sounded so careless with her future—*What you do is your business*—she admitted defeat. To him their weeks together had been a "liaison," to be shed like the leaves of a tree in season. Easy come, easy go. She was beginning to believe him.

Still, she couldn't change how she felt. She loved him —this maddening, cold, insensitive man who could also be so very gentle and caring if only he would let himself. However, that seemed to be her problem now. He was disclaiming all responsibility.

Another set of silent tears retraced the earlier paths, which soon were followed by another set and then another. Kathy tried to brush them away, but they would not be held back. There was nothing she could do about them, just as there was nothing she could do about the situation in which she now found herself a part.

Giving in to this reality, Kathy held his gaze for several long seconds before crossing to the door with unconscious dignity.

Her quiet tears were still falling, but now she didn't worry about them. She knew they were only a harbinger of what was to come.

The hollowness of his victory was excruciating to Peter. He had won. Only what was his prize? The knowledge that he had wounded her gravely? He gave an empty, mocking laugh. No, that was no prize. It was more of a penance—one he would have to live with for the rest of his life.

Peter walked into his bedroom and threw himself down on the bed. If he had had the energy, he would have cursed himself. But all he felt was drained.

He had done the right thing, made the only decision that was open to him. They couldn't have continued their relationship, so it was better to end it now. No matter what she said.

And he wasn't in love with her. It was infatuation.

Just as what she felt for him was infatuation. She *would* get over it.

He had seen his mother in the depths of despair one day and then the next, full of excitement because of a new prospective mate.

As he had told her, liaisons were fleeting, burning brightly for a time and then dulling into nothingness.

Having convinced himself of the merits of his decision, Peter got up and went to the closet for his robe. He needed a shower. He needed the hot stinging needles of water and steam.

But when he reached inside his closet, his hand brushed against something soft and satiny. One of Kathy's nightgowns!

A weakness flooded through him as he remembered the sweetness of her body, of her smile. His own body gave a haunting cry of wordless need. Then he was pushing the nightgown aside and swinging his robe over his arm.

CHAPTER ELEVEN

Somehow Kathy managed to exist for the rest of the week and through the weekend, but if she had been asked, she could not have told anyone what she did, how she had functioned. Mentally she had existed in a fog, performing her daily duties on autopilot. Her emotions were too tender to probe.

But when Monday morning arrived and she had the misfortune of running into Peter on the balcony as they both left for work, some of the ice that had been encasing her spirit shattered.

Her blue eyes were bruised as she stared across at him, her body frozen like a doe in the wood when confronted by a hunter. Her instinct was to run to ground, but unlike an animal that listened purely to its need for survival, she also knew pride as well. And she would not run.

Peter had hesitated, looking momentarily thunder-struck by this coincidence. Then he had assumed a facade of polite indifference. "Good morning," he said.

Kathy returned the greeting and then started for the stairs. All the way down she was aware of him close behind her. And then in the parking area she was aware of him veering for his BMW as she directed her steps toward her car.

Her hands had trembled as she grappled with the key, trying to insert it.

His car started instantly. He was having no similar difficulty.

Kathy's fragile shell of pride was sorely tested when he backed out and drove away, leaving her still sitting there, trying to insert the key. Through a haze of tears she had seen his profile in her rearview mirror as he passed. He didn't look at her. She might have been invisible.

When at last she finally got the car started, she had to wait a few minutes to recover. But her recovery was brittle, and when she arrived at work and Eric made a growling remark to her—himself looking as if he had had a bad week—she broke into a full avalanche of tears and had to flee to the bathroom to compose herself.

When she emerged, she found Eric leaning against the wall in the hall, waiting for her. Immediately, she apologized. "I'm sorry, Eric. That was really stupid."

"Hey, no problem. I shouldn't have tried to bite your head off."

Kathy tried to smile, her facial muscles having become unused to the action over the past days.

For the next few minutes their conversation consisted of bits and pieces of nonrevealing fluff, but Kathy gradually became aware that her partner was more subdued than usual.

She paused as they walked to the outside door. Today they were going to be part of a team that was going to concentrate on tagging more shrimp; so she knew that they would have little privacy once they stepped outside. She decided to make light of her own situation if that would help him open up.

"Neither of us is in too good a shape, are we?" She met his shielded gaze and offered, "I'll tell you my problem if you'll tell me yours."

Eric's ruggedly handsome features looked older somehow. He smiled slightly at her attempt to draw him out.

"Honey, you don't have enough hours in your day to listen to my problems."

She laughed but without amusement. "That's what you think."

Intelligent gray eyes examined her. Then he said slowly, "It sounds as if we *are* in the same boat. And I don't mean the skiff we usually share."

"You're having a problem with Sue?" She stated the obvious.

Eric raked a hand through his hair—a movement that echoed too closely the action Peter sometimes made. Kathy had to glance away.

"When am I not having a problem with Sue? The woman's a royal pain in the ass!" he said harshly. Then as some of his exasperation lessened, a hollowness entered his tone as he confided, "She left me, Kathy. She just up and left me."

"Oh, Eric!" she cried sympathetically.

"You have the right to say 'I told you so.'"

"But I didn't mean—"

"I realize that," he broke in. Then his eyes shifted to the clustering group of people outside. "Look—I think we both need to talk. Would it be all right with you if I come over to your place this evening? I'm sick of mine."

"Sure. That would be fine."

"Good," he said, then he leaned forward and opened the door.

197

That evening, over a quick meal of hot dogs and beans, Eric told Kathy about the most recent events in his life.

"My fatal error was in going with her to her mother's when she told her that she was pregnant. I like the woman—I really do! And I thought she liked me, even if she didn't necessarily approve of me. But when she found out that Sue was going to have a kid, she immediately started to apply pressure. To both of us.

"Then when we got home, Sue was in a tailspin. It seemed like all she could think about was that we had to get married. When I told her again that I didn't see any reason why we should, she blew up.

"That happened over and over, Kathy, until three mornings later I woke up and she was gone."

Kathy didn't pass judgment. She didn't feel that she had enough credentials. Sometimes problems went deeper than what lay on the surface. She had found that out for herself recently.

"Do you know where she is?" she asked.

"Take one guess," Eric answered sourly.

"At her mother's?"

"Bingo!"

Kathy poured Eric another glass of cola. Then she sat beside him on the couch.

"Eric?"

"What?" He was partially distracted, thinking about Sue.

"Do you love her?"

That got his attention. "Of course I do!"

"Then why won't you marry her?"

198

Hostile gray eyes turned and met hers. "Are you going to start nagging me, too?" he demanded.

"Of course not," she denied. "I'm just curious."

Eric settled down slowly. He took a sip of his drink and then answered. "I'm thirty-nine, Kathy. Did you know that?"

"Thirty-nine?" she repeated. He looked much younger.

Eric nodded. "And I've been married before."

"You have?"

He nodded again, not looking at her but at the far wall. "It wasn't a very pleasant experience. Messy divorce and all that kind of crap." He paused. "I've been happier with Sue than I ever was with Loretta. Ever!"

Kathy waited for him to say more, and when he didn't she concluded, "So you're afraid to get married again."

Eric moved restlessly on a soft cushion. "It's not exactly that. I'm not against marriage."

Kathy frowned. "Then what is it?"

An amused smile played about her friend's lips. "I'm warning you, sweetheart, I'm going to get mine back in a few minutes. If you can ask penetrating questions and expect answers, then so can I."

Kathy swallowed. He meant exactly what he was saying. Still she persevered. "I asked you a question."

Eric's smile lessened and he became serious. "Marriage does strange things to people sometimes, Kathy. It changes them."

"In what way?" She didn't remember either Jason or Ashley changing.

"Their true colors come out."

Kathy was silent, then she said. "I don't understand."

Eric sighed and stood up. He needed to move as he talked. "Loretta was such a sweet little thing when I met her. Sweet and innocent and I thought she needed me."

Kathy waited. In a moment he continued, "Shortly after we got married I went to Nam. And like an idiot I signed over all my paychecks to her. When I got back to the States, the money was gone and so was she. When I caught up with her, she was living with some guy in Pensacola."

Eric said no more, and Kathy was left to digest his tale. Finally she asked, "How old were you when you met your wife?"

"Twenty-three."

"Don't you think you've learned something in all these years?"

"I've learned to be leary of getting married again—that's what I've learned!"

"But you're not being fair to Sue!" she protested. Why did people always insist on making other people pay the cost of what they themselves had once paid? Innocent people. People like herself and Sue.

"I don't want to get married again," he said stubbornly.

"Then don't!" Kathy cried, feeling her own bruises coming to the surface. "But don't cry to me about your problems! Problems that you're creating yourself!"

Tears that had been in abeyance since this morning once again surfaced, and Eric was immediately at her side, putting a strong arm around her.

Kathy's head was down, her long blond hair covering

her face. Eric smoothed the golden strands. "Hush. It's all right. I'm just an unfeeling beast. Unloading all my problems on you when you have enough of your own. Hush now."

Kathy fumbled for a nearby box of tissues and wiped her eyes and blew her nose. Then she lifted her head while pushing some stray hairs away from her face.

She sniffed. "You're not a beast."

"How about a selfish pig?" he suggested.

Kathy gave a watery smile. "*That* I might settle for."

Eric squeezed her shoulder. "Now, it's your turn. Tell Father McMillen all about it."

Kathy reached for the fringed bullfighter pillow. If she had very many crises to go through, she was going to have to find a replacement pillow for the Sinclairs. She gently smoothed the embroidered cape with one finger.

"His name is Peter."

"That's a good start!" Eric said supportively.

Kathy gave an unsteady little laugh.

"And he lives next door."

"Convenient—or rather inconvenient!"

"Are you going to listen or lead cheers?"

"I'm sorry."

"We were close for a time," she continued.

"I figured that. Oops! Sorry."

Kathy forgave him his slip.

"But now we're not."

Eric started to say something else, but he decided not to.

"One day, after his mother paid a visit," she went on, "he suddenly changed his mind."

"His mother!" Eric nodded sagely, still stinging from

201

his own run-in with a mother. Then he cautioned seriously, "If he's a mamma's boy, you don't want him, Kathy. Maybe this is a good thing."

"It's not that," Kathy disclaimed. "He's not influenced by her in that way. More the opposite."

"That could be trouble, too. One's almost as bad as the other. If it pleases mamma, it displeases him."

"It's not that either!" She made an ineffectual movement with one hand. "Oh, it's so hard to explain! It's like—it's like there's all this garbage between them. A lot of years of hurt. They seem to have an argument whenever they see each other."

"So what's the problem? Where do you come into the picture?"

"As an innocent bystander, I guess. I love him, Eric. But he doesn't want to let me. He says he doesn't believe in love."

"Did he kick you out?" The question was brutally frank.

Kathy nodded. "He said it wouldn't work."

Eric stared at her steadily. "But you still love him."

"Yes." Her reply was a whisper.

"The man's an idiot," Eric concluded.

Kathy tried to smile. "Thank you. I think so, too."

Eric gave a shout of laughter. "Kathy, you're a treasure!"

He continued to laugh softly to himself for another few seconds, then he asked, "Are you going to try to get him to see reason?"

"I don't think it would do any good."

"Stubborn as hell, huh?"

"Just like someone else I know."

"Oh! Hey! That's a low blow!"

"You're right. I apologize." She hesitated, then added, "Even if it is the truth."

Eric looked at her archly. "I'm old enough to be your daddy, little girl. I could take you over my knee and show you a thing or two."

"Try it!" Kathy warned.

Eric immediately pretended to back down, glad that his teasing had put a little spark back in her eye. He pulled his arm away. "Nooo—thank you. I like my skin right where it is. I've got no wish to see it hanging on your wall." He motioned to Frederick's shrine. "This place is strange enough as it is."

Kathy giggled. She had told him about the Sinclairs and how she had come to live in this apartment.

"Is it what you expected?"

"No, it's worse!" He grinned. He motioned to the painting. "What kind of dog was he anyway?"

"A Shih Tzu, I think."

"Looks like a mean little booger."

"I've come to like him."

"*You* would!"

"Are you trying to say I have no taste?" She was looking at him with merry eyes, his gentle teasing having drawn her out of herself and away from her troubles.

"No," he returned, half in jest, half in earnest. "You're just like Will Rogers: you've never met a person you don't like. And that probably includes dogs."

Kathy thought for a moment and then said, "I read something about him once. He said he never *met* a person he didn't like. He was willing to give anybody a chance, but he didn't necessarily continue to like them."

"I bet that you do."

"Saint Kathy!" She laughed sarcastically and then remembered what Peter had said about her not canonizing him. Her laughter immediately vanished.

Eric sighed, noting her return to despair. "We're a matched pair, aren't we?"

Kathy looked into his sad eyes. "It looks like it."

"How would you feel about sticking together for a little while then? I mean"—he rushed on when she gave him a slightly shocked look—"as friends. Not anything else. More like misery liking company."

"Sure. I guess so," she agreed. She did feel better after talking with Eric. Not so alone in her plight. And maybe she would be able to help him.

"Then it's a deal," he said as he stood up. "I've got to push off for now, though. There are a few things I have to take care of before calling it a night."

Kathy walked with him to the door.

"I'm glad we're friends, Eric," she said softly, meaning every word.

He had reached for the knob but paused in turning it when he heard what she said. "Me, too, kid," he agreed quietly, "me, too."

Then he opened the door, and Kathy reached out to give his shoulder a friendly pat as he went out.

That was how Peter saw them. He was just coming back from his usual workout and was taking the last step up onto the balcony. His foot froze in midair as he watched a vaguely familiar, ruggedly handsome man come out of Kathy's apartment with a self-satisfied smile on his lips. Kathy was smiling as well, her hand resting lovingly on his shoulder. Peter didn't want to believe what his eyes were seeing! His foot slowly lowered to the cement.

When she looked across at Peter, Kathy froze as well, her eyes riveted on him.

Eric glanced from one to the other. He knew that this must be the stubborn, idiotic fool who was the object of her affection. There could be no mistake, not with the way they were looking at each other.

An imp of mischief made Eric turn back to Kathy. Under his breath he murmured, "We'll see just how serious the bastard is."

Then he kissed her.

Afterward, speaking loudly enough for the other man to hear, he said, "I've been around a lot, love, but you're the best. And to think that we've been working together for all these weeks and not known—"

He left the sentence hanging there and then turned away, whistling a happy little tune as he started for the stairs.

Kathy remained in the doorway, her eyes wide, her mouth partially open.

Peter had the sudden urge to reach out and trip the man as he passed. Then his heated glance switched to Kathy, causing her to immediately shut her mouth *and* her door.

Peter stared at the blank portal for another few seconds before stalking to his own door, which he slammed behind him with restrained fury.

She had done what he said! She had already found someone else! He expected it of his mother, but he hadn't truly expected it of her!

With a monumental force of will, he made himself

calm down. *I don't love her. She doesn't love me. She's free—just as I am. Nothing she does matters to me.*

But even as he thought those words, and try as he might to believe them, the niggling doubts that had been eating at him all along grew more insistent.

CHAPTER TWELVE

Over the next few days Eric became a regular visitor at Kathy's apartment. They spent most of their free hours away from work together; and by the end of the third day, Kathy knew Sue almost as well as Eric did. All he did was talk about her, but Kathy rarely talked about Peter, preferring instead to listen.

On Friday Eric decided that the time had come to pay back her hospitality by taking her out to dinner. At work he asked her the name of her favorite restaurant.

Both out of tenderness of heart and spirit, Kathy replied, "Claudio's."

She dressed casually for the meal, knowing that a nice pair of slacks and a pretty blouse would suffice.

Eric must have felt the same way about expending too much energy in making an impression—they had no need—and called for her in a faded pair of jeans and a western shirt.

"This is the place your sister owned, isn't it?" he asked as they turned into the parking area.

Kathy gazed at the familiar building. "Yes."

"It must have been fun working here while you were growing up."

"At times I didn't think so."

Eric laughed as they approached the front door. "Yeah, I'm sure. I bet I'd have loved it, though."

"There was a lot more to it than just waiting tables and talking with people. There was a lot of dirty work."

"Which you got stuck with."

Kathy thought back. "No, not a lot."

Eric reached for the door handle and pulled. It rattled, but nothing happened. He pulled again. Still nothing happened. Then Kathy saw the sign. It read: "Closed Indefinitely for Repairs."

She stared at it. Claudio's was closed!

When Eric read the sign aloud, the words penetrated, but she still turned blank eyes upon him.

"Did you know about this?" he asked.

Kathy shook her head.

Eric cupped his hands around his eyes and leaned into one of the small windows built into the door.

"Doesn't look like much is happening yet," he observed.

Kathy leaned forward to copy his movement. Everything was still the same. The rooms were just empty of people.

"The new owners were talking about changing the place, but I didn't think it would happen so soon," she said, sickened. *What's happened to Mary Morgan and Iris? Are they out of a job now? Oh, if only Ashley would come walking through that kitchen door! I miss her so—especially now. And Jason—I just want to see his understanding smile.*

Eric shifted away from the glass and Kathy followed suit.

"Well, where'd you like to go now," he asked, "since this place has cratered on us?"

Kathy mentally took issue with his term but didn't voice her displeasure. He didn't realize how she was feeling. "I don't know," she replied.

They started to walk back to his car.

He snapped his fingers. "Hey! I have a great idea! Why don't we have a barbecue? I have a hibachi I can bring over to your place, and I'll even supply the steaks. All you'll have to do is supply the view and maybe a potato chip or two."

"I'm not really very hungry, Eric."

"Oh, come on! You have to eat! And I make the best barbecue sauce in the state. Come on. You have to try it."

Kathy let herself be persuaded.

What Eric promised, he delivered. His sauce was one of the best Kathy had ever tasted. But all the while she picked at her meal she was conscious of growing problems. She wanted to call Mary Morgan to find out what had happened, to find out if Iris was well, and to complain to both of them that they hadn't kept her informed. A tiny pang of conscience told her that she hadn't done a very good job of keeping herself informed either, but she quickly subdued it. She couldn't be everywhere at once, and it wasn't as if she didn't have enough other problems in her life to think about. Like Peter.

As luck would have it, he had come upon her and Eric bent side by side on the balcony, laughing as Eric turned the cooking meat over above the glowing coals and applied more of his special sauce.

Her smile had instantly evaporated, but Eric, a rascal

by nature, had continued laughing and actually had the gall to greet Peter!

"Hello!" he had said with much cheer. "Nice evening, isn't it?"

Peter had mumbled a frigid reply that Kathy's ears had been unable to decipher.

After his stiff back disappeared into his apartment, it had taken Eric's joking whisper, "The man is *not* pleased!" to help her get back any appetite at all.

The next morning Kathy called Mary Morgan.

"When did it happen?" she asked, coming directly to the point.

"Just a few days ago." The waitress tried to sound unconcerned.

"Is it closed for a long time? Do you know when it will reopen?" Those questions were a delicate way of asking if she and Iris were going to be taken back on.

"Her ladyship didn't inform me," the woman sniffed. "Iris either. She just came in one day and said we were closing the next."

"But isn't she going to open it back up? As a 'fern bar,' or whatever Iris called it?"

"That's the last that I heard. But I also heard that her husband wants to tear the place down and use the land as a used car lot or something. Doesn't make sense to me, but then what those people do rarely makes sense to me!"

Kathy hesitated. This was a delicate subject. "How will you get along? Do you think you'll find another job soon?"

"In time. And so will Iris. We won't starve."

"But—"

210

Mary Morgan interrupted. "Don't worry about us so, Kathy. We're grown women. We can take care of ourselves."

"You'd worry about me if I were in your position. And I'm grown."

"Now, that's different."

"No, it's not," Kathy said decisively. "Now, listen. You're the one who found this place for me, so you know I'm not paying rent, which has let me save most of what I've earned in salary. So . . . and I don't want you to argue . . . I want you and Iris to have it if you need it."

"We won't let you do that!"

"All the same, it's here. I have money that's not doing anyone any good sitting in the bank!" At that statement she remembered Peter's explanation of what actually happened to the money she deposited in his bank. And it *was* in his bank. "At least do this"—she decided on another track, one she was going to use on Iris as well in application to Mary Morgan after she finished with this conversation—"at least promise me that you'll keep an eye on Iris. If she needs any help, you let me know. Agreed?"

"Agreed," Mary Morgan returned happily. They were like a family. One looked out after the other. And that reminded her of something she had meant to ask for quite some time. "Say, Kathy, that young man of yours—the one you came to Claudio's with shortly after you came back to stay—are you still seeing him? I'm only asking because I had the feeling that you kind of liked him special. Or was I wrong?"

Kathy felt her stomach tighten. "No, Mary Morgan, you weren't wrong," she replied.

"Are you still seeing him then? You don't sound happy."

Kathy sighed. Sometimes it wasn't pleasant being so transparent. But then Mary Morgan was specially attuned to her after all their years together. She had picked something up from her voice.

"I'm not seeing him," Kathy answered simply.

"But you'd like to be," the waitress guessed. "Well, let me give you some free advice since Ashley's not here to mother you: if you want him, go get him!"

It isn't that easy! Kathy thought. But she couldn't say that to Mary Morgan. She thought she was helping.

"I'll remember that," she promised.

"You do that," her friend replied.

Kathy hung up, and after a few minutes to collect herself, she called Iris to extract the same promise from her about watching out after Mary Morgan. Then she could stay in the apartment no longer. Eric was busy giving his car a tune-up, so she had the morning free. But she was not about to spend it cooped up inside.

She showered, changed into a pair of white shorts and a bright T-shirt, and brushed her hair until it shone. She was going to go for a walk—maybe along the marina, maybe to the small shopping center a short distance down the highway. She didn't care where. She just had to make her body move.

Peter paced in the confines of his living room. He wasn't positive, but he thought that he was going to go quietly mad. He couldn't get Kathy out of his mind!

He glanced at his door.

How many times had he wanted to go charging across that balcony, gather her into his arms, and then

212

come swinging out like Errol Flynn did in all the old swashbuckler movies?

Not less than a hundred, he answered his own question.

But if he did that, it would mean that he probably loved her.

No, I don't love her.

Somehow she had managed to implant herself in his brain, but he didn't love her. Love meant trust.

I don't trust any woman . . . especially not her—not with her new boyfriend.

Peter slammed a fist against a nearby wall in unrestrained response. Shocked by his action, he began to rub his knuckles. He had to get away! He couldn't stay inside any longer. He felt trapped, trapped with the memory of her. He had to find someplace where he could find peace.

Kathy had had a love affair with the water since she was a very young child. She loved the feel of it as it trickled gently through her fingers, as it lapped quietly against the moorings, as it roared to the coast in gigantic waves driven by hurricane-force winds.

And she also loved it in the form of rain. That was why, stepping outside this morning for the first time, she had not been put off by the gray, drizzly sky. An umbrella was all she would need.

An hour later she was still walking. The steady drizzle had turned into a fine mist. She had lowered the umbrella some minutes before, letting the minute droplets caress her skin. She would get damp but not wet, and she didn't care anyway.

This is the first time I've felt truly carefree since Peter and I—Kathy wouldn't let the thought complete itself. *No!* She had done enough thinking about him over the past week and a half to last her a thousand years! And thinking did little good. It only made her feel more miserable.

Then, in spite of herself, she once again remembered him as she had last seen him. Frowning, disapproving, and yet so breathtakingly handsome and familiar! Eric had said that he was displeased to see them together—which to him indicated that Peter cared for her. But Kathy didn't think that his feelings were from any deeper cause than the old I-don't-want-her-but-you-can't-have-her routine. He didn't care for her; otherwise he wouldn't have kept himself aloof for so long.

Kathy stepped mindlessly onto the condo's driveway, still lost in thought. The immediate, startling blare of a car's horn along with a loud squeal of brakes brought her abruptly to awareness that she had done something wrong.

A blue fender was only inches from her hip—the chassis was still rocking. Kathy was appalled by what had almost occurred! Then the car door flung open and a man jumped out.

To Kathy's disbelieving eyes, it was Peter!

With quick, deliberate steps he covered the distance between them, coming around the car's hood, and grabbed her arm in a none-too-gentle grasp.

His eyes were burning with anger. "Just what the hell were you trying to do? Make an offering of yourself in front of me?"

Kathy was still reeling from her shock. But at his angry, abusive words, she began to recover. She shook her arm free. "Of course not!"

"Then what would you call it?" he demanded.

"I'd say that I just wasn't looking where I was going!"

A sneer pulled at his lips. "Too busy thinking about the new boyfriend?"

"Eric's not—" she started to say, stopping herself. She owed him nothing. If she had almost killed herself by stepping in front of his car, it had been his fault! She had been thinking of him! "I don't want to talk about it," she said and started to turn away, but Peter blocked her retreat.

"It didn't take you long, did it?" he accused. "I didn't think that it would. I told you you'd find someone new."

Kathy lifted her chin. "Then what are you complaining about? That should make you happy!"

"I *am* happy!" he practically shouted.

"Well, so am I!" she returned with just as much passion.

They glared at each other for another few seconds until Peter, pushed beyond the point of reason, reached out to jerk Kathy against him, making her gasp in surprise.

His kiss, angry at first, mirrored his frustration. *She's so obstinate, so aggravating, so . . .* Then, as her startled body began to respond, his lips stopped their punishing assault, and a well-remembered sweetness flooded through him. It would be so easy to lose himself in the bliss that was Kathy's warm, willing body. It would be so easy. . . .

Kathy couldn't completely comprehend what was happening or the reasons for it. But she didn't care. After his cold withdrawal, after his angry words, all

215

that mattered was that he was now showing his need for her. She could have cried out at the achingly familiar feel of his arms, of his lips, of his hard body pressed to hers . . .

Until a car, wanting to pass but unable to because of the door Peter had left open on the BMW, gave a prompting tap of its horn and broke them apart.

Peter gazed down at her, his eyes glittering with shock, with desire, with anger.

Then the other driver impatiently tapped his horn again, and Peter pierced him with a raging look before directing it back at Kathy.

Kathy took an unconscious step back while he stalked wordlessly to his car.

With a quick, angry spurt Peter directed the BMW around the corner of the parking area and into its allotted space. But once he was there, his anger disappeared and he was left to deal with the aftereffects of his actions. His breathing was unstable, his heart pounding. He could still feel her softness drawn tightly against him, still feel the unabashed delight he had realized upon having her there. But he had to stop himself from calling upon that memory; he had to bring himself to task. What had happened wasn't suppose to have happened. He had just gone momentarily crazy.

Then he began to tremble—because of what *had* occurred and what *might* have occurred. He might have killed her! She had stepped right out in front of him! If he hadn't been watching where he was driving, if his mind hadn't been on what he was doing . . . And that kiss! If the other car hadn't come along at that precise moment, what would have happened next? Would he have allowed the embrace to unfold to its logical conclusion? Would he have been able to help himself? Certainly Kathy had put up no barriers, but then she never had. Whatever barriers existed between them were totally of his making.

Peter had to pry his fingers loose from the steering wheel in order to get out of the car.

Once he reached his apartment, he didn't remember the walk there. His mind was buzzing with so many conflicting thoughts; he was embroiled in so many confusing emotions.

The relaxing drive had turned into a fiasco. He couldn't find a small portion of peace even in a quiet corner of heaven! Especially not when at every turn Kathy was there to torment him.

The near accident had shaken Kathy, but what had followed had shaken her even more. Her lips were still stinging from his devastating kiss, her body alight with unfulfilled passion.

Kathy touched her mouth, her eyes wide, the light mist swirling around her on a gentle gust of wind.

She started to walk, her mind moving swiftly from one interesting proposition to the next. Peter was upset; he was angry. Was it possible that he *was* jealous, as Eric had suggested? And not out of spite, as she had thought, but because he cared for her? Really cared for her? He had certainly given her cause to think that. That hadn't been the kiss of a man who could take her or leave her, not from its angry start to its sensual aborted ending.

Kathy rounded the corner and moved along the sidewalk toward the stairs. When she finished mounting them, she paused on the balcony and threw a puzzled glance toward Peter's door.

Was it possible?

When Eric came over for an hour or so on Sunday morning, Kathy realized that he was beginning to wear a little thin on her nerves. She wanted to grab him by the shoulders, look him straight in the eye, and tell him that if he didn't go see Sue and put things right between them soon, she was going to start sharpening her knife for his skinning.

She had never met Sue—and from what Eric had said, she would probably like her very much indeed—but if she heard her name mentioned too many more times, she was going to scream!

When the knock sounded on her door later that evening, Kathy was tempted to pretend that she wasn't home. She knew who it would be.

Still, she attached a patient smile to her lips, opened the door, and before she saw who was there, started saying, "Well, Eric. Did you finally get your old junk heap running ri—"

But the last word died on her lips. It wasn't Eric who was standing there.

Kathy stared unbelievingly at the couple waiting on her doorstep.

The woman was a slightly older replica of herself, only her hair was cut short, forming wispy curls around her delicate features, and her eyes were a beautiful shade of violet.

The man was tall, lean, with thick brown hair that curled slightly on the ends, laughing blue eyes, and the most wonderful, warm, open smile.

Kathy stammered for a moment, her surprise complete. Then she said, "Ashley! Jason! What—"

The couple could remain still no longer. They both rushed forward and embraced Kathy in a group hug. Then they separated to take turns.

Her sister was laughing and crying at the same time. When she drew away, Kathy could see that the intervening years had agreed with her. Ashley was tanner now, making the color of her eyes even more startling. But she looked fit, younger even. And Jason. . . .

When his strong arms came around her, Kathy wanted to break into tears herself. And not only because she was glad to see them. Ashley had raised her, and she loved her for that. They could remember both good and bad times and share confidences and problems. But it was Jason, once an outsider, who had come to have a special place in Kathy's heart. He was the father and brother she had never had. Emotionally she needed to know that he was there. He had helped her so much during a turbulent period in her life and many times between then and now. Just knowing that he was here—that they were here—for her was the best thing that could happen right now.

Kathy had to wipe her cheeks when she was finally released. She hadn't known that tears were flowing, but they had been.

Deeply felt emotion wasn't just a feminine prerogative, though. Jason's wonderful, familiar voice was both husky and tight as he observed wryly, "We wanted to surprise you. I think we succeeded."

Ashley agreed. "I think we did, too!" Then she added enthusiastically, "Oh, Kathy, you've grown up so!"

Kathy squeezed the fingers of the hands she held—

one small and delicate; the other large and strong. Both were callused from all the work involved in maneuvering a large sailboat through the open sea.

"What are you doing here?" she asked at last when she had collected herself, closing the door and bringing them to the couch while she perched on a chair. "I thought . . . I thought you were in Tahiti!"

"We were," Ashley confirmed, clasping Jason's hands, "but we decided to come home for a time."

"But your letter—why didn't you let me know?"

"We did!" Ashley turned to Jason for concurrence. "We wrote to you just before we set sail."

"I never received it."

"We sent it to your address at the university," Jason inserted. "It must still be trying to catch up with you."

"And I wrote to give you my new address. Our letters must have crossed paths in the mail, and you left before you received mine." Kathy gave a delighted laugh. "So how did you locate me, then, if you didn't get my letter?"

"Who else?" Ashley asked. "Mary Morgan, of course. We went to see her just as soon as we docked. She told us where we could find you."

"Did she also tell you about Claudio's?"

"Yes! And I think it's awful!" Her sister's happy expression turned into a frown.

Jason's features started to cloud as well, but he made them brighten as he withdrew his hands from Ashley's and placed an arm about her shoulders, suggesting, "We'll have plenty of time to talk about that later. But right now"—his light-blue eyes began to twinkle—"tell us what's been happening with you, kid. We've come a long way to check up on you."

"Oh, not all that much," Kathy replied out loud but to herself added, *If you count falling in love, then being rejected as not being all that much!* But she couldn't unburden herself now. She didn't know if she ever could.

"Now *that* I don't believe," Jason teased. "Wherever you go, Kathy, action follows."

"No, really," Kathy denied, "I'm working at the institute, but you already knew I had secured that position. I'm certain you got that letter."

Ashley nodded.

"And do you enjoy it?" Jason asked, his eyes probing as his hand once more sought Ashley's.

"Very much. But what about you two? What made you come back? Did you get homesick?"

Kathy noticed the tightening of Ashley and Jason's intertwined fingers. She looked up to examine each face.

Ashley was blushing! And Jason—Kathy didn't think she'd ever seen him looking happier.

He met her puzzled gaze. "You might term it some sort of *sick,*" he said, "but the actual wording is *morning sickness.* You're going to be an aunt, Kathy. How does that sound to you?"

"A baby?" she breathed. "You're going to have a baby?"

Jason's handsome features beamed. "Yep. Or, more technically, Ashley is . . . in about five or six months."

"Oh, fantastic!" Kathy cried, rushing to her sister's side. She reached out to hug her and then Jason. "Oh, I'm so happy for you! For both of you!" Then she straightened. "Are you sure? I mean, have you checked?"

"Of course we're sure." Ashley smiled.

"That's why we came back," Jason chimed in.

"I still say we didn't have to. There were perfectly good doctors in Tahiti."

Jason shook his head decisively. "Oh, no. We decided not to take any chances, remember? And that if we were going to sail for port in the States, we might as well come home."

"A sound idea." Kathy took Jason's side.

Ashley grinned. "I think so, too. I can think of nothing better than to bring another little Texan into the world."

"His father is from Montana, don't forget," Jason reminded her.

"I never forget that," Ashley said softly, all the love she felt for him showing in her eyes.

Seeing her sister's emotions revealed so openly made Kathy look away. Not that she was ashamed to see the love they shared. It was because it reminded her all too forcefully of everything she was missing.

"So we've come back for at least the next year, possibly longer. Do you think you can stand to have us around again?" Jason teased.

Kathy hadn't known that he had broken away from his wife's loving gaze. She quickly reaffixed her happy smile.

"As long as you don't expect me to come swab the decks, or whatever the nautical term is," she returned. "You're going to stay on *Sunchaser,* aren't you?"

Jason was slow in answering. He had seen the glimmer of pain in her eyes before she could hide it. Kathy had never been able to hide her feelings from him.

"We aren't sure," he said at last, deciding not to

222

probe at this moment. "We'll stay on her for the time being—at least until it gets closer to the time for the baby to be born."

"Baby!" Kathy repeated and gave a squeal of delight. "I'm just so excited for you!" And then she suddenly remembered, "But what about your car? You'll need it."

Jason shrugged. "Eventually, maybe, but not right now."

"We don't want to take it away from you," Ashley said. "You need it and we don't."

Jason laughed. "We've gotten to be experts at being self-contained."

"But you're back here now," Kathy protested. "Ashley will need to go to the doctor. And you—"

Jason hushed her flow of words. "We'll let you know when she has an appointment, okay? Otherwise, we'll be fine."

"But—" Kathy still protested.

Ashley put on her mother face. "Kathy, listen to what Jason is saying. We'll be fine."

Kathy looked whimsically from one to the other for several long seconds before allowing her smile to broaden.

"The two of you can be royal pains," she decreed, "but I'm glad you're back."

"Thank you," Ashley acknowledged. "The compliment can be returned."

Kathy accepted it regally, then she began to giggle. Soon all of them were laughing purely from the joy of being together again.

Kathy went to sleep that night with a warm feeling of completion. They were back! They were home! She didn't have to feel so alone anymore.

Then she thought of Peter. And she knew that without him, she would always be alone. Her feelings hadn't changed; they never would.

CHAPTER THIRTEEN

Eric was the first person Kathy met at work the next morning. He was lying in wait for her as she came in the door.

"Kathy! I'm glad you finally got here. I have something important to tell you!"

Kathy had awakened with a horrible headache. There was no reason for it. It was just there, making her mind muzzy, her actions slow.

"What?" she asked, turning to him with squinting eyes.

Eric gave a low whistle. "Boy, do you look terrible!"

Kathy gave a mirthless laugh. "Be careful. Your compliments might turn my head."

He grinned sheepishly. "Sorry." Then he began to beam again and proceeded with what he had to say. "Remember how I told you I'd come back to your place last night?"

"I remember."

"Did you wonder why I didn't show up?"

Kathy sighed. One thing she had learned about Eric was that he loved to draw out suspense.

"To tell you the truth, no. My sister and brother-in-law came in from Tahiti."

"The sister who lives on a boat?"

"I only have one sister."

"Hey! That's great!"

"Mmmm," Kathy confirmed absently; completely preoccupied with the throbbing pain in her temples. She wished that she had taken something for her headache before leaving the apartment. Maybe it would have begun working by now. As it was, if she took an aspirin now, it would probably be another hour before she would start to feel like a human being. She began to rummage in her purse, admitting that the sooner she got a tablet inside her, the better.

Eric stilled her hand. She looked up at him. He was still beaming.

"I talked with Sue," he said, his emotion growing less restrained as he went on. "I started thinking about some of the things you said. About how I was making my own misery. About how Sue wasn't the same person as Loretta. About how a person can't run around being afraid to take a chance with love because someone has hurt them in the past. And I called her. I asked her if I could come over and talk . . . and she said yes.

"And what's come about is that she came back to me! She does love me, Kathy! And . . . well . . . she said that if I needed more time, she would understand. But"—Eric was breathless with happiness, his usual veneer of cocky assurance absent in his excitement—"we set a wedding date!"

"You did?" she said, smiling.

"A month from today!" he replied proudly.

"A month!"

Eric nodded. "She wants to have a real wedding. Church, flowers, cake . . . the works!" He swooped forward and gave her a resounding kiss.

"I'm sure going to do my best to make this work!" he vowed. Then upon seeing the shadows that lingered in Kathy's eyes, he said softly, "It'll work out for you, too. He'll come around. I'm sure he will."

Kathy shrugged.

"He *will!*" Eric repeated.

Kathy gave him the brave smile that he wanted, but she wasn't as sure about the future as he. She wasn't sure about it at all.

Peter's disposition descended to a new low. He did his best—he really did! But he had no patience with life's minor irritations. If he was put on hold while making a telephone call and some of that syrupy canned music was switched on for his listening displeasure, he would immediately hang up. If the guard at the bank clacked his false teeth together one more time when he walked in front of his office, Peter thought that he was going to go berserk and feed them to him! It didn't matter that the man was almost as much of an institution around the bank as the bank was an institution around him. Or that the guard was in his eighties. Or that he had met each of the man's five great-grandchildren just the week before. He would do it. And he would probably laugh maniacally as he was hauled off to jail.

Peter pushed away from his desk. What he needed was a drink of water.

Water.

Why did water remind him of Kathy? Why did everything remind him of Kathy?

He pushed his fingers through his hair in frustration.

Kathy spent the evening with Jason and Ashley on *Sunchaser.* It was a bit like coming home again. The long wooden sailboat was docked in the same marina and unbelievably in the same berth as it had been when Kathy first discovered it and Jason all those years before. Entering its narrow confines was similar to stepping back in time. She remembered the bologna sandwiches she had shared with Jason, the times she had confided her innermost secrets and problems.

Kathy fingered her glass that was partially filled with wine to celebrate the occasion and leaned back against the tiller. Ashley had gone below some minutes before, tired from the after effects of the long journey and sleepy from her pregnancy; Jason had accompanied her —". . . to tuck her in," he had said with a wink.

As she waited, a soft summer breeze caressed Kathy's skin and played gently with the long strands of her hair. She closed her eyes to let her senses appreciate it more. Then a step into the cockpit from below made her lids flutter open.

Jason smiled, his gaze going over her in approval.

"It's been a long time since you stood in that spot, brat."

"Two years," she replied.

"You came all the way home from Florida."

"It was an occasion. Not everyone has a pair of vagabonds for relatives. I had to see you off."

Jason laughed and hoisted himself onto one side of the cabin top.

"And now we're back."

"Three instead of two. Are you proud of yourself?"

"Naturally."

228

Kathy became serious. "Ashley's okay, isn't she? I mean, there's not some kind of complication."

"None that I know of. But we do have an appointment for her to get checked out tomorrow morning."

Kathy instantly volunteered the car. "I can get a ride to work. It won't be any problem."

Jason pretended a certain nonchalance. "With the boyfriend?"

Kathy's smile immediately cracked under her brother-in-law's penetrating look. But she pinned it back on again. She hadn't come here to confide her problems. Jason might want to put out to sea again if she started to bend his ear.

"Oh, I always have a spare boyfriend or two," she said brightly. Possibly too brightly.

"Kathy . . ."

He knew! From the way he said her name he knew that something was wrong. She had always been so easy for him to read. She had never been able to deceive him.

She gave a little groan and turned to hold onto the tiller, her fingers tightening on the smooth wood.

Jason hopped down from his perch and came to tip up her chin. "What's wrong, kid? I may have been away for two years, and you may have done a lot of growing up in that time, but I can still tell when something is troubling you."

Kathy sniffed and looked up at him with glistening eyes. "I'm as transparent as glass to you, aren't I?"

His pale eyes gazed down on her with love. "You don't have to tell me if you don't want to," he said softly.

Since that was exactly what she had been wanting to do even before their return, Kathy drew a halting

229

breath and let it out slowly. Then she said, "I'm in love, Jason."

"Who's the lucky man?"

"His name is Peter Maxwell. But I don't think he counts himself as lucky."

Jason frowned. "Why?"

"Because he doesn't love me. Or he says he doesn't."

"Do you believe him?" he asked quietly, watching her with careful concern.

Kathy blinked back quick tears of relief. Finally her dear Jason was there to talk to. He was so kind, so understanding.

"I don't know." She tried to sound as if it didn't hurt so much.

Jason anticipated Kathy's need to be held. He gathered her gently into his arms. Her fingers twisted into the material of his shirt as her cheek pressed against his chest. Talking with Eric was one thing, but talking with Jason was another. With Jason she had no need to hold anything back. She could be young and vulnerable and not feel as if she had let anyone down.

He held her for several long moments as she collected herself. Then he made her look at him.

"Is there anything I can do?" he asked, wishing that he had some kind of answer that would help her—answers like he used to give when she was a teen-ager in need of a steady hand. But this wasn't a teen-ager's problem. Not from the way she looked when she spoke.

"Not really." She gave a wobbly smile. "Not anymore than you already are."

Jason brushed a loose strand of hair away from her eyes.

"Is he here or in Florida?"

"Here. He's—he's my next-door neighbor."

"Right across the balcony?"

Kathy nodded.

"That was fairly quick. You haven't been here that long, have you?"

"No," Kathy whispered.

Jason said nothing for a minute and then called softly, "Brat!"

Kathy refocused on his face. Her mind had been away somewhere, thinking of Peter. "Yes?"

"Love doesn't have a time clock. I think I fell in love with Ashley the first time I set eyes on her."

She blinked. "But she was horrible to you! She practically called you a pervert when she thought that you and I—"

Jason shrugged. "It didn't matter," he said simply.

Kathy thought for a moment, remembering how she had reacted to Peter upon first seeing him.

"You're right," she agreed.

"Of course I'm right."

Jason's quick agreement amused her. "And smug!" she added.

"Of course."

Kathy took a playful swat at her brother-in-law's cheek, which he evaded with practiced skill.

"I may be an old married man," he claimed, "but I haven't forgotten all the moves."

A smile played about Kathy's lips. "No, I imagine not. Ashley probably keeps you on your toes. You must be horrible to live with!"

"I am!" he said happily, glad to have brought her out of her gloomy mood.

"A wicked little boy," she surmised.

231

"Sometimes," he agreed.

"And a wonderful husband." Kathy returned to seriousness. She was thinking of Ashley. "I'm sure you're aware of this . . . of how I feel . . . but I'll risk saying it again: I'm glad everything worked out the way it did. Ashley's lucky to have you."

Jason contradicted, "No, I'm lucky to have her. And you." He leaned down to plant a kiss on the tip of her nose. "You're a pretty good kid, for a brat!"

Impulsively Kathy gave him a quick hug, her throat tightening with emotion.

Jason inspected his car as they walked toward it. They had decided that since he and Ashley were going to use it tomorrow, he would come home with Kathy tonight and just drive it back to the boat dock.

He nodded his approval that there were no new dents to its sleek exterior. Then, as he settled into the driver's form-fitting seat and grasped the steering wheel, he completely succumbed to nostalgia at the familiar surroundings.

Finally he began to chuckle softly. "I might as well have been born a Texan, considering how much they love their cars. It must be modern man's substitute for the horse—like a cigarette is supposed to satisfy an adult's emotional need for a pacifier."

"I can just imagine you with a pacifier," Kathy retorted.

"Me, too. The baby and I can have fights over it."

When Kathy merely shook her head in mock dismay at his statement, Jason laughed and started the engine.

The marina was less than five miles from Kathy's apartment, and the distance was covered before either of them could do more than continue to smile at their earlier exchange.

When Jason drew the car into the parking area, Kathy expected him to merely drop her off. But it seemed that he had other ideas. His door opened at the same instant as hers.

"A gentleman always sees a lady to her door," he teased when she looked at him in surprise.

Kathy made a face. "You being a gentleman and me being a lady?"

"I should certainly hope so," he returned, purposefully missing her sarcastic tone.

Kathy shook her head and murmured, "Poor Ashley."

Jason laughed and placed a friendly arm about her shoulders as he walked with her toward her apartment. Their bantering continued as they moved down the sidewalk and up the stairs. It ended only when they arrived at her door.

"I'll bring the car back tomorrow evening," Jason said seriously at last.

Kathy regarded him earnestly. "I still wish you'd keep it."

"Nope," Jason smiled, "not yet at any rate. We'll see about later."

Then he yawned, the action taking him completely by surprise.

Kathy was grinning when he finished. "Ashley's not the only one who's tired."

Jason rubbed his jaw. "Somehow I have a feeling that you're right." He chucked her under the chin with one long finger and said, "Get a good night's rest, little one."

At the same instant as he started to turn away, Peter's door swung open.

Peter had been restless in his apartment all evening. Nothing seemed able to relax him anymore—not vigorous exercise, not the project he had been working on, not music. He finally could stand it no longer and decided to try taking a walk. Maybe by the end of it, he would be able to go to bed and sleep. And not think about Kathy.

His lips firmed into a thin line as he whipped open the door. He had to think about her in order not to think about her! It was a vicious circle!

Then, before he could take his first step outside, he saw the couple standing in the doorway across the balcony. One of them was Kathy. But the man! He was someone new. Peter had never seen him before. He was taller, more refined looking. And older, more mature.

A cold hard shaft of jealousy pierced Peter's chest. He had the sudden urge to go over there and knock the man straight off the balcony. But he contained it. Instead he gave a jerky nod, muttered an arctic hello, and then proceeded on his way—for the relaxing walk that he knew was doomed to failure from the start.

Kathy released her pent-up breath. She had never seen Peter look so furious, not even the time his mother came to visit.

Jason turned back to her, a puzzled look on his face. "Was that him?" he asked.

Kathy nodded. She felt too weak to do more.

Jason smiled faintly. "For a second there I had the distinct impression that I wasn't long for this world."

Kathy folded her fingers together for emotional support.

"He probably thinks you're someone new I'm seeing."

Jason's look was quizzical. "And you're not sure if he loves you?"

"He says he doesn't."

"What men say and what they feel are sometimes very different things."

All Kathy could do was shrug. If Jason said it, it was probably true. But she had no way of proving it.

A light entered her brother-in-law's eyes. "Maybe I should have a little chat with him," he mused.

Kathy immediately disagreed. "No! Don't do that, Jason."

"Why not?"

"Because I don't want you to. I can handle my life myself."

His pale-blue eyes were watching her carefully. Then he said slowly, "The most valuable lesson a parent or guardian learns is when to let go. It's not always so easy, Kathy."

Kathy reached up on tiptoe to kiss his cheek.

"I love you, Jason."

"The feeling's mutual, kid."

Then he completed the departure he had started once before.

Kathy closed her door and leaned against it. "Why can't my life be easy?" she asked the empty room. But then she supposed that if a person scratched the surface of any other person's life, they would find that what they thought was such a carefree existence might be something very different.

She took a deep breath and released it slowly.

Peter was haunted all the next day by the idea that Kathy was now seeing another man in addition to the first one he'd seen her with. As she had reminded him, he had even told her to find someone new. So why was it driving him crazy that she was doing what he said? Laughing with them, talking with them . . . possibly even sharing her sweet body with them! So when he came home from work that evening and found the unidentified man from the night before leaning against the balcony railing, watching him as he climbed the stairs, a dark rage took hold of his emotions.

He tried to brush past, to pretend that he wasn't there, but the man wouldn't let him.

"Nice day, isn't it?" Jason commented to Peter's profile.

Peter turned slowly, briefcase in hand. He met the pale eyes. "Yes," he answered coolly. Then he started to turn away again, key in hand, only to be stopped by a question.

"Is your name Peter Maxwell?"

Peter's back stiffened. Had she talked about him? Discussed one lover with another?

When he again met the lazy blue gaze, his own was frosty.

"Is that any of your business?" he challenged with dangerous quietness.

The man had the audacity to smile. "It might be."

Peter felt his free hand tighten into a fist. In the past he had always considered himself to lean more toward

236

nonviolence than violence. But over the past week or so he'd come to question that assumption.

Peter lowered his briefcase to the concrete, freeing himself for action. "Why?" he bit out. He hoped he would be given an excuse to hit him.

"Because I'm Kathy's brother-in-law," the man said at last, "and you might say I have a vested interest in her happiness."

Peter's mind started to reel. Her brother-in-law! Then he remembered what Kathy had told him about her family. His body remained taut. "That's impossible. Her brother-in-law is in Tahiti," he countered.

"Not anymore," the man returned with level assurance.

Peter felt his body loosen, only to stiffen once again. How much had Kathy told him? Was *he* going to be the one tossed over the side of the balcony?

But instead of meeting him with aggression, the older man reached out to shake his hand. "Jason Frazier," he said by way of introduction, and he was smiling.

Peter looked at the extended hand for a moment before extending his own. He nodded acknowledgment curtly.

An uneasy silence followed. Jason again took the initiative. "I understand that you and Kathy were once close," he said quietly.

Peter started to worry again. "For a time, yes." He decided on honesty. Maybe a sound thrashing would help him get over her.

Jason nodded and then looked out toward the marina that was only half filled with sailing boats.

"She's a very special young woman."

"Yes," Peter agreed stiffly.

237

"She won't tell me what happened. Will you?"

Some of Peter's anger came to the surface again. "You're taking a lot on yourself! What happened is between Kathy and me. It's none of your business!"

Jason slowly looked around, an eyebrow raised in appraisal. He chose to ignore everything but the first sentence. "Yes, I am. Aren't I?" he said calmly.

When Peter made no reply, Jason continued, "But when something hurts Kathy, it also hurts me and Ashley, her sister." He paused, letting the effect of his words sink in. "You didn't like me very much when you saw me last night, did you? You looked as if you wanted to do me some kind of bodily harm. Have you stopped to ask yourself the reason why?"

"I don't have to answer that," Peter snapped.

"I'm not asking you to," Jason returned patiently. "What I'm trying to do is to get you to examine how you feel. Deep inside where it counts. Then, if you still come to the same conclusion you obviously came to before, well, Kathy's better off without you. She's young. She'll bounce back."

Peter didn't know whether to go ahead and hit him because of his insistent interference in what was essentially none of his business or to do as the man said and think. But he had already thought. And Kathy had already made her own decision. She had been seeing another man.

"I don't believe you've really talked with Kathy. If you had, you'd know she's not exactly pining away."

Jason made a good guess. "Oh, him," he said offhandedly, "he's just a friend."

"A friend!" Peter's disbelieving laugh was tinged with insulting bitterness.

"Would you like to tell me exactly what you mean by that?"

Peter met his gaze. Gone was the lazy interest and in its place was the hardness a man would feel when the honor of someone close was questioned.

Peter drew a breath, preparing to make a sharp, cutting reply, but the opportunity to make it never came. As the two men stood looking at each other in equal stages of mounting aggression, Kathy arrived at the top of the stairs and discovered them.

Shock gripped her for several seconds, then her wounded gaze settled on Jason after touching fleetingly upon Peter. She had no need to ask what they'd been talking about. She could tell from their tensed positions. She had asked Jason not to confront him, and she felt betrayed, embarrassed, and humiliated.

Still, she couldn't hide her head and run, although at that moment it would have been very easy to do. She swallowed her pride and said, "I see that you two have met, so I won't bother with introductions. And since you also seem to have an interesting topic to discuss, I'll leave you to it. But, Jason, when you're through talking with Peter, don't bother to pay me a visit. I'm not interested in hearing anything you might have to say. And, Peter, don't take anything Jason tells you very seriously. He's stayed out in the sun too long over the last year or two and cooked his brain!"

And with those words she turned and let herself into her apartment.

Tension was suspended between Peter and Jason as they both stared at the closed door, but the angry aggression that had been hanging between them slowly drained away.

Jason was the first to break the frozen quiet. "Damn, I'm in trouble," he murmured.

Peter had to mentally shake himself. He couldn't get the look of hurt that had been in Kathy's beautiful eyes out of his mind! Then, without thinking, he returned quietly, "I've *been* in trouble!"

Jason gave a sympathetic laugh. "I know what you mean. I'm married to her sister."

Peter found himself starting to smile tightly in shared suffering, but then he withdrew. He and this man were not friends. They couldn't afford to be. *He* couldn't afford to be.

"The difference is," he qualified with unmistakable meaning, "I'm still free."

Jason pulled himself back as well, returning to the role of concerned guardian. What little camaraderie they might have shared was fractured. "Are you?" he asked, his eyes steady. "Are you really?"

Peter met the penetrating look. He wanted to answer yes. He wanted to claim he was as free as any man totally unencumbered by emotional needs. But he couldn't do it.

"Think about it," Jason said softly, then walked over to tap on Kathy's door.

He found that, as promised, he received no response.

CHAPTER FOURTEEN

Kathy was angry throughout most of the night and into the morning. But as she drove to the Institute, some of her anger began to abate. Jason had told her it was hard for a parent to let go. And he did see himself as a parent of sorts. He had only been doing what he thought was best for her—putting his nose in where it didn't belong! A spurt of anger returned but was quickly extinguished. She didn't like being angry with Jason. She had never *been* angry at him before.

She was almost to the Institute when she started to brake the car and turn around. She would go to the marina, wake them if she had to, and apologize for her unbending behavior. She had heard Jason's repeated knocks the evening before. She had just chosen to ignore them. But she stopped herself, her foot poised just above the brake pedal. She couldn't afford to be late to work again. If only there were a telephone hookup on the boat!

Her fingers tapped the steering wheel in indecision. Should she, or shouldn't she?

Kathy chose to drive on to work. Maybe she could convince Eric that they had to eat lunch at a particular fast-food place not too far from where the marina was situated. An apology wouldn't take long.

241

But when she entered the building, she found that her problem was solved. Eric was off for the morning, and she was assigned to a particular area along the East Bay to check out a proposed construction site—alone. She would be her own boss, and on her way back to the institute she could stop for lunch wherever she wanted.

This was the first time she had been assigned to anything in the field on her own since she had come to the Institute. First she was seining with Eric, then she was assigned the creel survey with Paula, and then she was checking out reported fish kills with Eric again. Was it that her superiors had finally begun to respect her abilities, or was this just a test? Whatever the case, Kathy was determined to do her best—both for her job and as a way to keep thoughts about the problems in her personal life to a minimum.

She hopped into one of the company pickups and, after checking the map, started to drive to her assigned area. A channel was proposed to be dredged on public land, a marshy area leading off the bay actually, and the Parks and Wildlife Department was to evaluate the environmental impact and recommend ways to preserve the natural habitat. A responsible job, she decided, but one she felt qualified to handle.

Jason sat on a narrow cushioned bench in the boat's cabin, leaning his elbows on an equally narrow table. His chin rested in his hands. Ashley was busy in the galley, but she soon turned with a steaming mug of coffee that she placed before her husband.

"Come on. Drink up," she urged.

Jason reached out, but instead of grasping the cup

handle, he grasped her wrist instead. He smiled lazily at her.

"What I really need is a little more of what I already had earlier this morning."

Ashley's violet eyes were warm with love. "You're an insatiable beast, Jason Frazier."

"Sure enough. But you knew that when you married me."

Ashley pulled her husband's head to her breast, holding him closely. "And I wouldn't change you for the world."

Jason liked where he was. He liked being anywhere near Ashley. Six years of marriage had not changed the way he felt about her—the constant, passionate need to be with her. His arms came out to encircle her waist. But to give lie to his words, his mind traveled on to another subject: Kathy. Had he done the right thing yesterday? Or had he alienated her forever?

Ashley sensed that his mind had wandered. And she knew exactly which direction it had taken. After coming back to her last night, he told her everything that had happened.

She gave a gentle sigh and smoothed back his vibrant hair. "Kathy will come around. You know she will."

"I'm not so sure."

"She will. She loves you."

"You might question that if you'd been there last night."

"You were only doing what you thought was best."

He pulled away slightly. "I thought I was. Now . . . I just don't know."

"Give her time, Jason."

Her palm settled on his cheek. He turned his head to kiss it.

"I hope you're right," he said softly as she began to caress his cheek once more.

Peter took the morning off. The project he'd been working on during his own time was almost complete. He just had to double-check the final corrections and make a printout, and it would be finished. Then he would be able to present it to the board as promised this afternoon. Originally he had planned to be done with it a few weeks ago, but then nothing lately had gone as he had expected. Kathy had come into his life, and his world had turned upside down.

Kathy—all the while he was trying to complete his project, he couldn't get her wounded expression out of his mind! Nor could he ignore her brother-in-law's sarcastic, "Are you really free?" remark and make it stop playing over and over in his consciousness.

He wanted to forget her! God, how he wanted to forget her! He wanted his life to fit back into the nice, neat little cubbyhole it had existed in before she came on the scene. But he couldn't forget what had happened between them. He couldn't forget how much she had come to mean to him—how happy he'd been. And as miraculous as that sounded, he *had* been happy! She had taken his initial reluctance and turned it around, not only with that delicious body of hers but with her spirit, her joy, her own happiness and sharing. During their time together he had found something he'd never known before—something he hadn't even known existed. Then his mother had come, and everything had been shattered.

Peter stared at the nearby wall, unaware of what he was seeing.

His mother had hurt him all his life—from the time of his earliest memories and even before when he wasn't old enough to realize what was taking place. *She* was the one who had caused all the upheavals in his life. Was he going to allow her to continue to do it now by reacting to her in such a way that he destroyed his chance at happiness?

Peter slowly closed his eyes, a vision of Kathy's delicate features forming in his mind. *Kathy!* Over and over he had tried to tell himself that what he felt for her was infatuation, that their relationship wouldn't last, that he couldn't make a commitment. But deep down, hadn't he known? Wasn't that why he had reacted as he had to the prospect that she was seeing other men? Peter remembered how he had felt—the black, gnawing jealousy.

A grim determination was in his sherry-colored eyes as he opened them. If he was ever to live a complete life, he was going to have to let go of the past. He couldn't continue to allow what had happened to him to influence the way he acted now. He couldn't remain suspicious and blind to his chance for love. Kathy had accused him of that once. *She's right,* he thought, *absolutely right.*

Peter thought about going to the Institute where she worked to talk to her. To try to find out if it wasn't too late for them. He would beg her if he had to! But then he remembered the meeting he had scheduled for one o'clock this afternoon, a meeting he had to attend. When he talked with her, he wanted them to have time with no interruptions. He had a feeling they might need it. They had a lot to discuss.

Kathy pulled the truck over to one side of the road and parked it. From the back she extracted a pair of rubber boots and, leaning against the rear panel, she exchanged them for the shoes she was wearing. Then she was ready to attack her job.

From where she was positioned, she couldn't see the water. But she could smell it and she could feel it. According to the map, if she walked about half a mile through a sea of coastal grass, she would eventually find the proposed site that already ran along the edge of a natural bayou. Kathy collected her clipboard and pen and started to make a pathway through the grass.

Thirty minutes later she was deep in thought as well as calf deep in water. She was walking near the edge of the bay in a marshy area where only moments before her arrival a pair of cranes had been standing, their long sticklike legs making the depth of the water look deceptive. She had explored one section of the area, and before going on to the next, she wanted to pause and jot down some of her thoughts.

As she finished writing the last word, a sound that she had not expected to hear in this particular part of deserted coastland floated to her ears along the wind. It was the muffled sound of people talking.

Fishermen, Kathy surmised at first, smiling slightly to herself. Then something—a harsh laugh, an angry word not coming from the direction of the bay—caused a frown to grow in place of her previous expression.

Kathy listened another moment, her face turned inland, and then she began to move slowly, cautiously, toward the source of the voices. Instinct told her that something was not as it should be.

A short time later, after having followed the bayou up its bending course, Kathy faded into the coastal grass as she neared her destination. The voices were becoming discernible now—just barely, because the men were now keeping their conversation low. But what Kathy saw as she came closer was enough to prove to her that she'd been justified in her cautious approach.

They're not fishermen. They're poachers—alligator poachers! But what are they doing here in broad daylight? Poachers usually do their dirty work at night!

Kathy hunched down even lower, praying that she hadn't been seen. Her heart was thumping soundly; a thin film of perspiration had broken out over her body. She had heard about department personnel happening upon lawbreakers in the past, but she hadn't expected it to happen to her! Not when she was so new at her job. She tried to decide what to do.

First she would get a count. She waited several seconds and then raised her head to take another look at the makeshift camp.

A small canvas tent was positioned on the high ground of the bayou's bank; nearby, a tarp was stretched between four poles.

She counted four men, two of whom were busy with the grisly job of skinning the remains of what must have been a record catch, while the other two were salting down hides and adding them to the already rolled bundles that were tossed in a heap under the tarp. Alligator carcasses were lying close to the bayou, ready either to be pushed in the water as a method of disposal or just left for nature's automatic clean-up crew: buzzards and flies and worms.

Kathy sank down behind the grass, her stomach heaving at the sight.

Then, collecting herself, she knew that she had to get away. The men were not there to attend a cotillion; they were a rough-looking group who undoubtedly meant business and wouldn't appreciate being spied upon.

Hoping that she would be able to leave as quietly as she had come, Kathy started to sneak away. She had to get help! She wasn't armed, and even if she was, she wasn't trained in police tactics. That meant that there was only one thing left for her to do: she had to make her way back to the truck, then to the little drive-in grocery store she had passed several miles down the highway; once there she would call her central command to alert them to the problem. They, in turn, would notify the game wardens, who would come and arrest the men. If her truck had a radio, the ordeal could be simplified a great deal, but since it didn't, there was no use wasting energy on wishful thinking!

The pickup looked welcome to her as she rushed up to its door. Her heart was pounding; her breathing was ragged from the run she had broken into as soon as she felt she was far enough away not to be detected. She didn't stop to change back into her shoes. There wasn't time. She didn't know how much longer the men would be there, and she didn't want them to get away.

As she raced down the highway, her mind was active with the picture she had observed—the bloody scene, the rough-looking men. Alligator poachers were a problem along the coast. She knew that the game wardens sometimes had their hands full trying to catch them as

248

they made their way into Louisiana waters so that they could claim their haul had been caught under more liberal laws.

But these poachers—brazen in their flagrant disregard for the game laws in Texas—weren't content with the recently enacted two week period in September when alligators could be hunted legally. And neither were they concerning themselves with transporting their catch before skinning them. They were so confident they wouldn't be caught that they had even set up camp. Kathy wondered how long they had been operating undetected, moving from one area to the next.

Her lips settled into a grim line even as they trembled slightly. *Well, they aren't going to get away with it any longer! Alligators are protected for fifty weeks of the year in this state, and I'm going to make sure that the poachers are apprehended!*

She ran into the store, made her phone call, and then hurried back out. Without a thought, other than that she had to keep watch on the men until the wardens arrived in twenty minutes or so, Kathy jumped back into the truck and retraced her previous journey.

She drew to a stop where she had been parked before and jumped out, leaving the clipboard on the front seat. She didn't want to be encumbered while she waited and watched.

The wait seemed to draw out forever. Kathy had positioned herself so that she could see the men's activities without being seen. She watched with mounting anxiety as they seemed to be breaking camp. They had finished with the skinning and salting and were now

249

ready to move on, having stored the skins in several large plastic coolers.

When they were almost done—the tent and tarp folded and stacked on the ground—she could wait no longer. Surely twenty minutes had passed! She would have to do something to keep them there just a little longer! She glanced down at the khaki shorts and shirt she was wearing. At least it wasn't her uniform. There was no way they would be able to connect her with the Parks and Wildlife Department.

Kathy willed her knees not to shake. Then she crept away until she could stand upright and not be seen. After that she searched for a long pole she could use as a walking stick. Finding one, she took a deep breath and started to walk along the edge of the bayou. She even began to whistle quietly. Was she whistling in the dark, as the old saying goes, to bolster her courage? Or was she using it simply as a backup in her subterfuge to convince them that she was merely a young woman enjoying a day's hike along the bay and adjoining bayous?

When she came upon the men, she mirrored their surprise. She made her eyes wide and blank looking. If this was to work, they would have to believe that she was rather simple as well. She would have to ignore the carcasses that were beginning to stink or, at the very least, pretend total innocence that anything was wrong.

"Oh! Hello!" she said. "I didn't expect to meet anyone here." She let her gaze pass over the carcasses without seeming to see them. She smiled. "My aunt said not to talk to strangers, but I think that's silly, don't you?"

The men had frozen at first and then, one by one, they broke out of their immobility. Three of them looked related, having the same blunt features and pale-blue eyes. The fourth was shorter than the other three, but his weasellike face showed more intelligence. He was the first to speak.

"Where'd you come from, girlie?" His gruff voice made a chill run up Kathy's spine. Maybe she should have waited longer.

She continued with her deception by waving vaguely to the right. "Over there. My aunt and uncle have a trailer."

"And what are you doing here?" The shorter one started to walk toward her. Kathy made herself stay put.

"I just came for a walk. I get tired of staying in the trailer all day."

Yellow eyes raked over her when the man halted a few feet away. He spat a stream of tobacco juice onto the sandy soil.

"And you just happened to come along this way."

Kathy nodded, keeping her eyes wide and innocent.

"Well, what do you think of what you found?"

Kathy pretended to be momentarily puzzled and then she smiled, a bright, happy, little smile.

"Some new friends? My aunt won't let me have any friends. She says they only take advantage of me."

The man's eyes ran over her body again, slowing several times in the process. She didn't like the gleam that sprang into their depths. But she figured she could play this for a little bit longer. The game wardens couldn't be far away.

"Oh, she does, does she?" He spat again and reached for her arm.

Kathy evaded his touch, but she smiled. "Who are

your friends?" she asked instead, diverting his attention from herself.

The men had slowly begun to come forward. They might have been triplets, so closely did they resemble each other. Their blunt features were harsh, unbecoming; their light eyes like small blue pebbles. Only their hair was different: one man was balding while the two younger men wore their hair clipped close to their heads in military fashion.

The first man turned to them as they approached. "We've got ourselves a live one," he murmured, breaking into a wide grin. The others broke into grins themselves, exposing teeth in varying degrees of neglect.

The weasel-faced man motioned first to one and then another. "This is John, this is Billy Joe, and this is Joel. I'm sure they'd like to be friends with you, too."

The men laughed, and it was all Kathy could do not to turn and run.

"But I saw you first," the shorter man said, breaking into the laughter, causing the others to stop.

There was some protest, but it was soon apparent who the boss was.

"I said I saw her first, and that's all there is to it! You get back over there and finish up. Haul that stuff to the van. By the time you're done, I will be, too. Then you can take your turns."

Kathy's fingers tightened on the pole. If she had to use it, she would.

While the other men moved away, grumbling, the first man turned back to her. His eyes once again ran over her body. He licked his lips.

"You're a right pretty little thing. Has anyone ever told you that?"

"A few," Kathy answered demurely.

He stepped forward, trying to gain possession of her arm again.

Kathy laughed and stepped aside. She motioned to the carcasses.

"Was there some kind of accident?" she asked ingenuously.

"You might say that," the man answered. He continued to come toward her as she continued to sidle toward the outskirts of the camp.

"Have you been here long?" she asked.

"A few days." What little patience he had was beginning to run out.

"And you're leaving now?" she asked, pretending sadness. "That's always the way it is with me. I just make a friend and then they go away."

She watched the trio struggle with the heavy coolers as they moved away from the camp.

She switched her gaze back to the first man and stuck out her lower lip, poutingly. "Men are mean sometimes. My aunt always says that." She evaded his touch by stepping over to the carcasses. Her stomach heaved, but she controlled it. "What *were* these?" she asked.

"Alligators," the man replied. He made a lunge for her that was on target. Her arm was caught and held by his dirty fingers.

"Alligators?" she echoed and frowned. "I thought alligators only lived at the zoo!"

"They do. But they live here, too." He tried to take the walking stick from her grasp.

Kathy turned away, keeping the stick just out of reach.

"They do? I didn't know that. Are they dangerous?"

The man laughed. "Not anymore."

"They don't look like alligators. They look like—like —dead things!"

"That's because they are!" He was really beginning to become annoyed. She was messing up his timetable. It would also put a dent in his reputation if the others came back and she was still no closer to being had than when they left.

"What happened to their skin?" she asked again.

His fingers tightened. "Stop asking so damn many questions!" He pulled her close, stick or no stick.

His hot breath was on her cheek; his filthy clothing was pressed against her. He stank to high heaven.

Kathy turned her face away, revolted. His lips found her neck, and if the contact had continued for even a few more seconds she was going to hit him as hard as she could with the end of the stick on any part of his body that was available and then she was going to run. She had done all that she could do.

But in that same instant, as she was ready to strike, one of the men came whooping back into camp.

"She's the law, Bailey! She's the law! Her truck's parked just up the road apiece . . . around a bend!"

The man called Bailey jumped away from her as if she suddenly had turned to fire, but he retained his grip on her arm. His yellow eyes narrowed first in fear and then in cunning.

"The law, huh?" He shook her arm. "Is that the truth, girlie? Are you the law?"

Kathy dropped all pretense of simpleness. "In a manner of speaking, yes. I'm with the Parks and Wildlife Department."

Bailey uttered a curse. He wiped his upper lip.

"What are we gonna do, Bailey? What are we gonna do?" the man who had returned asked in a panicky voice.

Bailey's eyes refocused on Kathy. "Just what did you think you were going to do by coming down here? Ask us to please stop?"

Kathy said nothing. She wouldn't mention that a warden was coming unless she absolutely had to.

But the man was ahead of her. "I bet you were killing time, weren't you. Killing our time. Somebody's coming, aren't they? The real law?" he guessed.

Kathy still said nothing.

The man cursed again and then barked out an order for the other man to finish gathering what was left at the camp site. His eyes returned to Kathy.

"And you! You're going to take a little ride with us. How does that sound? A nice little ride?"

"I'd rather not," Kathy tried. Who knew? Maybe it would work. Stranger things had been known to happen.

Bailey smiled a none-too-friendly smile. "Now isn't that just too bad. Here"—his voice became stern—"hand me that stick."

Kathy hesitated, but when the man's free hand reached for a scabbard on his belt and withdrew a long-bladed knife, she yielded.

"I thought you might change your mind," he said as he threw the stick into the bayou. "Come on," he ordered gruffly.

Kathy tried to get away, but the fingers on her arm gripped her like steel claws.

The man spoke again while he brandished the knife.

"Now look, you can either do this the easy way or the other way. It don't make no difference to me."

Kathy chose life. Or at least life at the moment. She was smart enough to realize that she might have to face another decision later. But as long as she was in one piece, there was the chance that she would live through this terrifying experience.

Each day Mary Morgan O'Day took time to watch her favorite afternoon program. It hadn't taken long for the habit to form. One look at a certain actor playing the role of a certain doctor and she was lost to the world of daytime soaps. And that afternoon was no different. She had puttered around her house all morning, doing the chores that needed to be done, circling the help-wanted ads in the local newspaper for the next day's try at finding a job, and now she was ready to forget her own troubles and take on someone else's. Only just before the soap opera began, there was one of those annoying local newsbreaks. Normally she didn't listen to them because they gave so little information, just teasing headlines. But today—*Maybe it was God's way of spreading the word about what had happened,* she later thought—she was in her favorite chair for that fateful minute.

And when it was over, she no longer had any inclination to watch her afternoon television show, no desire to see the young doctor who could make her swoon with one flashing look of his dark-blue eyes.

Today there was trouble that affected her family—at least her extended family—and she had to find Ashley to tell her.

Kathy was missing! Kidnapped! By some poachers

she had come upon in the course of her work! The maddening newscaster had said nothing more, but what he had said had been enough!

Mary Morgan rushed out of her house without locking it and slid into her car.

She had to tell Ashley and Jason!

Peter didn't hear the newsbreak himself. He gathered the information secondhand. He was in the process of going to his one o'clock meeting when he overheard a customer talking to one of the loan officers of the bank. He barely heard her words in passing, but the content was enough to rivet him to the spot.

"I know! It's the most exciting thing to happen in our area since NASA first started making space shots! A young woman who works for the Parks and Wildlife Department has been kidnapped! Can you believe it? And by alligator poachers! Why, my lands, I didn't think anything like that went on around here!"

Peter did not react with the usual reserved manner he affected at the bank. His meeting forgotten, he lunged across the space that separated him from the two women. His eyes were blazing with the hope that he had not heard them correctly. Reaching them, he demanded, "What did you say?"

The two women cringed back, startled.

"What did you say just now?" he demanded again, impatient with their cowering. "Please!" he added desperately.

That was the magic word. The women were still looking at him as if he were a mad apparition out of a Stephen King horror novel, but they at least decided that he wasn't going to strangle them.

"A—about what?" the loan officer stammered.

"About the woman—the young woman who was kidnapped. What was her name?"

The loan officer looked blankly toward the customer, who spoke up for the first time since Peter's precipitous arrival. "Why . . . Kathy something, I believe. But I'm not sure—"

Her last sentence was made to Peter's fast-disappearing back. He didn't pause to tell anyone what was happening, where he was going. At the moment he didn't care if he had a job to come back to or not. Only one thing mattered: Kathy!

This can't be happening. I love her! I haven't had a chance to tell her yet, but I do love her! God, what a fool I've been to have wasted so much time!

Ashley's face was stricken when Mary Morgan finished delivering her tale. She was sitting on the edge of a narrow cushion in the cabin of the boat. She and Jason had just been preparing to take a long walk.

"That's all they said. Her name and that she was missing when the authorities arrived at the scene. The only conclusion they can make is that the poachers took her with them!"

Jason spoke through a tight throat, trying to still his fear for all of their sakes. He remembered the last time Kathy had been in danger physically, when the car she was riding in had been involved in a wreck and she had been the only one to be badly hurt. He remembered the gut-wrenching worry he had shared with Ashley. And now it was happening again!

"What made them think that she was there?" he asked.

258

"I don't know. They didn't say. You know how those news teasers are. They don't seem to care if they upset people. Just tune in later at the regular news time and hear the rest. Ratings! That's all they're interested in!"

Ashley waved away Mary Morgan's indictment of television news, asking anxiously, "How can we find anything out? Who can we talk with?" She, too, was remembering Kathy's accident and the horrible hours of waiting that followed.

Jason answered before Mary Morgan had a chance. "We'll go down to the Institute where she works. They probably know more than anyone." He paused. "If they don't, we'll camp out at the police station until someone tells us something!"

"Good idea," Mary Morgan concurred.

Peter arrived at the Institute five minutes after leaving the bank. The BMW had broken several speed laws, but he didn't care. This was an emergency.

The first person he found was Eric. He no longer dwelled upon what had passed between the man and Kathy. It didn't matter. All he wanted was someone to give him some information—preferably that Kathy was safe or that the entire thing had been some kind of practical joke.

But that wasn't the case. Eric's face was cast with lines of worry. He wasn't surprised to see Peter.

"I had a feeling you'd be here if you heard the bulletin."

"It's true then?" Peter asked hoarsely.

Eric nodded. "It's true."

Peter wanted to do something physical to release the ball of panic that was burning in his stomach, but instead he sank into a nearby chair opposite the one Eric was slouched in.

"What happened?" he asked.

"As far as we can trace it back, Kathy came upon some alligator poachers who were still working their camp. She was in the wrong place at the wrong time. Then she left to call in a report. But instead of staying out of it and letting the game wardens do their job, she went back. The stupid little idiot! I'll wring her neck if I ever see her—" Eric stopped, quickly cutting off his words when he realized where the expression was taking him.

Peter tried not to finish the sentence in his mind. "What can I do?" His body felt like a coiled spring.

"Nothing. Same as me. The police and the game wardens are handling it now."

"But there has to be something!" Peter protested.

"Nope, not a thing. All we can do is . . . wait."

Peter wanted to hit him, and Eric must have realized it. He spread his hands in a helpless gesture of futility and said, "Hey, man! I'd be out there in a second if I thought it would help her!"

Peter's fists unclenched a bit. What he was saying was probably true.

"All we can do is wait," Eric repeated, breaking into his thoughts.

Peter was quiet for a second, staring at the pale-green linoleum tiles that made up the floor. Then he looked up. "What about her sister and brother-in-law? Do they know?"

Eric motioned with his head. "They're in with the director right now. He's probably telling them the same thing I'm telling you."

260

Dr. Clifford Smith sat with his hands folded tightly together on his desk. He had just finished giving the anxious people waiting before him all the information he had. He wished that he could tell them more, give them more assurances, but he couldn't.

"So the only thing we can do is wait," the man who had introduced himself as Jason Frazier, Kathy's brother-in-law, said quietly.

"I'm afraid that's all." Dr. Smith shrugged helplessly. "Let the authorities handle it."

The woman who looked so much like Kathy spoke for the first time. "Are—are the men thought to be dangerous?"

Jason's fingers tightened on Ashley's.

Dr. Smith answered carefully. "We don't know. Most of the time these people are only out to make a fast buck."

"But if Kathy interrupted them . . ." Ashley's voice trailed away.

"They might just have taken her to keep her quiet for a time."

Mary Morgan had stood all that she could. The tension and the worry had mounted, and she broke into a wailing rush of tears.

Ashley immediately hurried to her friend's side and began to murmur soothing words.

"I'm sorry. I'm sorry," the waitress repeated between sobs. "I should be the one taking care of you."

"Hush, Mary Morgan. It's all right. You've known about it longer, that's all."

Jason cleared his throat. When Ashley met his gaze

above the waitress's bent head, he saw her glistening tears and felt his own eyes water instantly in response.

Even Dr. Smith seemed to be affected. He brought a handkerchief from his pocket and began to clean his glasses in a nervous gesture. Then, as if calling himself to task, he reached into a desk drawer and withdrew a box of tissues, which he pushed over to Mary Morgan and Ashley.

Once his glasses were back in place, he regained his air of authority.

"If you'd like to wait here, there's a spare office you can use. Just ask anyone you see, and they'll be glad to get you coffee or anything you want."

"Thanks," Jason said mechanically. At that moment eating and drinking were low on his list of priorities.

He stood to accompany the women as Dr. Smith led them into the empty room.

Peter saw the group file out of the director's office. He was able to observe them for a moment or two without being noticed himself.

He recognized Jason Frazier, and then his gaze transferred to the slender woman at his side. She looked so much like Kathy it made his heart contract! Then he made himself examine the older woman who was walking with them. He didn't recognize her at first. Then a spark touched his memory and he remembered her as being the waitress at Claudio's who claimed that she had practically raised Kathy.

His gaze followed them until they were almost out of sight, and then Jason, possibly sensing that he was being watched, paused to look back. At first there was surprise, then challenge, and then acceptance as their eyes met. Jason excused himself from the small group as they proceeded down the hall.

Peter stood up to meet him.

"I see you've heard." Jason spoke first.

"Yes." Peter saw the specter of worry in the older man's eyes and knew it was a reflection of his own. She had to be all right!

Jason's gaze was penetrating. "Are you planning to stay?"

"Yes."

The one-syllable answer was accepted without need for embellishment.

"Then you might as well come with us."

Jason turned away and retraced his steps to the hall. Peter started to follow him, then hesitated long enough to acknowledge the man he had been sitting with.

"I appreciate your taking the time to talk with me. In your position, I don't know if I'd have done the same."

Eric frowned momentarily before saying, "Everyone here cares about Kathy."

"Some more than others," Peter said tightly.

The puzzled frown still remained on Eric's forehead until he realized just what the man standing across from him was actually saying. Then he began to grin broadly. "Hey, now! That's great! I told her it would work out!"

Peter stared at Eric uncomprehendingly. When no further words of enlightenment were offered, he followed the path Jason had taken.

The tension in the little room where they waited was palpable. Peter felt a complete outsider even after being introduced as a friend of Kathy's. A friend! When he was so much more than that! Yet he didn't have the right to claim a closer relationship.

Countless minutes passed, minutes that seemed to turn into hours. Finally Dr. Smith came rushing into the room.

"She's been found! She's shaken up a bit, but otherwise she's fine! It seems as if the poachers drove her off into the middle of nowhere and then set her free. She's been walking for the past three hours—just trying to find help. She's on her way here right now!"

"She's fine?" Ashley repeated, wanting to hear the words again.

"Absolutely!" The director gave a relieved chuckle. "In fact the sheriff's officer who found her said that she was spitting mad!"

Ashley laughed and then dissolved into tears. Jason held her against him, his face buried in her short curls.

Peter didn't know how or when it happened, but he found himself holding a woman as well—the waitress. She was hugging him, laughing and crying at the same instant. Peter's arms automatically wound around her.

She's safe! Kathy's safe! His mind accepted it, but his body didn't seem able to comprehend the news.

Dr. Smith went on. "He said she was upset that the poachers got away! Can you believe that?"

The waitress hurried over to Ashley's side as soon as Jason had released her. The two women hugged each other.

Jason and the director shook hands, their smiles showing their release from tension.

"Of course she should never have gone back to where the poachers were after she called our central command. She should have stayed put and waited," Dr.

264

Smith confided now that the emergency was over. "I'm going to have to have a little talk with her about that. It was a very foolish thing for her to do. She was taking too much of a chance."

Peter walked over to a bulletin board hanging on one wall and looked as if he were studying it—when in fact he wasn't. He didn't even see the myriad of papers littering its surface. All he heard was a repeat in his own mind of what the director had said. *She shouldn't have returned. She shouldn't have taken the chance.*

His fists clenched at his sides. He had finally come to love a woman, and she had played a game of folly with her life—the life he had come to hold so precious.

Without anyone being aware of what he was doing, Peter moved quietly from the room. He had to be alone for a time. She was safe. That should have made him weak with relief. But instead, what he felt was a numb kind of anger.

He slipped out a side entrance, the evening sun strong in his face. But he didn't notice it. He wasn't in the mood to notice much of anything.

Before too many more minutes had passed, several shouts could be heard coming from outside the small office. Then Kathy herself was in the room. She saw Jason and Ashley and Mary Morgan. It was only then that she realized the worry her capture had caused. The realization hadn't sunk in when the deputy sheriff told her of the extent of the search that had been launched for her. She couldn't believe it. But as she passed from one loving set of arms to another, some of the reality of the situation began to materialize for her.

For all the hours she had been walking, she had ex-

265

isted in a fury that Bailey and the other men had escaped. Of course, she was relieved that nothing more had happened. She knew the situation could have been much worse. But Bailey was smart enough to know that killing an employee of the state, even a lowly marine fisheries biologist, would bring a much harsher penalty if they were ever caught—which seemed unlikely because they had bound Kathy's hands and covered her eyes before dumping her unceremoniously on the black dirt of a lonely back road. It had taken her a full fifteen minutes to loosen the rope and then lift the tightly tied handkerchief from her eyes. By that time the van was long gone, and she had no way of identifying them other than by their faces, which she doubted she would ever see again.

Before much more could be said, several photographers and reporters pushed their way into the room. Questions were thrown on top of questions, and it was all Kathy could do to breathe.

Dr. Smith tried to maintain order, but pandemonium held sway until he insisted that the room be cleared. "We'll be out to talk with you shortly," he promised as the group was herded out the door. Then to Kathy and her family he said, "I didn't know they were going to do that. I knew they were here, but I didn't expect them to do that."

"It's okay," Kathy reassured him. Being besieged by the press contained the same unsubstantiality as the rest of her day.

Kathy caught Jason's smile of approval and then noticed that he had started to glance about the room as if expecting someone else to be there. Did he think that a reporter had managed to stay inside?

His gaze returned to her, seemingly asking her a question. She returned his look with one of puzzlement. But Dr. Smith claimed her attention again by telling her how relieved everyone was that she was safe, and she knew it would be later before she would have an opportunity to talk with Jason.

As promised, they did meet the press, both television and print media, and Kathy quickly concluded that it must have been a slow news day for her little contretemps to have gained so much attention.

Finally the ordeal was over, and the four of them walked out of the building into the parking lot.

"We were so worried about you, Kathy!" Ashley said as they moved through the door, her violet eyes still retaining some shadows of worried tension.

Kathy smiled, relieved to be able to do so. "And all the time I was only thinking about how maddening it was that those men got away!"

"Well, don't you ever do that again!" Ashley warned, dredging up her mother voice.

"I doubt I'll ever have cause. Discovering a group of poachers isn't something that happens every day."

"Still—" Ashley wanted a promise.

Kathy's smile grew. "All right. I promise. Is that satisfactory?"

It was. Ashley leaned closer to Jason, who automatically tucked his arm around her shoulders.

They paused beside Mary Morgan's car. Finally Jason spoke. "We weren't the only ones worried about you, brat." His words were lazy, but they held a lot of meaning.

Kathy switched her full attention to him. She had the

feeling he was going to tell her something important. "Oh?" she responded.

Jason nodded. "Peter was there. He waited with us the entire time."

"Peter?" Kathy echoed, her heart starting to beat faster.

Jason nodded again, a smile pulling at the corner of his lips.

Ashley looked from one to the other. "Was that his name? I didn't catch it." Her gaze centered on her sister. "Who is he, Kathy?"

"A friend," Kathy said softly.

Mary Morgan, who until that moment had not entered the conversation, did a credible imitation of Iris's disbelieving "Harrumph!"

Kathy glanced at her and then back at Jason, who was speaking. "He must have left before you arrived."

"But why would he do that?" Ashley asked.

Jason shrugged lightly and winked at Kathy.

"That's something Kathy's going to have to find out on her own. I've already talked to him once."

Ashley looked at her husband blankly for several seconds before murmuring an enlightened, "Oh! Him. *He's* the one?"

Jason gave a low chuckle and kissed the top of his wife's head. "He's the one, all right."

Kathy pretended to be offended. "A person can't have any secrets in this family."

"Nope. And it's only going to get worse," Jason informed her.

"What do you mean?" Kathy asked.

Jason and Ashley exchanged a quick glance. "We weren't going to tell you so soon," Ashley began.

"But you're going to have to put up with having us around a little longer than we originally planned," Jason finished.

"Because we're buying Claudio's back!"

"You're what?"

"Buying Claudio's," Jason repeated.

Mary Morgan let out a little squeal.

"But how?" Kathy asked. "Did you sell *Sunchaser* again?"

Jason shook his head. "Nope. But we did get a loan on her—enough for us to repurchase the restaurant."

"But I thought you wanted to go back to sea again," Kathy protested, not out of dislike for what they were doing but because she didn't want them to be unhappy.

"We do. But not for a few years yet," Jason said. "We thought we'd make sure the baby has its land legs before we expect it to live on board ship. And even when we do set sail, we know the place will be in good hands with Mary Morgan and Iris managing it."

Mary Morgan could remain quiet no longer. Her dark eyes were large as she asked, "Did I just hear what I thought I heard?"

"You certainly did," Jason answered.

A beautiful ecstatic smile lighted the waitress's features. "Prayers *do* get answered!" she exclaimed. Then she squealed, "Iris will be so happy when she finds out! I can't wait until she gets back from visiting her sister so I can tell her!"

Kathy watched as Mary Morgan did an impromptu little jig, and Jason and Ashley laughingly applauded. A smile touched her lips and then began to fade as she reflected upon the occurrences of the day. So much had happened. So much— And Peter had come. He had come!

CHAPTER FIFTEEN

It was achieved with some protest, but Kathy managed to get Ashley and Jason and Mary Morgan to let her drive to her apartment alone. She loved them. She truly did. And she appreciated their concern. But there was something else she had to do right then—something she might never have the opportunity to accomplish again in quite the same way. She had to see Peter as quickly as possible. And she had to see him alone.

As always Jason was her ally. "The kid's got her reasons," he told the two women. "Important ones."

"But she needs to get cleaned up," Ashley countered, "and I thought I'd fix something for her to eat while she—"

Her husband intervened. "I believe most of that is secondary at the moment, love."

Ashley subsided at her husband's words, her violet eyes moving over her younger sister's face. "Yes . . ." she said softly, beginning to understand.

Mary Morgan waited until Kathy was seated in her car to say her piece. "Go get him, tiger," she urged, which had the result of making Kathy laugh.

As she started to drive away, she waved to the small group standing close to Mary Morgan's ancient sedan.

"I'll get by to see you as soon as I can. Okay? And Mary Morgan . . . thanks!"

Jason gave her a thumbs-up signal, and Ashley blew her a kiss. With fortification like that, who could lose heart on their quest?

But Kathy almost did. The nearer she got to the condos, the more nervous she became. What if he had just happened to stop by the institute? What if bank business had sent him there?

Then she told herself that she was being stupid. He had come because she was missing. He had waited with her family. That had to mean something. Only why had he left?

The BMW was parked in its usual space as she pulled into her slot. So at least he was here.

Gathering up her courage, she moved along the sidewalk to the stairs. She didn't even think about going into her own apartment. Her steps led automatically to his.

Peter sat in his chair. For an hour he had driven around aimlessly, unsure of his direction, unsure of his emotions. He wanted to see Kathy and yet he didn't. He wanted to hold her and yet he didn't. He wanted to tell her of his love and yet he didn't.

The burning knot of fear that had been present in his stomach had abated, but it had been replaced by one of anger. It had grown and multiplied, and now it needed release. But he didn't know how to ease it. He was just sitting there. Waiting.

The knock that sounded on his door seemed to be a partial key. At least he moved to answer it.

The door swung inward, squeaking slightly, reminding Kathy of the first day she had met Peter. The manager still had not repaired it. She wondered if Peter had thought to complain again.

Then, those inane thoughts disappeared as she saw him. He was standing there looking at her with a slightly dazed expression on his handsome features. Love for him filled her heart.

"Hello," she said softly.

Peter said nothing.

"May I come in?" she asked.

For some seconds Peter gave no indication that he had heard her. Then he moved, backing out of the way so that she could enter.

As Kathy walked into the apartment, her tension increased. She turned to face him after he closed the door. She had formed a loose kind of strategic plan in preparation for this moment, but now, poised on the edge of it, she threw her predetermined dialogue away and decided to wing it on her own.

"I—ah—I understand that you know about what happened today?"

Peter's eyes were unreadable, but they were fixed on her face. Still he said nothing.

Kathy laughed uneasily. He wasn't making this easy for her.

"A lot of people were certainly excited. I didn't realize that half the state would be up in arms, or even know what had happened."

Peter moved stiffly, walking to the bar, even though all he did was move a glass from one position to another. Kathy's eyes remained on him. Why didn't he say something?

273

"To quote the famous play title: in my opinion it was 'very much ado about nothing!'"

Her last words seemed to penetrate Peter's soul. His body jerked and he swung around, impaling her with his eyes. "Nothing!" he repeated, his voice an angry rasp. "Nothing?"

Kathy reacted by taking a mental step backward. She had wanted to break through to him, cut through the wall he had built up around himself. But she hadn't expected this! She wanted him to kiss her, to hold her, to tell her that he had been worried sick about her while she was missing.

Peter could hardly contain himself. For too long he had held his emotions in check. For too long he had existed in a frozen world of half-truths and assumptions, not letting himself feel any true emotion, until finally, in spite of his desire not to, he had come to love the woman who was standing before him. His surrender hadn't been easy. He had put up an exhausting emotional battle. But in the end he had been forced to admit that he didn't want to continue his life without her. Then she had done something so stupid—taking a chance with her very life! And now she had the audacity to stand there before him and make it into a joke! Something inside of Peter snapped, and he reached out to take rough possession of her arms. He began to shake her.

Kathy stared up at him when he had stopped, her eyes huge.

"You think it was nothing?" Peter demanded, his voice still tight with anger. "You almost get yourself killed and it's *nothing?*"

Kathy tried to defend herself. She wanted to cry. He

was reacting so differently than what she had hoped. "I wasn't almost killed. I wasn't even hurt!"

"Oh, no? Well, look at yourself! Your blouse is torn. You have dirt all over you. And your knees—look at them!"

Kathy tried to loosen his grip. It was tight and beginning to hurt. When she wasn't successful, she looked down to where he indicated. Each knee was caked with dried blood and dirt, but she hadn't noticed them before. She didn't remember hurting them—although at the time she had been so angry when Bailey threw her out of the van that she wouldn't have noticed a broken leg!

"I didn't know—" she began to say, only to be interrupted.

"You don't know anything, Kathy!" He was furious. "Just who the hell do you think you are? Clint Eastwood or something? Just mosey on in and round those poachers up by yourself! You and your .44 Magnum!"

"I didn't have a gun!" she returned, getting angry herself in the face of his accusations.

"No gun. My God! You're even more stupid than I thought! Why didn't you wait? Why in God's name didn't you wait? The game wardens were coming. You didn't have to wade in and play hero! The director of your Institute said you shouldn't have done it. You took a chance with your life, Kathy. A stupid chance with your life!" He gave her another shake. "You worried your family, not to mention your friends, and all because you just had to go back out there and see for yourself!"

Kathy's anger disappeared as quickly as it came. Tears sprang into her eyes. He was being so unfair. She had been through a lot today. She didn't expect a medal, but she had hoped for some tenderness. He had come! He had waited!

Her gaze went over his tightly drawn features. He looked so much older. His eyes had a hollowness, his mouth lines of worry. On occasion when she had done something to particularly worry Ashley, her sister had reacted to her relief in anger. Was that what Peter was doing? Did he really care for her so very much? Was that what he was trying to tell her?

Kathy decided that she had little to lose and much to gain. She licked her lips reflexively and asked in a voice that was barely above a whisper, "And you, Peter? Were you worried about me?"

Peter's sherry-colored eyes were blazing stones. They remained that way for several heartbeats. Then the anger in him began to drain away. His face contorted; his shoulders bent. Suddenly he looked to be a man who was defeated by his own emotions.

He drew a ragged breath. Kathy could feel the way his fingers had started to tremble against her arms.

She could stand it no longer. She cried his name. "Peter!"

Peter looked at her as if she had gone to the edge of her grave and come back. And now she was here, ready to be held, but he was afraid to do it because she might disappear.

"Peter, please!" she cried again, tears streaming down her face. "Please hold me." The last was a broken whisper that seemed to crack his rigid spell.

He groaned something indecipherable and then pulled her tightly against him, his arms crushing her,

276

his body straining her close. Kathy wasn't sure, but he might have been crying. She knew she was.

"I love you, Peter," she whispered achingly.

If it were possible, he held her tighter.

They stayed that way for a long time, just holding each other. Then Peter pulled his head away from where it was resting against hers. But it was only to find her lips.

Kathy's mouth melted against his. She loved him so!

When he pulled partially away again, his cheeks were damp. Kathy saw the wetness, and her love swelled for him.

Peter looked down into the blueness of her eyes. "I thought I'd lost you, Kathy," he confided huskily.

Kathy shook her head.

He didn't give her time to speak. "At work I heard about what happened, and I came directly to the institute . . . and then I couldn't do anything more. I just had to sit there and wait. And worry. I've never been so frightened in my life!"

"It really wasn't that bad, Peter."

"For you, maybe!"

Kathy was repentant. "I'm sorry."

Peter moved to cradle her face in his hands. He looked at her, his eyes serious. "Don't you ever do that to me again, woman. If you do, I won't be responsible for how I react."

Kathy loved the feel of his hands. She loved the closeness to him. She loved the way he was looking down at her. All of this, added to his previous actions, emboldened her to prompt, "You haven't told me why yet."

"Why what?" he questioned with a slight frown. It didn't seem real to him that she was here, in his arms, but she was. He could feel the warmth of her body, see the softness of her lips, taste the sweetness of her breath.

"Why you were upset."

Peter was silent, then he said, "I've said it in everything but words."

Kathy grinned slowly. "I'd like to hear them."

One long thumb moved to stroke the sensual curve of her bottom lip. "I love you, Kathy. I've loved you for a long time, but I didn't know it. I only realized it today. Before I heard that you were missing. That was what made it all so—"

Kathy hushed him by saying, "Forget about it now, Peter. It's over. All that matters is that you love me."

"I do!"

"I know."

As Peter lowered his head to kiss her, her hands automatically curved around his neck, keeping him there, trapping him. But he didn't protest. He was more than happy where he was. With Kathy. Where he should be . . . for the rest of his life.

When their lips parted, he smiled down at her and said softly, "I've missed you."

She smoothed his hair. "And I've missed you. Every day, every night."

He cocked his head. "What about Eric?" He had told himself at the institute that it didn't matter. And it didn't. If she had had an affair with the man, he would just have to take it. He loved her and, as she said, that was all that mattered. If she refused to answer, he wouldn't press.

Kathy smiled. "Eric is a friend. Nothing more. The entire time you thought we were making wild, passionate love, he was crying on my shoulder about the trouble he was having with the woman *he* loves. They're getting married soon. We'll probably be invited to the wedding."

Peter swallowed with relief. It wouldn't have mattered, but he was glad that she had stayed loyal to him. It meant a great deal to him.

He looked down at her, and for the first time since his anger abated he was reminded about the bedraggled state she was in. The hair that had come loose from her french braid was tangled; she was dirty—streaks of grime and black dirt were on her face, on her clothes. And her knees!

Peter made a small sound of distress. Kathy followed the direction of his gaze.

"It doesn't hurt," she assured him.

"But they need to be cleaned." He picked her up and carried her into his bathroom. Once there, he began a gentle cleaning of the mud-encrusted blood.

As he bent to his task, Kathy watched him lovingly. He was her man—the man she had waited for. Only now he knew it, too, just as she had all along.

His touch continued to be caring as he removed her soiled clothing while drawing a tub of warm water. Then using the same gentleness as he had before, he picked her up and placed her in the tub.

Tears of happiness came into Kathy's eyes as he began to bathe her, using slow, easy motions, rejecting the washcloth for his bare hands. He saw the tears and kissed her tenderly.

After cleansing her, he lifted her from the tub and began to towel her dry.

Kathy didn't reject his ministrations—she wanted them, she needed them. She needed the healing comfort of his loving touch. Only as the water was removed from her body, some of the delicious sensations that had started when he was smoothing soap over her breasts and stomach and thighs increased in potency.

Peter's fingers stilled as he met her glowing gaze. A fire raced through him. He had held himself separate from his emotions, cutting them off as he took care of her, wanting her to see the degree of his love. He would do anything for her! But as he looked at her now, saw her expression change from gratitude to desire, he no longer held himself in check. The towel dropped unheeded to the floor.

Kathy closed her eyes as his lips slid over the sensitive skin of her neck. She felt herself begin to tremble. It had been so long since they had touched in just this way. So long since passion had flared between them. She gave herself up to the ecstasy of feeling him near.

Peter's hands repeated the path they had traveled earlier, rediscovering the rounded perfection of her breasts, the curve of her hips and stomach.

Kathy gave a soft moan as he continued to touch her, bringing her body to tingling life. Then her feet were lifted from the floor and he carried her into the bedroom they had once shared.

As her golden hair spread on his pillow, she whispered, "I love you, Peter."

Peter looked down at her, at the woman he cared for above all else, and answered huskily, "Almost as much as I love you."

He removed his clothing before stretching out beside her. In some ways what was happening didn't seem real to him. So much had taken place that day—over all the days.

Kathy ran an appreciative hand over the deep muscles of his chest, a very real hand that caused an eruption of feeling within him. Then she smiled that wonderful Kathy smile that had intrigued him from the first, and he was lost, just as he had been then.

He drew her body closer, burying himself deeper in the softness and growing heat of her smooth, damp skin, while their mouths, heeding only their need, sought and found each other, melding, blending, becoming one in preparation for the more complete union that was to follow—a union that was as natural for the two of them as if each had been waiting for the other from the beginning of time.

EPILOGUE

Kathy hurried up the stairs to her apartment. Once inside she called her husband's name. "Peter! Peter? Where are you?"

Peter came out of the bedroom he still used as an office. As always when he saw his wife, a gentleness touched his handsome features. "I'm here, love. What's up?"

Kathy rushed into his arms, ignoring the papers he was holding. She gave him a big, wonderful kiss and then leaned away, still keeping possession of his neck with her arms.

"Guess what?" she asked brightly.

"What?" he answered dutifully. Living with Kathy had taught him to delight in the unexpected.

"You'll never guess who's back!"

"Who?" Peter returned, pretending to growl. He bent to nuzzle the soft, sensitive skin of her neck. Kathy laughed happily, enjoying his preoccupation. Then following her original path of thought, she said,

"The Sinclairs! They're finally back from Australia! I saw them in the parking lot. They were upset because you're still parking the BMW in *their* parking place!"

"Oh, my God," Peter murmured, his head lifting immediately. He could just envision the battle that was

282

going to start up again. And it was all for nothing. If they could just be made to see that they were the culprits in the affair.

"I set them straight!" Kathy said proudly. Her blue eyes began to gleam as she teased, "All you have to do is explain things to them."

Peter groaned. "I've tried!" Then he looked at her archly. "Maybe the solution is that a person has to be on their wavelength."

Kathy took a playful nip at his chin.

"You know what this means, don't you?" she murmured, her lips roaming tantalizingly closer to his.

"What?" Peter's level head always deserted him when he was near Kathy. He existed purely on sensual sensation, his body and mind responding as they pleased, which didn't bother him in the least. In fact he rather had come to enjoy it. He didn't miss his bachelor days or the "freedom to order his life as he pleased" that he had once valued so highly.

She pulled away slightly and grinned at him. "Frederick is all theirs again! I won't have to go over to their apartment and baby-sit him each night!"

"Hallelujah!" Peter exclaimed.

"And they really are a nice couple. Just wait and see."

"I'd rather not," Peter demured.

"Just wait!" Kathy directed before breaking away to hurry into their bedroom to stand at the closet door. "What do you think I should wear tonight?"

Peter came up behind her, placing the sheaf of computer paper on the nearby end table. He couldn't resist kissing her again. His lips feathered against her neck, causing goose bumps to break out over her body, his hands lifting to take gentle possession of her breasts.

"Peter!" she cried a protest, but she leaned back against him, her body becoming warm in response. "We're going to be late if I don't get changed out of this uniform."

"I'll help take it off," Peter volunteered softly.

Kathy giggled as she tried to make him stop playing with her hardening nipples. Finally she was successful in dragging his hands to her waist.

"Now, Peter. Ashley and Jason are expecting us. They want us to help toast the baby. And we don't want to be late for that, do we?"

"Why not?" Peter questioned, nibbling on her earlobe, causing Kathy to gasp slightly.

"Because it's a celebration. He's been a member of the family for two whole weeks now! Patrick Wayne Frazier. Never 'Pat,' Ashley warned. Always 'Patrick.' I like it!"

"I do, too. But can't his aunt and uncle be a little late this once?"

"Absolutely not!"

Peter sighed and made as if to pull away, but Kathy stopped him. She turned in his arms and brought his head down until she could kiss him.

When she drew away, she promised tenderly, "We'll come home early. How does that sound?"

"Perfect," Peter said, smiling.

He watched as his wife began to search through a succession of dresses.

"Why don't you wear the red one?" he suggested.

"Do you think it will be warm enough?" she asked, holding the dress out for inspection.

"We're only going to Claudio's—not the North Pole."

"But it's going to get cold tonight—at least according to the weatherman, it is. No more easy winter for us!"

Peter laughed. "You'd better get used to it. When we go visit Mother in Japan, it will really be cold there."

"I didn't think it got cold over there."

That drew another laugh from Peter. "You're probably too young to remember, but the Winter Olympics were held there not too many years ago. And that's exactly the area of Japan where Mother has decided to settle for a while."

"Yes, Father Time," she retorted, then mused thoughtfully, "I'm glad you decided to go see her. I think she needs you more than you think she does."

"After marriage number eight cratered."

A touch of bitterness had entered his voice. Kathy pretended not to notice. She was determined that Peter and his mother would come to some kind of understanding.

"Yes, poor thing," she said. "I wish she could be happy like we are."

Peter gazed at his wife. He knew what she was doing. He had known all along. She wasn't exactly the epitome of subtlety. But then she never had been. Kathy went her own way, loving people, trying to reach out to them, trying to help them.

He was afraid his mother was beyond her help, though. But then, maybe not. He had once thought that he was, too. And look what happened.

Kathy moved in front of him, slipping her uniform off as she made her way across the room toward the bathroom. He watched appreciatively as the smooth, healthy glow of her body was revealed until only small wisps of underclothing were left to conceal certain parts.

"I love you, Kathy," he said softly.

She turned and smiled at him. "And I love you, too, Peter. More and more with each passing day."

Then, wrinkling her nose at him, she went into the bathroom and turned on the shower.

Peter stood where he was, listening to the running water. He heard the small sound the stall door gave when it opened and closed.

Then, smiling roguishly to himself, he copied her path toward the room that was quickly filling with steam.

Patrick Wayne Frazier can wait, he decided as he removed his clothing in the hall. He was sure that Jason and Ashley would understand.

A startled squeal met his arrival in the cubicle, followed by a flirting giggle. Then came a soft, low moan of pleasure as his roving hands and mouth sought and found the most sensitive areas of her body.

"Oh, Peter!" Kathy's voice could be heard above the sound of the rushing water. "Do that again and you'll have a slave forever!"

Peter laughed.

And from the next sound she made, he must have taken her up on her amazing offer.

—You can reserve December's—

Candlelights

before they're published!

- ♥ You'll have copies set aside for *you* the instant they come off press.
- ♥ You'll save yourself precious shopping time by arranging for *home delivery*.
- ♥ You'll feel proud and efficient about organizing a system that *guarantees* delivery.
- ♥ You'll avoid the disappointment of not finding *every* title you want and need.

ECSTASY SUPREMES $2.75 each

- ☐ 101 **ONE STEP AHEAD**, Donna Kimel Vitek 16723-X-11
- ☐ 102 **FIRE IN PARADISE**, Betty Henrichs 12519-7-18
- ☐ 103 **AN INVINCIBLE LOVE**, Anne Silverlock 14126-5-27
- ☐ 104 **A LUST FOR DANGER**, Margaret Malkind . . . 15118-X-24

ECSTASY ROMANCES $2.25 each

- ☐ 386 **A STROKE OF GENIUS**, Helen Conrad 18345-6-23
- ☐ 387 **THROUGH THE EYES OF LOVE**,
  Jo Calloway 18672-2-18
- ☐ 388 **STRONGER THAN PASSION**, Emily Elliott . . 18369-3-24
- ☐ 389 **THE CATCH OF THE SEASON**, Jackie Black . . 11107-2-26
- ☐ 390 **MISTLETOE MAGIC**, Lynn Patrick 15635-1-10
- ☐ 391 **POWER AND SEDUCTION**, Amii Lorin 17038-9-19
- ☐ 392 **THE LOVE WAR**, Paula Hamilton 15017-5-18
- ☐ 393 **EVENING THE SCORE**, Eleanor Woods 12390-9-12

At your local bookstore or use this handy coupon for ordering:

DELL READERS SERVICE—DEPT. B852A
P.O. BOX 1000, PINE BROOK, N.J. 07058

Please send me the above title(s). I am enclosing $_____$ (please add 75c per copy to cover postage and handling). Send check or money order—no cash or CODs. Please allow 3-4 weeks for shipment.
<u>CANADIAN ORDERS:</u> please submit in U.S. dollars.

Ms./Mrs./Mr._____

Address_____

City/State_____ Zip_____